BURN THE NIGHT

A Max Strong Thriller

MIKE DONOHUE

For my sister –

The first author in the family and still the only award winner.
It's never too late to start again.

I know you have stories to tell.

Well, it may be the devil or it may be the Lord
But you're gonna have to serve somebody.

— BOB DYLAN

BURN THE NIGHT

CHAPTER ONE

She tasted smoke and fire. The oily fumes and the suffocating air surrounded her. Other than the urge—the urge was always there—the acrid tastes were her constant companions. And the darkness. The darkness was always there, too. Sometimes the darkness was warm and inviting, like a shallow lake warmed by the summer sun. Other times, it was cold and sharp as an ice pick.

Hot or cold, in the dark, she learned that memory was a slippery thing. She could remember her childhood, helping her mother make rice, or running through the red dust down by the river, or working with Tio, but she couldn't recall anything about yesterday. Those details slipped through her fingers like mist.

She could remember each wrinkle and line of her mother's face, surely now long dead, but not the face of the man who brought the fruit and water bottles each morning. He let her out and sat with her on the rocks while she ate and drank. He talked about his childhood and the sea. She listened to the passing boats. The ferry always chugged past with a short, two-note blast. She squinted into the harsh light after so many hours of darkness. She smelled the nearby saltwater and she smelled his rich, pungent coffee, but she never saw his face. Not clearly. Just when her eyes stopped watering and the blurry shapes gained edges and corners, he took her by the arm and led her back. Then there was the prick of the needle.

Time had become a disjointed jigsaw puzzle, scattered throughout her broken mind. She could pick up the pieces and examine them, but some were foreign to her, images from a different life, maybe a different person. She might have imagined them. Some were blank. Just empty holes taking up space. Others, the ones she'd learned to fear and did her best to avoid, were sharp and so clear that they could pierce her deep down where she could still feel. That always surprised her. And made the pain worse. She thought she was empty, any emotion long carved out of her, but sometimes it still slipped in. Humanity was a strange and stubborn species.

Something scratched at her face, but skittered away again when she lifted her head. Or had she imagined it? She touched a finger to the crusted blood around her nose. She flexed her hands until the bones ached and the cuts and bruises blurred into a single point of pain. What had she done? Was it her blood? Then she relaxed. There was no point in trying to remember. It would all end soon enough. One more time, maybe two, and she would be used up. No longer useful. The man did not keep useless things. She could feel the demons crouching in the dark. Their teeth were sharp, but they were patient. They could wait a little longer.

She knew that the man, like the string of other men before him, thought she had one use, but she had been down that road and thoroughly explored it. She didn't allow it this time. She had broken teeth and bones to make sure they didn't try again. She thought that was her way out, a way to end it, that they would simply find her too much trouble to be useful, but she proved to be *too* good at fighting back. The man saw an opportunity to still make use of his asset. If she did well, she earned a needle. That was how she spent her time now. She worked and bled for his ambition, and then she waited, and lay in the dark.

If you had asked her then about her childhood, she would have said it was normal. She wouldn't have known any differently. Her house was a little bigger than some of her friends' houses. Carla and Tio were around to help. They never went to sleep hungry and always had clean clothes, but didn't everyone? She dropped her head onto the rough carpet and looked into the black. She didn't see her mother this time, but her father.

He wore his work clothes: a linen suit, white shirt, and thin, solid-colored tie. They were a little more wrinkled and mussed than they'd been at the start of the day when he'd kissed them on the head as they sat at the breakfast table. He held a sweating bottle of beer in his hand, the condensation dripping off the bottle onto the rug. He leaned in the doorway of his small office. She hadn't heard him. He could be quiet when he wanted to be. The office was just off the kitchen, down a short hallway next to the little bathroom with just a sink and toilet. The office was the one room in the house he forbid her to enter. She was standing by the desk in the corner under the double-wide windows that looked out over the rolling hills and farmland behind the house. She'd found the key under the cup of pens on the desk blotter. How does a curious child resist a locked drawer? She had opened it and looked inside.

The truth can have terrible power. And a terrible cost.

CHAPTER TWO

Ash didn't count on the music. He didn't count on any of it at first. It all seemed like a dream. Money, new clothes, a bed. He couldn't remember the last time he had one, never mind all three. It felt like he'd won the lottery. But he knew from rehab and some trippy DTs that pleasant dreams had a way of shapeshifting into a nightmarish hellscape when you least expected it, and he was beginning to suspect that the truck's endless music loop was the devil's personal mixtape. Now he understood why Uncle Sam thought music was an effective psychological weapon. When he'd been in Afghanistan, he'd heard stories from other guys about what the psyops people did with the prisoners, but he'd mostly written it off as beer-time bravado. Most of the talkers were regular enlisted boots like him. What did they know? He still wasn't sure if they'd been lying, but after driving the truck for just three days he knew, if given a choice, he'd have his eyes gouged out rather than lose any more of his mind to this maniacal music.

He'd noticed that he'd started hearing it when he wasn't driving. He'd hopped up off the bed last night, cheap springs screaming, and ran to the window, then opened the door, looking for the source, sure someone was playing a joke on him. Nothing. The hooker that worked two doors down had been smoking outside, wrapped in a purple terrycloth robe, talking on her cell phone. The street was empty. She raised one painted eyebrow, flicked the cigarette away, and disappeared inside her room. She'd probably seen weirder things at the hot sheet motel than a strung-out junkie in new bright-white briefs bursting out the door. He'd gone back inside and turned up the volume on the *Leave It to Beaver* re-run.

He'd been coming down but still floating along, not feeling too much pain yet, when the man had approached him outside McDonald's. He'd been tucked into his usual spot, between the big HVAC outflow vent that kept him warm and the chain link fence that surrounded the trash bins. He was waiting for the night shift to finish and lock up. Sometimes they would toss him a few leftover burgers or chicken nuggets. A couple of employees were mean about it. Throwing the food at him like he was an animal in a cage. Others, usually the older ones, were nicer. It didn't matter to Ash. He ate it either way.

He was hoping for a burger tonight. Put enough ketchup on it and it didn't matter if the burger was three hours old. That was his first thought when the shadow fell over him. The man was just a dark, blurry patch against the bright overhead parking lot floodlights. Ash put his hand out for the food. He wasn't hungry, not right then, but knew he would be in a few hours and some food in his stomach could help make the turbulent ride back to reality a little smoother. But instead of cold burgers or a box of dried-out chicken parts, he held a thin piece of paper in his fingers.

He pushed himself more or less upright against the back

wall of the restaurant and tried to focus. It wasn't easy. He brought his hand closer to his face. Not paper. It was money. A lot of money. A one-hundred-dollar bill. He hadn't held that much money in ... a long time.

The man said something. Ash looked up. "What?"

"Interested in a job?"

Too good to be true. He knew it. It wasn't the first time it had happened. He held the money out. He wasn't that far gone or desperate. Not today. He hoped not ever, but Ash had hoped for a lot of things in the past. "I don't do sex stuff. Not with dudes."

"I'm not a fag." The man took a step back. "You know how to drive?"

"I can drive."

"Can you stay sober and off the shit for four hours a day?"

"For a hundred bucks I can."

"Okay, follow me."

The man turned and walked toward the only car left in the lot. Had the restaurant closed? Was it later than he thought? Ash's head felt like it was filled with warm sand. He sat for a moment, trying to get his mind straight. Was this a good idea? It could still be a fucked-up situation. Why would this guy pick him? Why would he approach him in the middle of the night? How did he know where to find him? He wasn't exactly sleeping in the middle of Rittenhouse Square. No one could see him from the street. This wasn't even his favorite McDonald's. The one on Lombard had a better view and more leftover food, but kept their dumpster area locked at night. Shit, he was getting off track.

His eyes moved back to the money still clutched in his hand and the questions faded to background static. Had he finally reached the bottom and the money was the first rung on the way back up? He stood, folded the bill, and put it care-fully in his front pocket, the left one, the one without the hole, where he kept the picture of Maggie, and followed the man across the lot. He knew he was lying to himself. He'd had chances before and always ended up back on his ass, a dumpster not far away, but he always believed it at the moment. The junkie's creed.

The man was standing by the driver's side door. It was a nice sedan. It was too dark, and Ash was still too scrambled, to tell exactly what kind, a Mercedes or BMW, but it was sleek and large and powerful. Ash approached the passenger's side door, but the man waved him back.

"Hold up. Damn, you stink. I thought it was the trash back there, but I can smell you from here. No way you're getting in my car." The man looked around and rubbed a hand over his head. This stretch of South 20th Street was a commercial strip filled with fast-food joints, gas stations, self-storage facilities, and other low-rent places that could be found near highway interchanges and industrial districts. "C'mon, let's walk."

They traveled two blocks south, under the Schuylkill Expressway, and crossed the five-point intersection where Ash sometimes tried panhandling during the morning or evening rush hours. Next to a diner, just before the area transitioned into cheap cookie-cutter condos and duplex housing developments, the man stopped in the parking lot for the 76 Motor Lodge. Ash had seen it before, many times, but even a cheap flophouse was beyond his means.

"Wait here." He disappeared inside the small turret of an office on the far end and returned two minutes later with a keycard. He studied the doors that opened onto the parking lot and then walked to the second to last one and opened the door with the card.

Ash was getting nervous despite the man's previous assurances that he wasn't homosexual. He looked around. He still didn't know what time it was but traffic on the Schuylkill was light, and down here at street level it was nonexistent. While Ash was at least a head taller, he was in no condition to fight. The man could probably pin him with one arm. He was thinking about bolting or at least walking away, he wasn't sure he could still run, when the man turned and held out the keycard along with more cash.

"I'll stop back tomorrow at some point. Clean yourself up and get some new clothes. Be sober when I get back and we can talk about the job."

A day later, the man had dropped the keys in his palm along with a cheap mobile phone. "Keep the phone on you. It won't dial out, but I can call you." Ash put it in his pocket, then started up the truck and smiled, even hummed along a little to the music. Everyone knew that tune. This felt like a new chapter for him. It really did.

CHAPTER THREE

Max had merged onto the highway, headed back downtown, when he realized what had happened. He sighed, checked his mirrors, and got off at the next exit. He'd dropped the three women off at an old Victorian in Manayunk. It was clear the three were intoxicated when he picked them up outside the bar, but only one of the three seemed very drunk. The fare from Center City was high enough that Max thought it was worth the risk that he'd be cleaning up puke before he made the address. All three also seemed very young and it was getting late. He'd let them in the car.

The drunkest girl had been predictably obnoxious and, given the increasingly sour faces of her friends as the trip progressed, Max guessed she was getting on their nerves, too. But, by the time he pulled up outside the slightly dilapidated, pink and white gingerbread on Carson, she'd kept down whatever she ate and drank that night. If it came up again, well, it would soon be someone else's problem. He'd stayed and watched as her friends supported the woman up the steep set of stairs onto the house's sagging front porch and navigated her inside.

It was only now, approaching the city again from the northwest on 76E, with the dark expanse of treetops from Fairmont Park to his right, that he realized she hadn't kept everything in. She'd urinated all over the back seat. Max could almost see the statue of old Billy Penn shaking his head from atop City Hall at Max's rookie mistake. It explained the friends' demeanors. With the drunk girl sandwiched in the middle, it must have gotten on both of them, as well. At least he had their address and could get the flat fifty dollar cleanup fee added to their fare.

As he exited the expressway and turned left into a gas station at the end of the ramp, he once again silently thanked Liam for installing the wipe-away upholstery fabric on the car's back seats. It wasn't the most elegant look, but it was smart business when at least half their revenue came from inebriated passengers. He popped the trunk and took out the cleaning supplies: bleach wipes, gloves, trash bags, and a bucket. He spent five minutes wiping everything down and getting the car back in order. He wadded up the used wipes and put them in a garbage bag. The scent still lingered if you knew it was there, but now it mostly smelled like Max had showered in lemon bleach or had terrible taste in aftershave.

It could have been worse. Vomit was definitely worse, more colorful and more difficult to clean up, even with the stain-free seats, but as he walked to the set of garbage cans near the gas pumps, he thought there was something animal and atavistic about urination that left him feeling violated. Any sympathy he'd had earlier in the night for the three girls disappeared. He would get that fifty bucks. He dumped the garbage in the can and continued inside to the small convenience store. He nodded to the sleepy clerk, listlessly paging through a magazine, and found the coffee machine. There was a half-inch of black sludge in one pot. He detoured to the refrigerated case and chose a Coke instead.

When he returned to the car, the two-way radio was beeping. It was after two a.m. now and the bars were closed, a time of night when the calls typically tailed off. He considered ignoring it but knew that Terry, the night dispatcher, would quickly switch over to his personal cell phone if he didn't answer. He was relentless. When Max had brought it up one day with Liam, after Terry had tracked him down on his off hours about a potential pickup from six hours earlier, he'd been told Terry used to be a driver but had been injured in a nasty accident that left his brain muddled. Sometimes he got stuck on things. He was too much of a risk for driving, but it made him a great dispatcher, Liam had laughed.

Max picked up the radio from the cup holder. "This is Max. What's up, Terry?"

"Got a request for a pickup at Whiskey's off Ritt Square. You're closest. You know it?"

"I know it." It was a chic little place off 18th Street near the affluent Rittenhouse Square. It had an unmarked entrance and fashioned itself a speakeasy. Not Max's style but also, he thought, not drunk twenty-somethings' style either. A single cocktail probably ran in the double figures. There were much cheaper nearby places to get drunk. He didn't think he'd be running the risk of a second cleaning fee client in one night.

"Where are they going?"

"Didn't say. The bar called it in. One of the places Liam has a deal with."

Not knowing where he was going gave him pause, but it was too early to pull the plug on his shift yet. "Nothing else?"

"No, not until a five a.m. airport run."

"All right, I'm on it."

Ten minutes later, he pulled up in front of a brick building sandwiched between a Greek diner and a local chain coffee shop. It was now well past closing time, and the streets were emptying. Not just the revelers but the night shift too. He idled at the curb and was about to hop out and jog down the short flight to the bar's entrance to see if his fare had skipped, or grabbed a passing yellow cab, when he saw two men, one wearing kitchen whites, the other sporting the manicured facial hair that said he might be a bartender, half carrying, half supporting a woman up the stairs. Her eyes were unfocused and her face slack with drink but Max thought when she was sober she might be very attractive. She was slim with shoulder-length curly blonde hair and high cheekbones. She wore a green dress that was expensive enough that Max didn't worry about the credit card clearing on the fare, with or without an additional cleaning fee tacked on.

But what he mostly saw was more trouble. He blew out a long breath and opened the rear door.

"What's the story, guys?" he asked.

"Uh, found her in a back booth when we were closing up."

"No one noticed her before that?"

"Look at her. She's a tiny thing and it's dark in there. Lucky we didn't lock her in overnight."

She suddenly laughed, then listed to port. The bartender on the left propped her back up. Max put a hand on her head so it wouldn't clip the door and they slid her inside. "Take me home, please," she said before her eyes closed.

"Did either of you get an address out of her?"

The cook handed Max a light tan coat and a small black purse. "These were next to her in the booth. Couple business cards and an ID in the wallet. Looks like a valid driver's license with an address out in Merion."

Max rubbed a hand over the purse. Leather and not cheap. "These would match her clothes," Max said, looking back into the car. The woman's head was tilted back against the headrest and her mouth was wide open. Merion was on the Main Line, a wealthy suburb ringing Philadelphia. The two men started walking away. "Hold on. You're my witnesses." Max opened the purse and checked the address so he could plug it into the car's nav system. "Forty bucks in cash. Lipstick tube. Compact. License. ATM card and business cards. That's it." He held it out so they could see inside. He opened the slim case of business cards, glanced at the info, then checked it against the ID. The names at least matched. "Erica Childs. Works at Brennan and Waites. She's a lawyer. She calls to complain, or claim I robbed her, you guys better vouch for me."

"Man, she's not gonna remember any of this. The way she was drinking, she'll be lucky to remember any of last week. I can still smell the gin from over here."

In the car, he tried to rouse the woman, but she was comatose. The entire situation made him nervous. He wanted her out of his car, quickly but safely. He had a general idea where he was going but plugged the address into the GPS for guidance on the last couple of miles and put the car in drive. He turned the radio to an all-night talk station and listened to the host and callers ramble back and forth about the upcoming local election and the rising gang violence in certain sections of the city. He checked the rearview mirror every few minutes, but the woman's position rarely changed. Her soft snores told Max she was at least still breathing.

Thirty minutes later, he exited the expressway, turned off the radio, and turned up the GPS prompts. He followed the directions down dark roads and eventually pulled the car into a driveway that matched the address on the license.

Then things got weird.

Max got Erica Childs out of the car and helped her down the brick walk beside the neatly landscaped shrubbery and fall flower beds. A light snapped on by the front door and he spotted a head in a downstairs window. He was relieved someone was home. He had spotted no keys when he'd searched her purse back at the bar. He wasn't sure what he would have done if no one had been home and the doors were locked. And the doors would certainly be locked in this neighborhood.

He stood in the halo of light, an arm around Erica, who was still mostly unconscious, so whoever was inside could get a clear look. When nothing happened for ten seconds, Max cleared his throat and said loudly, "I'm the car service driver. I picked Erica up in the city. She's had, mmm, some drinks. This was the address on her driver's license?" He realized this last bit came out as a question. Something wasn't right here.

After another pause, Max heard the locks turning and then the door opened. The man who stepped out was tall and angular with thinning hair. He wore blue scrub pants and a gray T-shirt. He looked over his shoulder, then quietly pulled the door closed.

Max took a step forward and shifted Erica's weight toward the man, but he just held up both hands.

"Whoa, buddy, that's not my wife."

"What?"

"That's my ex-wife. We divorced three years ago. My current wife is upstairs in bed and I'd prefer not to wake her."

"You're joking."

"No, I'm sorry. Her ... drinking was the major reason our marriage fell apart."

"Well, what am I supposed to do with her?"

"Last I heard, she was living with her parents in Cheltenham. That's probably your best bet. Hold on, I've got an address." He disappeared back inside and reappeared three minutes later with a scrap of torn paper. Cheltenham was only ten or fifteen miles away, but it would be a circuitous trip over a mix of roads even at this time of night.

It could have been worse. She could have lived somewhere in Jersey.

The ex-husband helped load her back in the car and then kissed her lightly on the forehead before shutting the door. Max drove and Erica Childs snored. Her sour breath mixed with the scent of the lemon bleach. He rarely saw another car.

An older man wearing a bathrobe and slippers was waiting. Maybe the ex-husband had called. Or maybe he always kept vigil. The only thing he said was 'thanks' then took his daughter in his arms and led her inside.

Max had taken the driving job because he needed something to occupy his time, and it helped him learn this new city. He hadn't counted on these intimate glimpses into people's lives. He rolled onto 76E again, feeling empty and hollowed out.

CHAPTER FOUR

Max had passed Love Park with the iconic Robert Indiana sculpture and skirted around City Hall Plaza onto South Broad Street when the two-way rattled in the cup holder again. He'd already made his nut on the weekly lease from Liam. He was in the black and the college kids and Erica Childs had drained his energy. He didn't need to push any more fares tonight. He'd planned to turn in the keys and head home. He was looking forward to a cold beer, some hockey highlights, and then some sleep.

But Terry had other plans. The radio vibrated again like an angry insect. Max picked it up with a sigh and keyed the transmit button. "I'm not up for that airport run, Terry. Find someone else." Airport runs were heavy with city tariffs and fees and were highly profitable for the drivers. Terry would have no problem finding someone else.

"Already got that one covered. This is a different job."

"I'm five minutes from the house. I was going to call it a night. Anyone else available?"

"I know where you are. That's why I'm calling. The fare is right on Ellsworth at Federal by the subway stop. You almost have to drive by it to get to the house. And she's only going back up to The Clyde. Twenty minutes tops. Easy money."

"Did she sound drunk? I can't take any more drunks tonight. I've had my fill, believe me."

"No, she just sounded tired."

"What's the name?"

"Uh, she didn't leave a name. Said she'd be on the steps of the shrine and you'd know her when you saw her."

That was cryptic, but even with only six weeks on the job and discounting his lapse in judgment with the girls earlier, Max felt like a grizzled veteran. He'd already heard it all driving the night shift.

"Okay, I'll take it."

The dead leaves and scattered trash blew along in the gutters and across the city sidewalks in swirling eddies. At four thirty a.m., on a cold October night, Ellsworth Street in South Philadelphia was quiet and deserted. Three, four a.m. It was the only time the city truly seemed at rest. In less than an hour, lights would turn on, coffee would start percolating, and people would start moving, but for now, everything still belonged to the shadows.

Max pulled the car to the curb in front of the white and tan sandstone Baroque shrine to St. Cascia. The broad steps were empty, but then a shape moved out from behind a large pillar on the left. She passed through the dim lights mounted over the shrine's doors and walked toward the car.

She wore a classic white wedding dress with a scuffed leather bag slung over one shoulder.

Max shook his head. He thought he was hallucinating. He'd heard about other drivers seeing strange things on the road, especially at night. He would have been less surprised if the Virgin Mary had floated down the stairs.

He glanced around to see if there was anyone else to witness this strange apparition, but the street remained empty. When he looked back, she was still there, still in the dress, crossing the sidewalk, steps from the car.

She was tall and lithe and moved with a grace and surety that made Max think of a dancer or athlete. She kept one arm tight against her side. Max watched her do her own quick check of the street as she approached. She opened the door and climbed in behind Max. He heard her put the satchel in the footwell. She blew on her hands and rubbed at her bare arms. A sleeveless dress, even a bulky gown, was no match for the October air. Max bumped up the heat a few notches and waited as she buckled her seatbelt. Up close, the dress was dirty and torn in places along the edge. He could see a few places dotted with dark stains. She looked up and met his eyes in the mirror.

"The Clyde Hotel?" Max asked.

"By City Hall, in Center City. You know it, yes?" Her voice was deeper than he expected and tinged with an accent.

Max shook off the strangeness and put the car in gear. Do the job, then get home for that beer. "Yes, I know it. It will be a quick trip."

He turned left at the end of the block, headed south on 15th before a second left on Wharton and finally north again on Broad Street toward the cluster of hotels around City Hall and the various historical buildings, like the Constitution Center, that attracted millions of people each year.

Max usually let the customer drive the interaction. If they wanted to talk, fine, he could do small talk or sports or a little business. If they wanted quiet to read the paper or scroll through their phone or just stare out the window, that was fine, too. But the dress and utter strangeness of the encounter made his curiosity get the better of him. While the woman looked out at the empty sidewalks and passing buildings, he broke the silence. "Coming from a party?"

Their eyes caught in the mirror again. "Excuse me?"

"The dress. Halloween isn't too far away. I was just wondering if you were coming from a costume party."

The woman looked down at her dress and almost seemed as bewildered as Max at what she was wearing.

"Something like that."

He watched a small trickle of blood drip from behind her ear and down her neck. She didn't appear to notice.

Max cleared his throat, and she looked up again. "You've got, ah, something ..." He moved his own hand across his ear and down his neck.

She mimicked the gesture and then looked at the blood smeared on her palm. She didn't seem surprised and instead leaned down and took a small cloth from the bag at her feet and pressed it to her head. "Thank you." She didn't offer any more explanation and returned to staring out the window.

He tried to study her in the mirror without being obvious about it. She wasn't conventionally beautiful. She had an oval face and dark arching eyebrows over brown eyes set a little too close together. He could see that her nose had been broken at one time. There were two thin, white, horizontal scars running parallel to each other just over her left eyebrow. Twin comet trails on her dark skin. Not beautiful, but the overall effect was striking. She wasn't someone you looked at and forgot two minutes later. He also noted the circles under those large eyes. This woman was tired, maybe exhausted. Was she chasing something or running from something? She caught him looking at her at a red light and held his eyes until the light changed. Max looked back at the road, feeling his cheeks flush in embarrassment. He now felt her watching him during the rest of the ride. He didn't meet her gaze, just stayed focused on his driving.

He braked to a stop in front of The Clyde. The woman climbed out after saying a soft thank you and picking up her bag. She declined a receipt. A doorman in a green and gold brocaded jacket stepped outside and held the hotel door open for her. He gave no reaction to her appearance. Either he was a veteran of the night shift or he was very good at his job. The bride gave him a quick nod and then disappeared into the hotel.

Max stared after her. What had she been doing out there alone, in that dress, with the creatures of the night?

CHAPTER FIVE

He decided it wasn't a question he was going to solve. Not right now. Right now, he needed his own cold beer and then some sleep. He didn't believe in omens but this shift had put him on edge, and he wasn't one to press his luck. Three drunk college students, an alcoholic lawyer, and a bride. Sounded like the opening to an Andy Kaufman joke that most people wouldn't understand. No need to add any more players on stage. Time to call it a night. He turned the dial on the handheld radio to the off position. He'd see Terry in the office in five minutes. He wouldn't give the man another opportunity to send him off into the night.

Philadelphia Private Car Service, LLC was on the edge of an old neighborhood called Fitler's Square on the bank of the Schuylkill River and in the shadows of Route 76, the primary interstate into the city from the west.

Liam O'Brian had picked a smart and convenient location when he purchased the building and started the business in the mid-eighties. It was close to the expressway, the historical sites, downtown office buildings, and not far from the airport or the occasional trips to southern Jersey.

It was a simple, mostly corrugated sheet metal building painted bright-blue. There was a three-bay garage to the left and a short, stubby two-story building on the right that served as the office and dispatch center. The bright-blue building had become a bit of a local landmark. Liam had bought it from a bankrupt pest extermination company and didn't have the money at the time to repaint it. He removed the giant pair of plastic ants from the roof. The old company's slogan ('We send the ants marching!') eventually faded, but the electric blue paint job remained.

Max turned off Lombard and hit the button on the remote clipped to the passenger visor. The lot's security gate rolled back. He noticed a black Suburban SUV idling at the corner as he drove past, the shadows of two heads visible in the front seat behind smoked window glass. Unusual for this time of night and this street. PPCS was the only business open on this stretch after typical business hours. Max paid attention to the unusual. He drove through the gate and made sure it rattled closed behind him.

The remaining area of the PPCS lot was used for fleet and personal parking and was ringed with a chain link fence and inward-facing barbed wire arms at the top. The barbed wire was almost comical and had become a point of ribbing between the drivers and Liam in the last few months. What had once been a rundown and ragged section of Southwest Philly near the river was going through a dramatic change. The centuries-old Irish American neighborhood was being plowed under and gentrified by an expanding downtown, real estate development, and a major expansion of the nearby Children's Hospital. The hospital project was pricing working-class people out of adjacent apartments and affordable row homes, but how do you fight a hospital that treats children?

Max parked the Town Car at the end of a line of three identical cars. The current fleet was at eight, so four cars were still out doing jobs. Not bad for a Thursday night in October. Liam was making money in his sleep. If you have to work for it, that's the way to do it, Max thought. He grabbed his bag and small cooler from the passenger footwell, picked up the empty Coke bottle, and then glanced in the back seat. He almost didn't see it as it had partially slid under the seat. Maybe that was why she'd missed it herself when she got out. He knew it was from his last passenger. He'd cleaned back there after the drunk girls and another passenger would have said something earlier in the night. He stretched his arm over the seat and grabbed it.

It was a small, rectangular wooden box. Max sat back down in the driver's seat so he could see it better under the car's dome light. It was approximately two inches high, five or six inches long, and three inches wide. It was the size and shape of two paperback novels stacked on top of each other. The wood was a deep golden brown with the grain and knots showing through the lacquer stain. Simple, straight lines cut a quarter-inch deep across the box on all sides, both vertical and horizontal. Max turned it over and studied the bottom. Something shifted inside when he flipped it, but there was no obvious way to open it. No latch or lock or keyhole. He shook the box gently. There was definitely something inside. He pressed on the sides and back but found nothing helpful. No soft spots. It was solid. He studied all the sides again, moving it around in the low light to see better. On the bottom, he spotted a small, dark, dried smear in one corner. He picked at it with a fingernail and some of it flaked off. Red and a little tacky. He didn't need a lab or better light to tell him what the stain was. Max had seen plenty of blood in his day, too much, and this stain wasn't that old.

He thought about the blood dripping down the bride's neck and then slipped the box into his bag, climbed out of the car, and headed toward the dispatch office. As he pulled open the front door, he glanced up the street. The SUV was gone. Something else to think about.

The PPCS dispatch center was a glorified closet tucked into the far left corner of the first floor. He could see Terry on the phone through the open door. Two other doors lined the back wall. One went up to a pair of offices for Liam and Fiona, his wife, who did the company's books and payroll. She also handled any necessary HR functions for the company, which mostly boiled down to periodic drug tests mandated by the city and any hiring and firing decisions. She was a no-nonsense woman and most of the drivers were much more afraid of dealing with her than Liam, who was a softer touch.

The second door led to the garage and repair bays. Liam spent far more time there than up in his office behind the desk. The right corner held the single bathroom. A small kitchenette took up the rest of the right side with a microwave, refrigerator, dual coffee pot, and a sink that was always filled with Terry's week-old dirty dishes. A motley assortment of tables and chairs from the land of lost and broken furniture filled up the middle of the room. Occasional card games would break out, but it was most often used by drivers grabbing a quick bite to eat or filling out various paperwork before starting or ending their shifts.

Max sat in a cracked green leather armchair that leaked stuffing from the back and waited for Terry to finish his call so he could turn in the keys and sign out. At least, he knew that's what he should do. But his thoughts kept turning back to the bride and the box. People left many things in the cars. There was an entire drawer inside Terry's office filled with old cell phones, wallets, glasses, keys, books, and fifty other examples of the detritus people carry around in their daily lives.

He heard Terry hang up and then his chair creak as he leaned back to look out the office door. "That you, Max?"

"It's me." Max stood and walked over to the office, leaning against the doorway. Just tell Terry about the box, turn in the keys, sign off on this strange night, Max thought.

"Pulling the pin?" Terry asked. He was somewhere in his sixties with a drinker's nose and a fringe of white whiskers that covered his face and most of his pink head. His speech still carried the strong inflection of his native Galway accent, even though he'd called Philly home for over forty years.

"I think so. One of those nights. Already made my nut. Don't want to push it."

"Ah, I've been there. A wise choice. Don't tempt the banshees and the pookas, my friend. The tricksters and demons enjoy the night. Wish I'd listened to my own advice."

He pushed the big ledger book across the desk. Fiona would later translate it over to the computer, but she didn't trust Liam, Terry, or any of the drivers not to crash the time and accounting system if left on their own. Max signed his name and added the time.

Max was about to drop the keys into Terry's open, waiting palm when he stopped and asked, "How's the morning look? Busy?"

Terry frowned, then glanced back at the call board on his monitor. "Not too bad. Four scheduled at the moment. Usually pick up a couple more unscheduled."

"You think Liam would mind me keeping the car?" Liam occasionally let the guys keep one of the cars if they needed some wheels. Liam favored drivers that were new to the city, immigrants, or guys trying to get back on their feet. They rarely had a lot of extra cash for personal vehicles. Max had never had a reason to keep a ride, but he knew other drivers did it occasionally.

"You're not running jobs off the books, are you?"

"No, no, nothing like that. I was thinking of running over to Big Lots and grabbing some furniture for the apartment."

"You will not fit a sofa in the back of those Town Cars."

"Nothing that big. Just tired of using moving boxes for end tables. Little things."

Terry looked at him for a beat, then said, "Sure, I don't see why not. You know the deal, right? Fill it up before you bring it back and make sure you don't total it. Insurance doesn't cover you when you're off the clock."

Max put the keys in his pocket. "Thanks. You here tomorrow night?"

"I'll be here. I'm always here. I'm the PPCS's own leprechaun."

Max walked back outside. People left a lot of things in the cars, but usually not stained with blood. Maybe it was nothing. But maybe it was something. Maybe she needed help. Maybe Max could be that person. He'd return the box and ask her.

That would turn out to be much harder than he expected.

CHAPTER SIX

I t was the same doorman or porter, whatever they called
them at The Clyde, as before. Tall, pot-bellied, slightly
stooped, perhaps from a career of lifting luggage and
pulling open doors. It had been less than an hour since the
drop-off and Max was sure the overnight crew was bare
bones. At this hour, how many people did it take to keep a
place like The Clyde running? Three? Maybe four or five max,
depending on if the hotel offered 24-hour room service.

Had to be the same guy. Max approached the hotel doors
and tried to appear relaxed and friendly. The orange coils of
the heat lamps glowed under the short entry portico and gave
off an insect-like buzz. The guy was a decade or so older than
Max, but still showed a thick shock of dark hair under his
green and gold Pershing cap. He matched Max's smile and
gave off a vibe of solid hospitality, despite the hour which
made his lying, or sudden amnesia, even more perplexing.

"Hi, I was the guy driving the black Town Car that
dropped off the woman wearing the wedding dress about an
hour ago?"

The guy kept the smile, but his forehead creased, "Sorry?"

"You don't remember holding the door tonight for a young Latina woman wearing a dirty wedding dress?"

"No, I'm afraid not."

"I'm not looking to get anyone in trouble. I'm not a cop. I'm just a driver, like I said. I'm looking to return some property she left in my car." He held up his backpack with the box inside.

"Sir?" He spoke with a slight accented lisp.

"Are you the only doorman?"

"Yes."

Max was losing his patience. Or his sanity. It had been a long night. His eyelids felt like sandpaper. His knees and ankles were stiff. "She was wearing a goddam wedding dress."

"I'm not sure what to tell you, sir. Are you sure it was this hotel? Lots of them in this area."

"Yes, I'm sure. Are you sure you don't have an identical twin brother also working the door? Can I talk to him?"

The man didn't budge from his story. "You're welcome to talk to Miranda. She's the night manager. I believe she's inside at the front desk."

He opened the door and held it with a benign smile on his face.

Miranda was not at the front desk, but Max could see a light through the door behind the desk and heard the soft click of computer keys echoing out into the quiet, deserted lobby. From a small, discreet footprint on the outside, the first floor of The Clyde bloomed open in opulent style once you were inside. The architect had designed it to impress, and it did the job in Max's opinion. A grand staircase led up two stories to an exposed old-fashioned elevator that traveled up a further two stories before disappearing into a gold-gilded ceiling. The furnishings around the staircase were muted, but the marble and leather all spoke of buttery richness and luxury.

Max spotted the entrance to the restaurant and bar in the back right, now dark. He turned left, past an empty concierge stand to the reception desk. There was a small silver bell next to a tall vase of irises and freesias. He felt ridiculous ringing the little bell, but he did it and heard a chair push back in the office and a moment later a woman appeared in the doorway. She had on a similar uniform to the doorman, though it looked much better on her. Black blazer with small gold buttons over a starched white shirt and black pants. A name tag with 'Miranda' in a simple sans serif font was pinned to the left side over the hotel's crest. She had shoulder-length hair and thin eyebrows that framed her light blue eyes. She wore little makeup and didn't need it. She smiled and stepped up behind the desk.

"Checking in?"

Max was scruffy and haggard in comparison to Miranda and wanted to take a step back and apologize, sure she could detect the girl's urine he'd had to clean up earlier. He momentarily forgot why he was there. "Excuse me?"

She tilted her head slightly and gave him a curious look. "Are you checking in?"

Max shook his head and ran a hand through his hair. "Sorry, spaced out there for a second. Long night."

"Of course." She smiled back, still waiting.

"Uh, no, not checking in. I'm wondering about a guest." He glanced over his shoulder. The doorman stood behind the concierge kiosk near the doors. He was looking down, maybe at his phone, and didn't appear to be paying them any attention. He'd been polite, if oddly obtuse, and passed the problem on to the manager. Job done. "I'm a driver. For a local car service. A passenger left something in my car. I dropped her off here. I was hoping to return it."

"Oh, that's thoughtful. What was the passenger's name?"

"I don't know. She didn't give a name."

"Hmm. That makes it more difficult."

"I dropped her off less than an hour ago. Right outside. She was alone and wearing a wedding dress."

The woman frowned and tilted her head again, this time to the other side. "A wedding dress?"

"Yes, she was quite memorable."

"Gabriel wasn't able to help you?"

"He's the doorman?"

"Yes."

"No, he couldn't help. He says he doesn't remember anyone like that coming into the hotel."

"Huh. Gabe is very reliable."

"You didn't see her either?"

"No, I'm sorry." She caught his expression. "But I probably wouldn't notice an elephant walking through unless it rang the bell." She smiled in sympathy, but it was clear that she thought he was mistaken. He didn't blame her. She knew Gabe, probably trusted him, and if he didn't see this person, how likely was it to have happened? It was all so bizarre. Why deny all of it? Max couldn't figure it. "It's likely I was back in the office." Miranda continued, "Unless a guest needs something or rings the bell, I spend most of my time back there during night shifts. Would you like to leave the property here?"

Max didn't think that was a good idea. Something told him to hold onto the box. "No, that's all right. Could I leave a card? In case she shows up and asks."

"Sure, that's a good idea. I'll leave a note for the day shift as well."

He pulled two slightly battered cards from his wallet, clients occasionally asked for them, even though the information was easily looked up on a phone or computer. "I'll put my cell phone on the back. Might be faster than calling the main number." He put the first one on the cream and marble check-in counter. He handed the second one to Gabe as he left. "In case your memory comes back."

"Of course, sir."

Max returned to the car and sat for a moment. The entire exchange felt surreal and left him confused. He rubbed at the grit in his eyes and zippered open the backpack. The box was still inside. He wasn't crazy. It existed. It had happened.

He could see Gabe looking out through the doors at him. Max put the car in gear and drove off. He was tired, but he wasn't ready to give up on The Clyde for the night. He didn't like to be played for a fool. He followed the series of one-way downtown streets until he could loop back around behind the hotel. But he soon learned the hotel only took up half the block. The back half was a financial company. He drove down a connecting street until he came to an alleyway splitting the block. Blue and green dumpsters, smaller overflow trash and linen bins, exhaust pipes, and scattered homeless encampments cluttered the narrow space.

He parked the car on the street with a view of the alley's opening. He hoped someone from the hotel would come out. A cook. A maid. Some other service personnel. Max wasn't sure who else worked overnight in a hotel. Someone else might know the bride and be more forthcoming.

Max sat and alternated between checking the alley and checking the street. Philly was a working-class city. The sidewalks, streets, and buildings were mostly old, nicked up, and cracked, but it wore it all with fierce pride. He liked that. He'd only been here six weeks, but he identified with the city's underdog spirit. It had a similar pugnaciousness to his hometown of Boston, but without the blue blood entitlement that sometimes crept into Beantown. Right now, everything was quiet. No one in the alley. No one on the street. Even the most dedicated hustlers were asleep.

He pulled out his phone. His friend Lawrence had set him up with it and anytime they talked, he still gave Max crap about using it mostly to listen to music and watch NHL highlights.

"You've got a pocket-sized computer in your pocket and you use it like it's a Canadian Walkman from 1985."

"I make calls, too."

"Fine. A Walkman and a cordless phone. Congrats, you've time-traveled to 1992. Would you like some Crystal Pepsi?"

Lawrence was only half-joking. Max used it for a little more than just music and calls, but not much. When he wasn't driving, he spent most of his free time reading in his apartment or working out at the nearby boxing gym. He was okay with that. It was a quiet life. And he liked it most of the time. He wasn't looking for more distractions or more connections through a phone or a computer.

He did like the ability to call up any music he might want to listen to. He might have left Prince Edward Island and Canada behind, but he had picked up an unexpected appreciation for French pop music. His friend Mose had occasionally put it on when they were working on an old Chevy pickup in his yard, and it sort of worked its way into his brain. The phone showed a strong signal in the middle of the city and he was quickly able to get the streaming music for a Quebec radio station playing on his phone. While he couldn't speak a word of French, he thought the best songs were musically intricate yet kept a mood of nostalgia or longing. He didn't need to understand the words.

He listened to the music, waited thirty minutes more, but still saw no one. Everybody and everything was stubbornly asleep. When his own eyelids started drifting down, he got out of the car and stood for a moment to let the crisp air revive him. He walked into the alley. He wasn't even sure The Clyde had doors back here. They might have a place to receive deliveries on one of the side streets. If he came back to watch again, it would be good to check now so he didn't waste more time.

The alley stank like every alley Max had ever set foot in: spoiled food, standing water, urine, and wet cardboard. He passed two homeless people sleeping underneath the warm steam of an exhaust pipe. If Max disturbed them, they didn't show it. He walked halfway down the alley until he found a line of six trash bins and two brown steel doors with the name and address of the hotel stamped in white paint in a rough block font. There was a lock inset on each but no handle for the doors. He couldn't think of anything else to do. He knew now that The Clyde had a delivery slip and trash pickup in the alley. Shouldn't take too long during normal business hours to find someone coming out one of those doors. He walked farther down the alley, but there were no more doors for the hotel.

Like a lot of kids growing up in Boston, Max played hockey as a kid. He was good. The coaches and other players often marveled at Max's sixth sense to know where his teammates and the puck were going to end up. That anticipation and uncanny sense to see a few seconds into the future was his biggest talent, and for a long time it allowed him to compete against bigger, stronger, and more physically gifted players. Eventually, it wasn't enough to compensate and he gave up the sport. But he never quite lost that skill. And it saved him now.

He sensed the movement before he saw it. A rustling disturbance of the air at his back. He twisted sideways. Not enough to avoid the blow altogether, but enough to save him from a nasty concussion, or worse. He took the brunt of the impact on his shoulder. The sharp impact on his deltoid ran down his arm and paralyzed the right side of his body. A follow-up kick to his ribs blew the air out of his lungs and knocked him down. He scrambled to get up but couldn't get any leverage with his numb arm. He rolled to his knees when another kick to his side put him flat on the ground again, with pain radiating through his lower back and up to his chest. A knee pressed on his back and hands lightly moved over his body, checking his pockets. He tried to crane his head around to see his attacker but couldn't. He caught the scent of something vaguely familiar, not more garbage, not from the alley, but it slipped away. Then there was nothing but a soft emptiness.

He woke up with a jolt and immediately regretted trying to move. He laid his head back down on the pavement and took a moment to move his fingers and toes. He gingerly pushed up onto all fours and paused again as he scanned the damage to his body. His right side was tingling with pins and needles, but the numbness was fading. He got to his feet and his head swam. The dumpsters started sliding sideways, and he thought he was going back down, but then they shifted back in the other direction. He was reminded of standing on the deck of *The Miss Ashely* in rough weather off PEI. His ribs and lower back pulsed where he'd been kicked. He knew those spots would get worse in the morning. When the ground stopped swaying and the building walls stayed upright, he hobbled back to his car. He had to stop once and dry heave, but he eventually made it. He checked his pockets and was relieved to find the car keys still there. He checked his other pockets. His wallet was still there. He flipped through it. ID, money, bank card. He'd left the phone in the car. He'd been jumped but not mugged.

CHAPTER SEVEN

L eonard Ross sat behind and to the left of Deke in a cheap folding chair against thin, warped wood paneling that was likely older than he was. He fidgeted in his seat, picking at the weave of his pants, and tried not to rip his collared shirt and tie off. There were four of them crammed in the small back room of Watts's campaign offices on the corner of 22nd and Tasker. Watts, his chief of staff and primary hatchet man, Michael Youngblood, Deke, and himself.

The room was stuffy. A drop of sweat ran down his back. It wasn't the first. The sweet sauce of the spareribs from the King Wok takeout restaurant next door leeched through the walls. Deke said something, and Leonard realized he'd lost the thread of the conversation again. He tried to tune back in.

"Look, all I'm asking is for a fair shake when the contracts and licenses come up for the parcel on the west side of 76 next year," Deke said.

Watts nodded along, but even Leonard could hear the

careful tap dancing. "Of course, of course. You understand, I can't guarantee anything. Right? This isn't a rubber stamp. It will have to go through the committee and you need to see it from their perspective."

"What's that mean?"

Watts dropped the smile a few notches. "That means, Deacon, that you have a history and a reputation. People know your name. Whether or not you like it, that will be a consideration. You can't hide from that."

"I'm not trying to hide. I'm asking people to check the numbers. Our financing and cash flow are in order. You can get the goddam FBI to go through the books. I've got nothing to hide there."

"Okay, okay." Watts held up his hands in what looked like a practiced stump speech gesture. "No need to get heated. I know you and I know what you've been doing recently. I'm just saying reputations fade slowly. One coat of paint doesn't cover up the graffiti on a subway car. It takes time. You need to be patient."

Leonard knew Deke would not like that comparison, and he watched his friend stiffen and sit forward. "That's why I'm here, Curtis. You're another coat of paint. You are going to vouch for me, and I am going to deliver the votes from Gray's Ferry. Do you know what also happens to subway cars? Besides the paint job? They get old and breakdown. A newer model comes along and replaces it. I know you're up on Walters, but it's close. Closest it's been in years. Bet you weren't expecting that."

Youngblood jumped in. "No reason for threats. We can keep it civil."

Deke sat back. "Good. Glad to hear it. And that wasn't a threat."

Leonard enjoyed seeing Deke let out some of that old fire.

In Leonard's opinion, it didn't happen often enough anymore. And it still had an impact. Leonard watched Watts and Youngblood digest everything Deke had said and didn't say and reach a decision.

"I'm sure we can come to a mutually beneficial understanding," Watts said.

The tension in the room dropped back a few notches and the conversation continued into the current council makeup and how best to curry favor and votes when the time came. Leonard drifted off again. Politics bored him. He wasn't the type to sit still in a chair. He pushed his short legs out in front of him, then pulled them back in. He couldn't get comfortable and the temperature in the small room kept rising. He felt like an animal in the zoo. He wiped the damp from his brow and over his top lip. He glanced at Deke as he talked. As cool as a cucumber and as dry as the desert. The man gave no sign of wanting to be anywhere else. He probably didn't. Deke's gift had always been to first find a way to fit in and then rise up and stand out in any situation.

If you glossed over a few chapters, Deacon James would be a Southeast Philly success story. His father was killed when he was three and his mother raised him on her own in the Ferry Estates. Leonard knew Deke's mom had more interest in pills and liquor than Deke and that he'd mostly raised himself, but the story Deke spun now played better with the single mom angle. He was an academic and three-sport star at West Philly High, liked by just about everyone. He had his pick of scholarships when he graduated but stayed local, going to UPenn for both undergraduate and later returning for an MBA. And the whole time he was building up, consolidating, and running a drug organization that sprawled over most of south Philadelphia. He took perfect advantage of all the brainpower and all that charisma to dance circles around law enforcement and the few competitors who tried to step up. And the few times that he couldn't outsmart them? Well, that's why he had his friend Len.

Leonard had made it halfway through ninth grade and when the coach cut him from the basketball team, he decided school wasn't worth the effort anymore. He wasn't a dumb man. You didn't survive this long, in this neighborhood, without some intelligence. He just wasn't school smart or book smart, whatever you wanted to call it, like Deke. What had the juvenile counselor said? He had a propensity to reach for violence as his first instinct in solving a problem. And hell, that man had been right. Len preferred being on the move, on the make. He enjoyed being out on the streets. He liked the action and the energy and using his fists. That's what felt right to him. That was when he felt most like himself. The streets were his natural habitat.

He glanced up. The other three men were standing, shaking hands and exchanging plastic smiles, all teeth and no meaning. Leonard stood, relieved to have the meeting over. No one offered to shake his hand, and he followed Deke out of the office and down a hallway to the back door. Leonard hadn't liked that when they arrived.

"We're sneaking around like a couple of bitches."

But Deke had shaken it off like Leonard knew he would. "Save that righteousness for something that matters, Len. No reason for everyone to know we've got Watts in our pocket yet. We'll own the whole goddam block next year and we'll walk in the front door to pick up the rent check. I'll insist Watts hand it over personally."

They pushed out the building's rear door, the hinges screamed, and stepped into the alley that ran behind the short business block. The narrow space stank of rotting produce and fry oil from the Chinese restaurant. Cherry was waiting, leaning against the back panel of the car. Leonard wondered how the big man could stand the stench, but he gave no indication that it bothered him. Or that he even noticed. Cherry had been with Deke almost as long as Leonard, and the man remained mostly an enigma. Leonard knew he could eat two large pizzas by himself. He also liked video games, classic comics, and good weed. He still lived with his mother in their public housing apartment where he'd grown up. He didn't drink and he didn't do small talk. Everything else was a mystery.

He opened the door as they approached. Deke climbed in first, then Leonard, and Cherry shut the door. The air inside was blessedly cool and the stink of fetid food receded. Leonard yanked off his tie and undid the first three buttons on his shirt. He felt like he could breathe for the first time in an hour.

Deke glanced at the clip-on tie. "Gonna have to teach you to wear a proper tie at some point. You're not six anymore."

"Fuck that. I don't mind being the heavy and watching your back in a couple of meetings, but we gotta figure out a different uniform."

Deke shook his head, but he was smiling. "If you want to be in the game, you gotta wear the uniform." He smoothed his blue silk tie as if to underline the point.

Leonard wanted to be in the game, he just wasn't sure if it was the same game Deke wanted to play. After leading his double life and getting away with it for almost fifteen years, Deke now wanted to go legit and had spent the last two years laying the groundwork for what he called his next act. The one where he didn't need to go in any back doors and didn't need to buy up strip mall businesses just to launder drug money. The one where he'd spend all his days in a suit and tie. The one he assumed Leonard wanted, too.

Deke was trying to get his people off the streets. As part of the groundwork for his next act, he'd started offering members investment opportunities. A way to earn that didn't involve drugs or dodging bullets. Len knew most of the guys thought it was crazy, but some had signed up out of loyalty to Deke. And you know what? Deke delivered. He started cutting dividend checks. And it didn't make a damn lick of difference. Sure, the guys were happy to get it, but it changed nothing. The checks were just a new income stream, and they spent it on the same things they always did: clothes, cars, guns, and more drugs.

"Might work for you, but if there's trouble, that tie could hang you. Literally." Len flicked the small metal clip. "Someone tries to strangle me with his, they're going to get a surprise."

Deke gave him a glance. That's right, I might be just a little smarter than you realize, Len thought.

"Take us on the tour, Cherry," Deke said.

They inched out of the alley and waited for a city bus to pass, then took the one-way Tasker west before doubling back and heading south on 23rd Street. It wasn't the major thorough-fare through Southwest Philly. It was a tight one-way street bordered on each side by aging brick row homes, but it was arguably the most well-known to the residents. It was certainly the bloodiest. For decades, small rival street gangs had been killing each other with 23rd being the arbitrary dividing line. Most of the killings now were just an endless cycle of retribution. Whatever reason had kicked up the initial turf war had been forgotten. Deke's father was one early casualty. It rarely interfered with Deke's businesses, most of the gangs were just loose groups of rival teenagers, but it was the one piece of messy business that Deke wanted to end before he jumped into that bloodless second act.

"Any news from Bishop?"

Bishop Allen was the leader, or at least the current public face, of the faction east of 23rd. Deke had been trying to reach out and find some way to parlay with the kid and hash out a resolution to end the shootings. So far, each polite inquiry had been met with sneering disdain. Deke was trying to remain patient, but the fact that he'd sent Leonard to deliver the last message was a message itself. Deacon James's patience only extended so far.

"No, not yet, but I got with his boy Scootch last night. I know Bishop got the message."

"All right."

"You want me to push it?"

Deke looked at him. They both knew what he meant by push it. It was what Leonard did best. Leonard was a battering ram. He didn't think Deke was there yet and wasn't surprised when he shook his head.

"No, give him a day."

But he was getting close. Leonard said nothing else, just closed his fists until the skin was stretched tight over his scarred knuckles.

They crossed Point Breeze Avenue and Cherry steered the car smoothly through the intersection and kept going south until they neared Passyunk, the unofficial border of Deke's little kingdom. Leonard could see the bright blue cinder block building that everyone used as a landmark just under the shadows of Route 76. Cherry turned down Snyder and then weaved his way back north on 30th. Leonard looked at the cars flowing past them on 76 and wondered where everyone was going. He'd never been out of Philly. He'd barely been out of Gray's Ferry. Was he missing out? Was there something better waiting for him out there? Did he just need the courage to go get it? He didn't know but anytime he tried to stretch his mind beyond the neighborhood the world loomed up and the sheer size of it, the vastness, was too big to comprehend and he always retreated.

He was a battering ram, a tool with a purpose but limited use.

CHAPTER EIGHT

He woke up blinking in the late morning light and thinking about the bride. He'd come home, swallowed six aspirin, and fell into bed. He didn't dream, and he was thankful for that. He reached out and took his phone off the nightstand. No texts or voicemails. Not surprising, but he thought if Miranda had passed on his message that someone on the day shift might have gotten in touch. No luck. He put the phone down and picked up the strange wooden box. Like everything else, the box kept generating more questions than answers.

He scrutinized it, now in the bright sunshine instead of the dim car's interior. He spotted nothing new. It was a wooden box with a concealed way to open it. He thought it was old, but he didn't know that for sure. It was a gut reaction, something about the wood. It felt like it carried the weight of time in the twisting grains. There were no other markings beyond the crisscrossing cuts. He tried pressing various squares, but nothing moved.

He gave up and put the box aside. He had more pressing

issues. He sat up and winced at the pain that lanced across his lower back. He took a deep breath. No additional pain. He probed his side carefully with his fingers and while it hurt, and would eventually produce a helluva bruise, he didn't think the attack had broken any ribs. He raised his right arm over his head. His shoulder was stiff and sore, but again, not broken. He'd been lucky. He'd recently recovered from a concussion and it wasn't a pleasant experience. He didn't think a second one in three months would be any better. He'd trade a week of sore muscles and a stiff back to avoid a head injury. He stood. No dizziness. Another positive. There was one last thing to check. He limped into the bathroom. There was no blood in his urine. He didn't relish the thought of spending a day at emergency care getting scanned for internal bleeding and filing a police report on the assault. His day was already improving.

He stood under the shower nozzle until the water had scorched his skin to a medium-rare and loosened up his lower back. He toweled off, swallowed more aspirin, dressed, and grabbed his gym bag from the floor near the door. Given his current state, working out might not be the best idea, but he was afraid if he sat down for any length of time, he would stiffen back up. Once in motion, best to keep in motion.

Ronnie Shelton's RSG Elite Boxing was across the street from Max's apartment. It was on the second floor of an old mill building that was now divided up into different spaces for different businesses. In addition to Ronnie's gym, the tenant directory on the hand-painted sign out front listed an Asian import/export company, a fine arts photography studio, a commercial real estate office, a hair and nail salon, a holistic psychotherapist, and a law office. It made for an eclectic clientele, and Max thought it summed up the scruffy, mixed-up little neighborhood.

The first night in his new apartment, he'd left the window open and he woke up like he was lying on a slab in a morgue. The morning wind whipped in off the Schuylkill with an angry bite. He was shivering under his thin blanket, his breath visibly puffing out like an SOS signal. He'd closed the window, but not before he heard music, shouting, and the angry slap of skin on skin. He tracked the sounds to the open windows across the street. Not skin, leather. He could see people boxing, sweating, and working out. He'd grabbed his jacket and returned to bed. But the next day he wandered over to the gym and met Ronnie.

Ronnie Shelton was a retired cornerman/cutman who had been in the fight game for half a century and had trained up many useless lumps to world champs. Or they would have been world champs if they'd just listened to Ronnie. Ronnie could be anywhere between sixty-five and ninety-five. He was whippet thin. Five-foot-six and shrinking. Even in his prime, he would have struggled to make it as a bantamweight. He had a short fringe of graying hair framing a flat nose and bent ears. Max wasn't sure how many champs, or even pros, Ronnie had worked with, but his face didn't lie. The man had been in the fight game for a long time.

He'd looked Max over the first day and asked, "Why you wanna fight?"

"I don't want to fight, but if I have to, I want to be the guy standing at the end."

"Hmmph." He reached out a bony hand and pinched Max's waist. "Could lose a few pounds, too."

Max didn't disagree. After the damage to his lungs from dealing with Carter and then his concussion up in Prince Edward Island, he'd gotten a little soft while he let his body heal up. "That too."

"You ever been in a fight?"

"Played hockey growing up."

"Hmmph." Max would quickly come to learn that this was Ronnie's default pejorative. "So, you shoved guys around while wearing figure skates." But his eyes sparked.

"Something like that."

"Better than those guys that think they're MMA fighters because they watched the *Karate Kid* on TV." He pointed to a door in the corner. "Showers and lockers over there. Go change up and let's see if you can last an hour with me."

Max had lasted the hour. Barely. Ronnie's orientation was designed to get the weak and the pretenders out the door before they wasted more of each other's time. Jumping rope, squats, push-ups, crunches, a three-mile run, then shadow boxing, and then time on the heavy bag. Then repeat it all. In the end, Max's shirt, shorts, and shoes were soaked with sweat and he couldn't lift his arms. But he was still standing.

"Not bad. Fifty bucks a month gets you three workouts a week to start. Sound good?"

Max wasn't sure if he could take three workouts like that each week, but he agreed and so far he hadn't missed one.

He walked in today carrying his bag and trying not to show all his aches, but he didn't fool the old man. Ronnie eyed him up from across the room then called out, "Why are you walking like my momma the morning after a Saturday night at the Downbeat?"

Max tried to deflect. "I didn't know your momma was into jazz?"

"She wasn't. She was into drinking, and dancing, and traveling horn sections. Can you play the trumpet?"

"No sir."

"Then you're safe."

"She sounds like quite a woman."

"She's been dead for thirty years, but if she was alive, she'd agree. Terrible mother, quite a woman." The old man cackled as he walked up to Max. He shrugged. "She didn't do any permanent damage. Now, those nuns at St. Catherine's? Those hellhounds will keep chasing me to my grave."

"I might not be a brass man, but I can relate to the horrors of a Catholic school education."

"Stop trying to distract me, boy." He poked a finger into Max's side and Max winced. "I knew it. I've spent years watching men get hit in the ring and try to hide how much it hurts. You ain't special and you ain't very good at it. Now, what happened?"

Max told him the story of getting jumped behind The Clyde.

Ronnie was shaking his head by the end. "I knew a couple of guys worked at The Clyde back in the eighties. Not sure I know anyone up there now."

"I don't think it had anything to do with the hotel."

"You sure?"

Max thought about it. He wasn't sure. If it was connected to his questioning of Gabe and Miranda, it was an awfully fast response. "I don't think so. I think I was just stupid and let my guard down and someone tried to mug me." But they hadn't, he thought. Someone had knocked him senseless, searched him, and then left him. Why? "Then got interrupted halfway through the job. Or distracted. I don't know."

"Probably hoping you were carrying," Ronnie said, providing as good an answer as any.

"Right downtown there? Thought that was all up in the northeast. In Kensington." PPCS didn't get many calls up there, but Max read the papers and watched the news. Kensington was ground zero for drugs in Philadelphia.

"You buying that badlands crap? Sure, it's in Kensington and everywhere else, man. Creeping into all the neighborhoods like an invasive weed. Can't keep it out. Used to be I could count on thirty or forty kids in here after school or on the weekends. Now? I'm lucky if I need two hands to count them all. Too much easy money and easy addiction. Hmmph! Don't get me started. Doc says I gotta watch my heart, so I'm gonna accept the story that you got sucker punched and rolled in an alley and not that you got your clock cleaned in something as pedestrian as a bar fight. That would just be an insult to my tutelage. Go change up and I'll think about going easy on you today."

Max usually headed into work around six and would sleep until close to noon, so he never saw many other people in the gym. He assumed early mornings or early evenings were the peak times. One exception was a young black kid who was there so much Max assumed for a long time that he worked there or slept under the ring at night. He was thirteen or fourteen if Max had to guess, with the hard chiseled arms and chest of a man but the softer cheeks and jaws of a kid. He'd come in while Max was talking to Ronnie and was warming up with the jump rope, skipping clean and fast. He gave Max a nod as Max walked into the locker rooms.

The Skyline Diner was not in the old mill with the gym but just next door in a prefab rectangle with dented and dull chrome edging. The entire structure collectively leaned slightly to the left. Inside, three cracked vinyl booths lined the windows that fronted the street. There were eight stools along a counter in front of a hulking flat top griddle. Regulars got their choice of the stools. Sherrod worked the griddle and his wife, Nia, worked the floor. Sherrod was a goddam wizard with breakfast food and burgers. Max wasn't sure how The Skyline passed inspection and stayed open, but they had the best fried egg and scrapple sandwich that Max had found inside the city limits.

Scrapple was a strange and indigenous food to the Philly area. A mix of meat, usually pork, but sometimes deer or rabbit if a restaurant got creative, plus spices, and cornmeal. Originally brought over by Dutch settlers, it stuck, though it didn't exactly take off across the rest of the country. It was an acquired taste but sandwiched between slices of wheat toast, cheddar cheese, and eggs, he'd found it an excellent recovery food after Ronnie's lung-melting workouts. The Skyline served breakfast all day, and it had become his Friday ritual and reward for making it through another week in one piece.

He had finished the sandwich, not feeling the least bit guilty after the 'easy' workout that Ronnie had put him through and had accepted a second refill of coffee from Nia when his phone rang. He received so few calls that it rang five times before he realized the sound was coming from his pocket. Nia's eyes burned into him from across the room. She did not like cell phones in her restaurant. He pulled it out, quickly silenced it, and looked at the number. It wasn't Lawrence or the community phone Mose used to call him occasionally. He had a quick pang of regret. Mose had left a message earlier in the week and Max hadn't returned his call yet. He pushed the emotion aside. It could be the day manager at The Clyde. He'd risk Nia's wrath to find out. He swiped to accept.

"Hello?"

"Stop asking about me."

She didn't need to introduce herself, and he didn't need to ask.

"I've got your box. It fell out of your bag. It was in the back seat."

There was a pause. "Leave it with Gabriel. Then forget about me."

"I can help."

But she was already gone.

Back at his apartment, he picked up the box again and turned it over in his hands. Why couldn't he let it go? Just take the box back to the hotel and hand it off to Gabriel as she had asked. He didn't even need to get out of the car. He could roll down the window and be done with it. He looked at the dried splotch of blood on the bottom. The woman in his car the previous night had looked calm. She hadn't looked scared, though she looked tired. More than tired. Exhausted. He thought about the drops of blood and dirt on the white dress. She looked like a woman running out of ideas. And running out of time.

He took out his phone and hit redial from the call log. There was a pause, then it connected. He let it ring ten, twenty times and then disconnected. No voicemail. Likely a disposable phone. Maybe bought just to call him. Or perhaps bought for some other purpose, but not one where you'd need to get messages. He waited five minutes and tried again. Same result.

He took his sweaty workout clothes and the other assorted laundry from the week down into the basement where there were washers and dryers for use. He separated the lights and darks and then paused over the T-shirt he'd worn last night. There was a tear in the side and a small, dark stain. He fit a finger through the hole. Something dark uncoiled inside him and warmed his blood.

Maybe getting jumped in the alley wasn't connected to his visit to the hotel. Maybe it was all a coincidence. A painful lesson learned in a dark alley. Maybe she didn't need help. Maybe he was just getting in the way. Making things harder.

Maybe it was a mistake to get involved.

He closed the lid on the washer and tossed the T-shirt in the trash. He'd return the box, but he thought he'd earned a few answers of his own.

Mistakes always did feel pretty good.

CHAPTER NINE

After finishing the laundry and cleaning his already spartan apartment, he decided to just go to work early and pick up a couple of extra fares or, if there were no reservations on the book, use the time to drop by and see Gabriel. See if his memory had improved at all with some sleep.

Normally, he'd read in the afternoon or walk down to the Queens branch of the Philly library or stop by a local bookstore to see if they had any new pulps in stock. Today, after Ronnie's workout, he wasn't up for walking and if he was just going to sit and stiffen up, he might as well be earning some money.

He took a folded white T-shirt out of his dresser, took a clean no-iron white shirt off a hanger from the closet, and slipped into one of his two pairs of black pants. Liam's only request for drivers was clean-shaven, white top, dark pants. That was it in terms of expectations or dress code. Max didn't have an issue with it. He thought it was a fair trade-off for the loose oversight and flexibility that came with the rest of the job.

He made two turkey sandwiches with spicy mustard for dinner, put them in his cooler, then added an apple and two cans of Coke. He chewed four more aspirin, grimacing against the bitter tang of the acid, and then threw the rest of the bottle into his bag along with his latest paperback, *Police at the Funeral* by Margery Allingham, one of the rare Golden Age mysteries written by a woman.

Finally, he wrapped the mystery box in a dishtowel and put that in his bag before zipping it up, grabbing the cooler, and locking his door.

Unlike his last stop on Prince Edward Island, where seasons changed slowly with a largesse that matched the easygoing attitude of the population, Philly was much closer to Boston. Spring and summer might drip in slowly but fall snapped shut like a trap. The day had been bright and sunny, but the air had a bite and as the sun dipped and shadows grew, people were pulling their lightweight coats tight and hustling to their destinations.

Max guided the Town Car into the lot and its assigned space and headed for the front door. The two men coming out the front door of PPCS looked like a matched set and Max had to look twice to make sure they weren't twins. Each man stood about five-seven with all the lift that their clean white sneakers could provide. Unmoved by the temperature, they wore identical plain T-shirts with stiffly starched jeans and long, colored cloth belts around their waists. They each had thick, curly black hair and a wisp of a goatee covering their chins. The same hair and clothes, but not identical. One was missing half his left ear. The other had a long scar from the back of his jaw wrapping around to the middle of his throat.

As he passed them, it was like tuning into a shared

frequency. They were young, barely into their twenties, but their eyes were twice as old. They were dangerous. They had earned those scars. They had each likely killed. Max could see the mirrored recognition as their eyes passed over him. Max stopped by the door and watched them walk out the open gate and get into a black SUV parked in front of a hydrant. The same car as the previous night? Max couldn't be sure, but he thought it might be.

Inside, the typically boisterous office area was almost silent. No laughter or banter. No hustling card games with shouted taunts and insults. The only sounds were men chewing, eyes downcast, or the rustle of papers or pages being turned. The atmosphere was tense and brittle. No one was looking at each other.

Then everyone turned to stare at him and then just as quickly they looked away again as if ashamed or caught doing something embarrassing. Max was still new and worked the night shift. He recognized a few faces, but he had no real friends or even acquaintances here. He walked through the room to the dispatch office in the back. Carlee was behind the desk. She ran the day shift until Terry came on at six.

"What happened? It's like a funeral in there." Max asked, even though it didn't take a genius to figure it out, but he wanted to hear what Carlee said.

She shrugged. "None of my business. Two guys came in and went up to see Liam. All I know." She found something interesting to read on the call screen.

Carlee had been with Liam from almost the beginning. She'd chain-smoked her way through three boys, single motherhood, and 12-hour shifts. Her voice sounded like a steel brush on dirty grill grates. She didn't spook easily, but she was scared now. She was tight with Fiona as the only other woman in the office, and Max was sure she knew more than she was telling. He let it go for now.

"Wondering if you could get a number for me? A call last night, late, around four."

She seemed relieved Max had changed the subject. "Was she good-looking?"

"Huh?"

"The only time guys come in here asking for a number is because they want to cook up some excuse to call the fare and try to finagle a date."

"Oh, no, that's not it. Something fell out of her bag last night and it looks valuable. I thought I'd try to call and arrange a way to return it."

Carlee gave a smile that said she wasn't buying his story, but she also turned to the screen and clicked a few buttons. "At 4:17 a.m.? Pick up on Ellsworth? Huh, no name. That's interesting, but probably few people waiting at that time of night. Sound right?"

"That's the one. I took her up to The Clyde."

She grabbed a scrap of paper and jotted down the number and handed it to Max. "Good luck."

He looked at the slip of paper. It was the same number she'd called him from that afternoon. He'd been hoping for a different number. Some other way of tracking her down.

"Any problems with the payment?"

Carlee frowned at the follow-up question but glanced back at her screen. "If she's got a room at The Clyde, I doubt it. Yeah, no issues, right through on a Visa."

"Thanks." He didn't ask for the card number. She wouldn't give it to him, and it would only raise her suspicions higher than they were. If he needed it, he could get it another way.

Outside the dispatch office, the noise was returning, like a tide slowly creeping back up the shore. If you walked in now, you might pick up that something was a little off, maybe two guys got into a beef over cards or a scheduled fare, but you'd most likely forget about it after ten seconds, like adjusting to a foul smell. Nothing like the nervous fear that had draped the room ten minutes prior.

Max took the stairs and knocked on the door to Liam's office.

"Come in."

"Hey, boss."

Liam was a big, square man who had spread as he aged. He was now more a polygon than a square. He had a mashed nose and clipped ears. He let his white hair grow long to cover up his ears. A mechanic and tinkerer at heart, he still retained the thick forearms and shoulders from a lifetime of squeeze wrenches and tightening clamps. His handshake was like a vise.

"Hi, Max."

"Just wanted to say thanks for letting me keep a car last night. Made the day a lot easier."

Liam waved him off. "Not a problem as long as it doesn't get in the way of business. Happy to help. Get what you needed?"

"Yes."

"Good." He flipped the parts catalog closed and put it aside and grabbed the remaining stack of yesterday's mail that was rubber-banded together on the corner of his desk. The tops of the envelopes were already sliced open. Fiona paid the bills, but Liam liked to check the invoices. It made him feel more involved now that he wasn't driving or working on the cars as much. "A life of leisure doesn't suit men like my husband," Fiona had told him once.

He flicked his eyes up at Max as he sorted through the envelopes. "Anything else?"

"Saw those two guys leaving as I was coming in." He

paused. Liam put down the stack of bills but said nothing. Max continued, "Didn't look like they were applying for jobs."

"They weren't."

"Anything I can do?"

"No. Not your problem and not the first time guys like that have come through my office. I'm getting old so maybe it will be the last, but I doubt it."

"Racket as old as time, huh?"

"Something like that."

Max knocked on the wood frame. "All right then. Let me know if you change your mind."

"Thanks, Max. But this too shall pass, as they say."

Max moved down the stairs thinking about the unfamiliar emotion he'd seen in his boss's eyes, a shakiness that belied his gruff words. Every fighter thinks he can answer the next bell until the round that he can't.

It was after five when he came back down the stairs into the common room. Most of the drivers had departed. There were no set hours. That was part of what made the job appealing, especially as a second job. The flexible hours could paper over other gaps in a patchwork schedule to make ends meet. Max was one of the lucky few where this was his only gig. He knew everyone else was hustling daily to cover rent, health insurance, alimony, child support, or just food and gas. When you signed on, you let Fiona know your hour prefer- ences. The dispatchers parceled out any advanced bookings based on seniority and preference. Being new, Max was near the bottom of the list, but he didn't mind. Cash wasn't a priority. This job was about staying busy and keeping other thoughts at bay.

As he walked toward the door, he heard Carlee call out to him.

"Yes?" He stopped and turned.

"Late-breaking airport pickup at 5:45 with a run out to Conshohocken. If you hustle, you can make it. You want it?"

"Sure, I'll take it."

"I'll send the details to your phone."

An hour later, he was second-guessing his decision and getting a reminder of why he preferred driving in the middle of the night. He was jammed up in bumper-to-bumper traffic at the tail end of rush hour, and what would normally be a half-hour run up 476 was looking like it would take at least an hour. Thankfully, he was not stuck in the car with intoxicated, incontinent college girls but a middle-aged businessman who kept his head down poking at his phone.

Inching along four feet at a time, his mind kept slipping back to the previous night. The dead of night pickup at the St. Cascia shrine. The blood-speckled wedding gown. The box. Fresh blood on her neck. The Clyde. Gabriel the doorman developing convenient amnesia. And then the alley.

A mile later, Max inched past a two-car fender-bender north of Swarthmore where Route 1 crossed 476. A red Dodge Ram rear-ended an older model maroon Saab. Two men were standing among the shattered brake light glass and crumpled bumpers yelling at each other. No police were yet on the scene and Max thought if they didn't arrive soon they would have an assault to deal with and the traffic accident. Max hit the gas and settled back into his seat as the road opened up.

Getting jumped in that alley. He was embarrassed at that memory. He thought of himself as careful and calculating. His free hand drifted to the sore spot on his ribs. He'd blundered into that alley and never saw the attack coming until it was too late to do anything but try to cover up and survive. Just a random incident like he'd told Ronnie? The laws of averages and crime statistics catching up to him in America's fifth largest city? Or something more deliberate?

Then, the bride's call this morning warning him to back off and forget it.

So why wasn't he listening to her? Why was he still carrying around the box? She was an adult. She didn't need to be saved, especially by a strange limo driver. She could make her own decisions. He thought of her sitting in the back of his car, her face turned and looking out the window. He wasn't letting it go because he knew that look. She might be good at hiding it, but this was someone on or right near the edge. Max knew he'd at least partly blame himself if he walked away now and later found out something had happened to her. This was what he did. The new life he'd set out for himself. It was how he kept the ghosts quiet. He tried to help and in some small way make amends and balance all the wrong choices he'd made in the past.

He slammed on the brakes and veered slightly left into the breakdown lane and just missed clipping a white Pathfinder that had stopped in front of him. Traffic had backed up again, and he'd been so deep in his head he'd missed it. The passenger's phone in the back had flown out of his hand and he'd been slammed against the seatbelt from the sudden stop.

Max reached across to the passenger footwell and retrieved it. "Sorry," he said as he handed it back.

The guy nodded and took the phone but said nothing.

Max forced any more thoughts about the woman, the box, or the alley from his mind and stayed focused on what was in front of him. The rest of the trip passed without incident. For now, at least. If the guy was a regular customer, he might complain. Or, if he used the PPCS app to schedule, there was a way to rate your driver and experience. Max wasn't sure if Liam or Fiona did anything with the information or ratings, but he didn't like the idea that his carelessness had almost cost him. A hot spur burned in his gut and he clenched the steering wheel tight until it began to bend. He'd avoided an accident. But barely. Careless and stupid. An accident meant police, and police meant incident reports and personal information. He couldn't afford to do anything that drew attention to himself. He lived his life in the shadows now. A creature of the night couldn't forget that.

CHAPTER TEN

She'd expected her father to be angry. He was a man of extremes. He spent much of his time at home sitting near his family, quietly watching or smiling as his wife and daughters continued their daily routines. He seemed like a man content and happy with his lot in life. Her mother was the voluble one. She filled the house with her talking and laughter. But occasionally, like the fast-moving thunderstorms that raced across the arroyos, her father's mood would darken and he would lash out with a fury completely out of measure with whatever offense had set him off.

She had learned to spot the signs, like seeing the distant flash of the heat lightning in the hills as the storm approached. She tightened her shoulders now in anticipation as she watched a glint flash through his eyes. But it passed. There was no anger or recriminations for her snooping. His shoulders slumped. He took a long swallow from his beer and then told her to follow him.

They walked through the kitchen. Her mother was stirring a pot at the stove and humming to herself. She looked at them and raised her eyebrows in question, but her father just kept walking. They walked to the long, low barn behind the house. Rafael was working with one of the new horses. He was a vaquero and had lived most of his life on horseback. He worked with the small stable of animals and did other necessary jobs around the house for her father. She didn't know how old he was. In her youth, anyone older than her father was simply very old. He was deeply tanned with a face that looked like soft leather. Sometimes he'd bring out his guitar at night and sing old folk songs in a clear tenor. She called him Tio Rafa. He'd been around as long as she could remember.

He tied the two-year-old speckled white Azteca that they called Cancion to the rail near the water trough and walked over to where she and her father stood. Whatever his age, he still moved with the fluidity of a dancer. He climbed over the wooden rails and stood before her father.

"Si?"

"She knows. I need you to teach her. She needs to be ready. To have a chance."

Tio Rafa looked at her. The slap was so hard and so quick that she was on the ground before she knew what had happened. She was too stunned and surprised to cry. She looked at Rafa, then at her father. He stared back but said nothing, just turned and walked back toward the house.

It would take her years to recognize that the expression on her father's face that day was relief. As if he'd been holding a terrible secret inside as long as he could, and now it was free.

For better or worse.

CHAPTER ELEVEN

Michael Youngblood looked out over the hotel ballroom. It was three-quarters full. A good turnout for a weeknight. He saw a mix of new and old faces. He feared it was more old than new and that was a problem that increasingly occupied his mind. Was this just a blip to be overcome, or was Watts stagnating? The answer to that would determine if Youngblood had wasted the last ten years of his life. He watched Watts work the room. He looked good tonight. The smile was out. So was the charisma. Youngblood saw the room responding. People were being drawn toward Watts like a magnet.

He passed the temporary bar in the corner and took a glass of wine. He sipped it and tried to hide his grimace. They needed to win and keep moving up the slippery pole of Philly politics, if only to improve the liquor and appetizers at these functions. His stomach ulcer was bad enough without enduring cheap merlot three nights a week.

He drifted around the edges of the crowd. He shook hands but didn't allow himself to be drawn into any long conversations. He kept an eye on his candidate. He'd need to intervene soon. Make sure the councilman didn't get stuck. Make sure everyone got their fair share of that smile. Not everyone in the room was on board yet, and this time around they would likely need every vote.

It was just a blip. It had to be. James Watts had the gift of gab. The man could talk a dog out of eating a porkchop. Some men were born to fly jets, some were destined for board rooms, some to play football in front of thousands of people. Every person had their talent. James Watts was a born talker. A born politician. He was the reason Youngblood hadn't given up on politics. Youngblood had run bigger campaigns. He'd run more successful campaigns. But he'd never had a candidate as good as Watts. He possessed that rare talent to make you feel like he was genuinely connecting with you. That you were the only person in the room worth talking to. That you might go out and get a beer and start a beautiful friendship. Even if you knew it was all bullshit, you were powerless to resist.

This was Youngblood's second time through the campaign wringer with Watts. He'd joined up when he was in town with a freshman House rep from Colorado for some symposium that he'd now long forgotten, and he'd seen Watts speak at an outdoor rally. Watts was supposed to just warm up the crowd for the national, more well-known speakers, but he eclipsed that duty. He had the crowd eating out of his hand and veteran politicos asking who the hell he was. If Watts won this year, it would be his third term. A third term would cement his name and reputation with the voters. Youngblood knew Watts would be the natural choice for council president and from there Youngblood saw the path taking shape to mayor, governor, or beyond. Watts inspired that kind of dreaming.

If it was a blip.

Youngblood knew every person also had a fatal flaw. Watts liked to talk, but he didn't like to be challenged. He had a temper. Jeannette Walters, who initially looked like a novice pushover, was proving to be very adept at getting under Watts's skin. The more she did it, the more he became distracted by it. The more he became distracted, the more he seemed to lose interest in campaigning. He became a little boy. He wanted to take his ball and go home. In Youngblood's experience, that wasn't a unique reaction among politicians, but Watts, for all his charm and charisma, wasn't so good at hiding it.

He worked his way closer to Watts and started slowly nudging him toward the door. It was a balancing act. You had to make the donors feel needed. You wanted them to walk away feeling as if they had gotten their money's worth. But you also had to make the candidate look busy and purposeful. You didn't want a donor's final image of the candidate to be him sipping wine and looking satisfied. Arrive a little late, leave a little early was the way to go.

Watts continued to shake hands, press flesh, and slap backs as Youngblood bored a hole through the crowd toward the exit. Outside, the air felt bracing and fresh after the recycled fug of the ballroom. A reporter that Youngblood recognized from the city beat of the *Inquirer* crushed out a cigarette when he saw Watts and hustled over. Youngblood hadn't gauged Watts's mood or how much wine he'd had and tried to wave him off. He didn't need to spend the rest of the night putting out any inadvertent fires, but the reporter was already talking.

"Councilman, do you have a response to Ms. Walters's claim—"

Watts turned and Youngblood watched the big, toothy smile switch on, but he also noticed Watts's eyes were cold, hard marbles. "Jeanette Walters can—"

Youngblood jumped in, stepping between Watts and the reporter's small recorder. "Sorry, not right now, Chris. Catch me tomorrow and we'll set something up. The councilman will give you all the quotes you need." The reporter frowned and looked like he wanted to argue, but a campaign was long and city politics even longer. You had to carefully pick the times you wanted to rock the boat. Alone, outside a Radisson, apparently didn't qualify. The reporter nodded and walked back inside the hotel.

Watts' car pulled to the curb and Youngblood got Watts inside, then collapsed into the seat next to him as the driver took off.

"Relax, Michael," Watts said. "You'll get an ulcer. I was just messing with you. I had it under control."

Youngblood wanted to scream and shake the complacency out of him. How did he not see he was on the verge of blowing it? How did he not sense the precarious position they were in?

Instead, he said, "We need to talk more about Deacon James."

CHAPTER TWELVE

He turned the big sedan carefully onto the access road and drove a quarter mile down the crushed gravel and stone path toward the caretaker's shack. After dropping off the businessman in Conshohocken, he'd been heading for the interchange with 476 and a trip back to the city. He didn't have another fare scheduled and any ad hoc pickup was unlikely to be this far from the airport or downtown; it made sense to head back south, then he passed the cemetery and decided to eat. Eat when you can was one of his personal rules that he learned growing up with Joyce and her sometimes infrequent trips to the grocery store. He didn't eat with clients in the car and didn't like to eat while driving, so when he had downtime, he took advantage of it.

Past the caretaker's shed, he spotted a small parking area. He pulled the car into a spot, grabbed his cooler and the two-way radio, and stepped outside into the cool October evening. He looked around. This was an odd spot to find a cemetery. There appeared to be no nearby church. The whole thing appeared to be a mistake. A weird misprint in the middle of a residential neighborhood. In the distance, over the bordering trees, Max saw the grim retaining wall for 476. To the east, was a thicket of tall signs promising a commercial shopping district on the horizon.

Security lights on the shed and two on the edge of the parking lot gave him enough light to see. The paved lot divided the burial space in half. The plots toward the front, where he'd turned in, were nicely maintained, grass clipped, stones tended, old ornaments or flowers taken care of. There was a large crypt or mausoleum in the center with a crucifix scene towering over the other graves. The back half still had a lot of room. There were just a few scattered markers dotting the green grass. Max felt an odd sympathy for the dead over there and walked in that direction. He chose a spot and sat a respectful distance from the marker of Lillian Wolfe who'd passed away five years prior and whose nearest neighbor was two hundred yards away.

Max liked cemeteries. From experience, he knew that ghosts haunted the living and had no reason to hang out with the dead. He found that being here, in the silence, helped chase away his own ghosts. They didn't much like the reminder of eternal sleep, either.

He ate one sandwich and thought again about the bride. She was like a splinter caught under his fingernail. If he was determined to help, and Max knew himself well enough that he knew he was going to try, how was he going to find her? He thought he had two options. Use the box as bait. Return it to Gabriel at The Clyde, like she'd asked, and see what happened. She'd either show up for the box or Gabriel would take it to her, but would Max be around to see it? He had a job and he was only one man. It would be impossible for him to watch The Clyde at all times. There were people he might ask for help, even a man with a solitary life like his had friends, but he wasn't sure he wanted to do that. Not yet. Not until he was sure of what he was dealing with.

The second option was to still ask for help, but from afar. He had the incoming number the bride had called from to warn him off and to make her car reservation. Maybe that might lead somewhere? He still believed it was most likely a disposable burner that led nowhere except a dead end, but you didn't know until you asked and when it was your only lead, what choice did you have?

He put his trash back in the cooler and pulled out his phone.

"You know, I was just thinking it had been over a month and my boy Max hasn't called. It's about time he got into some more trouble."

"Am I that predictable?"

"In a good way. You only call when you need something. And I like trouble. Trouble usually means money for me. And I definitely like money."

Max felt a small pang of regret for how he treated his friends. They'd met at the RFK juvenile youth facility when they were kids and bonded over an unlikely love of books. They lost touch when Lawrence transferred out and hadn't seen each other until the previous year when Max needed some help in Boston. It had been a mutually beneficial partnership. He knew Lawrence worked in a barbershop now and invested in real estate. That was it. The rest was all rumor and conjecture, and Max didn't need to know. And Lawrence didn't offer. He knew that whatever else Lawrence did, he was very good at it.

"I was wondering if Eddie could do a quick look-up for me. A phone number."

"Hold on a second. When I saw your number, I started upstairs. I'm almost there."

Eddie was Lawrence's half-brother, a savant with computers and networks, who lived in an apartment upstairs from Lawrence. He was somewhere on the spectrum and preferred the company of machines to people. Lawrence typically acted as a protective shield and go-between with the world at large.

"All right, go ahead. He says he's in the middle of something but is sure whatever you want is going to be simple."

"Did he just try to burn me?" Max asked.

Lawrence laughed. "Yeah, I suppose that counts as a dig from Eddie. You're making progress."

"I'll take it."

"All right, feed me the number."

Max read off the bride's number and heard the rapid clicking of keys as Eddie chased it down. A moment later Lawrence came back. "It's a burner."

"I figured but had to check. Can you tell me anything about who bought it?" Max thought certain types of phones might require registration or a credit card. That might lead somewhere.

"Eddie says no. Not on this one. It was a prepaid burner. Nothing was required except cash up front. He can see that it is still active, so whoever is using it hasn't dumped it yet."

"Can you figure out where they bought it? That might be useful."

There was a whispering conversation that Max couldn't quite make out and then Lawrence said, "Eddie can trace the lot number on the phone and can find the store that sold it. He thinks he can also get a call log, but it's going to take some time. Most of these burner companies rent time on larger networks and he'll have to sort through each to find the right one. He also says it's going to cost you."

"All right, I'll pay, but I've got something else. Can you check for an address on a credit card number?"

"Sure, that's easy. Credit check should show that."

"Good, only I don't have the number, but I know where it is." He relayed the details of the bride's reservation in the PPCS system to Lawrence who grunted an acknowledgment.

"Shouldn't take too long."

"Usual price?"

"Yeah."

"He want anything in particular?"

"No, he says he'll leave that up to you. He likes your taste. Damn, Max, have you guys been talking behind my back? First a dig and now a compliment."

"Tell him I'll find something and send a package within a week."

"I'll do that, and I'll call you back or email any details he finds on this."

They disconnected and Max laid on his back and watched the first stars come out overhead. When he'd been up north in Canada, he occasionally witnessed the green and purple swirls of the northern lights. The carpet of stars outside his small trailer had been awe-inspiring every time. Down here, there was too much light pollution from the city to see much, but even a glimpse of the larger galaxy was sometimes enough.

After a few minutes of contemplating the cosmos and the question of intelligent design, he picked up his phone again. It was an hour earlier in Chicago. Someone might still pick up. He had to look up the general office number on the Internet, which he was able to do, despite what Lawrence might think. He tapped the link, and the phone dialed. After a moment of circuitry silence, there was a brief ring and then a female voice answered. "Willis & Moreno Investigations."

So, Kate had made Jaimie a partner, Max thought. Might explain why she was at the office late. Or perhaps that's just who Jaimie always was. He'd never spoken to or seen Jaimie Moreno, but he'd heard plenty about Kate's assistant, and now partner. He'd seen her research skills up close when she and Kate had tracked him down in Chicago a few years ago.

"Is Kate in?"

"May I ask who's calling?"

"An old friend."

There was a pause. "Is this about a job?"

"Not exactly."

"Then I'm going to need more than that." Partner and gatekeeper.

"It's Max." He figured that would be enough and after another pause, longer this time, he was right.

"One moment."

He'd never been to their office, Kate had come to him last time, but he knew from their time together that Kate's apartment was across the hall from the office in a loft building south of the city with a view of the Chicago skyline. He wondered if Jaimie was knocking on her door or if Kate was standing next to the phone deciding what to do. They'd left on good terms, but it had been a messy, bloody affair from start to finish.

Ten seconds passed. There was no fancy hold music. Probably no need for it. How many times did private investigators need to put someone on hold? Probably not often, so not worth the extra cost. Max waited and listened to the silence from 750 miles east, an hour later, on his back, in a graveyard. Twenty seconds ticked closer to thirty. Either a very hurried, but intense discussion, or Kate was in the shower. He tried not to think about that and looked up at the stars. He had no place to be at the moment. He glanced over at the headstone to his right. Neither did Lillian.

After nearly a minute, Kate picked up. "Are you lost, Max? Did you need me to find you again?"

Max smiled. Kate always came out swinging. "No, you don't need to find me. I'm pretty happy where I am."

"Last I checked, you were still on the list."

"Yeah, I think I am. Not sure how hard they're still looking, but that status probably won't change soon."

They lapsed into silence, but it wasn't uncomfortable. Max was about to get to the reason for his call when Kate continued. "It's good to hear your voice. I'm glad you're okay. We heard some rumors about Boston and Carter but nothing about you, and Jaimie looked."

"And she's thorough."

"She is."

"What can I tell you? Any rumors of my death were greatly exaggerated. Boston helped rid a few of the people on my tail, but not them. My relationship with the FBI remains the longest and most stable thing in my life."

"And you're okay?"

"For the moment. Have Jaimie check tomorrow."

"Oh, she's one of your biggest fans, I don't think I'll even have to ask. So, you're okay, not lost, and don't need to be found. Why exactly are you calling?"

"I need some advice. I need to find someone myself."

"This isn't for …" She trailed off.

"No, nothing like that. You won't end up as an accessory to any crime. Jesus, Kate, who do you think I am?"

"A wanted fugitive for one." She said it in a joking manner, but Max also noticed she didn't exactly answer the question. Max might be working for his redemption, but he still had a long and well-earned reputation. One that Kate was very familiar with. He quickly filled her in on the bride, the box, the hotel, and the phone message.

"It's a prepaid burner. I've got a friend trying to chase down where it might've been sold, but even if they get that info, I'm not sure how much that will help," Max finished.

"It might. In a missing person or hiding person case, every bit of string helps. Typically, we have a name or date of birth or social to start with. With any of those you can usually pull a credit report or driver's license, either of which will have more of the personal information that you might be missing, sometimes including an address." Max remembered Kate liked to talk her way through a problem, and he almost heard her mind grinding through the phone. "Okay, if digital is mostly out, I think the old school methods might be your best bet."

"What are those?"

"Right up your alley, Max. Money, menace, or monitoring. The only solid thing you have is the hotel and how the doorman reacted to her arriving in a wedding dress, alone, in the middle of the night. People know her there, and probably more than just that doorman. Use some cash or some muscle to get someone to talk. You don't want to do that? Then you're going to have to sit on the place and hope she shows up again."

CHAPTER THIRTEEN

The two-way radio crackled to life after he hung up with Kate, and Max was busy for the next three hours with quick pickups and drop-offs, mostly runs from the different college campuses to various city hot spots for drinking and dining. He didn't have time to detour over to The Clyde until after ten. He expected he had only a few hours before the calls picked back up again and he ferried people in the opposite direction. And that was the problem. He would not have time to do any meaningful surveillance. He was fortunate that The Clyde was centrally located and close to where he did a lot of driving, but he would still be unable to spend a lot of time sitting and watching. To spot her, he'd have to get very lucky. Then there was the GPS responder on the car. Terry might wonder why he was idling outside the hotel for so long. PPCS didn't do cab lines.

Long-term surveillance was out. It just wouldn't work. He needed a shortcut. That left Kate's other suggestion. Money or muscle. Max steered the car south down 17th, across Samson, past the front entrance to the hotel, and saw the tall, recognizable outline of Gabriel behind his bellhop station.

Max had hoped to slip into the lobby and find someone new to question about the bride, but that wouldn't be an option with Gabriel manning the doors. He could wait until the man went on break or was busy with a guest, but Max didn't know how long that might be. He might have just returned from his allotted fifteen minutes. Or hell, didn't even take a break. He struck Max as the type of man who would sniff at the idea of a break from work. That left the alley.

He turned left on the one-way Walnut, then right onto 18th, traveled north for three blocks before turning right again and parked in the same spot as the previous night. He looked down the cramped alley. Trash, rusted piping, cardboard, and the homeless. Nothing had changed. He rubbed his shoulder. Max had to hope that at least he had a different experience.

He noticed a camera mounted on the decorative stone cornice that ran around the first floor of the building, but it angled outward toward the street and likely covered the sidewalk and steakhouse entrance on this side of the block. It wouldn't have captured any of the action the previous night. He didn't think there were many moments he was driving through the city streets that he wasn't on camera. He glanced around, but it was too dark to pick any more cameras out.

A pile of blankets shuddered and moved just inside the alley's entrance. A hand emerged and groped around until it found the zipper on a battered suitcase. Max watched as the hand unzipped the suitcase's front pocket, pulled out a single cigarette, red plastic lighter, and a half-liter liquor bottle, then disappeared back into the nest of blankets. It was clearly not the first time the disembodied hand had performed that maneuver.

Around the corner, just yards from the homeless encampment, Max watched a couple exit the restaurant. The man helped the woman into a long coat. A moment later, a valet pulled up in a late model silver BMW. The man held the door for the woman. The valet held the door for the man. He slipped the valet a tip, and they disappeared into the night. Smooth and slick. Not the first time that maneuver had been performed, either. Max thought there was likely some symbolism in the two worlds bumping up against each other, but maybe not. Maybe it was just the world we'd created. The haves and have nots right next to each other but also blind to each other. Or almost blind. As the BMW sped away, Max watched the valet look up and down the street, then down the short flight of steps into the restaurant. Nothing moved. Nothing to do. The street was quiet. The valet took a pack of cigarettes from his back pocket. He shook out one and lit it, then walked to the corner and laid the second one on top of the old suitcase.

Max waited ten minutes. The valet finished his smoke and went back inside. The pile of blankets remained still. The occasional car passed. He shifted his weight to open the door and his bruised ribs barked at him. He gingerly turned in his seat and grabbed the bottle of aspirin from where he'd stuck it in the cupholder. He turned the bottle in his hands, looking for the dosage information in the dim light from the street. Then realized there was no point. He'd been chewing them like Tic Tacs for most of the day. He took two more. He'd rather be able to breathe without pain and live with a little liver damage than the opposite.

He zipped his coat against the crisp air and took it slow. He watched his back. He did all the things he should have done the previous night. He walked the length of the alley, past the dented and fetid-smelling dumpsters, past the drainpipes and outflow vents, past the stenciled back doors. Other than the homeless pile of blankets, it was empty of life. He walked it twice. He listened. He was sure. He walked back and waited opposite The Clyde's door. Then he inched down a little, giving whoever came out a little more space and a little more time to notice him. He kept his hands visible and tried to adopt a relaxed pose. He thought of it like fishing, casting out his line and watching it bob in the water. He shifted positions slightly, putting more weight on his left leg, to relax the stress on his injured shoulder and ribs. He waited twenty minutes without a bite and was thinking he'd have to come back later when the door opened.

As the hinge pivoted and the door swung open, he realized that if it was Gabriel, he wasn't sure what he was going to say. But it wasn't Gabriel. It wasn't a porter, housekeeper, or someone from the front of the house. The guy was short and wiry with tired eyes. Max spotted the ends of tattoos on both wrists peeking out from his cuffs. His dark hair was slicked back and covered in a net. He was a cook, or sous chef, or kitchen manager judging by the hairnet and the rest of his clothes: black clogs, white coat over checkered pants.

He was carrying two bulging black trash bags. He clocked Max standing against the wall and paused in the doorway. Max held up his hands.

"I'm not going to jump you. Got a couple of questions about a guest or maybe someone that works here."

The guy didn't respond but hooked his foot around a plastic milk carton and used it to prop the door open, then stepped out of the doorway and over to the nearest dumpster. He didn't turn his back on Max as he flipped open the lid and tossed the bags inside. The bins must have been emptied recently. The bags hit the bottom and the trash inside smashed in a cacophony of broken glass. It was loud in the tight confines of the alley.

The guy moved back toward The Clyde's door, keeping as much distance as possible between himself and Max. Maybe something bad had happened to him before in the alley. Or maybe he was just cautious by nature. Maybe Max could learn something from his alley behavior. He wouldn't get sucker punched from behind. He pulled a pack of cigarettes from his coat, tapped the pack against his leg, then unwrapped the cellophane and dropped it at his feet. He took out a cigarette, lighted it, and slid the pack back into an internal pocket in his cook's jacket.

The man looked Hispanic, and Max was wondering if he spoke English. Kate hadn't covered the need to bring an interpreter. But then he tapped some ash from his smoke and asked, "Which is it? A guest or someone that works here? I rarely see the guests unless they make a wrong turn and end up in the kitchen." If the guy was originally from somewhere south of the border, he'd lost any trace of an accent. His speech was pure Philly. "I don't see much of the rest of the staff either unless they work the food somehow," the guy continued.

"I'm not sure. It's a woman. I drive a car. I dropped her off here the other night. She left something in my car. I'm trying to get it back to her."

The guy shrugged. "Ask inside. Leave it at the desk."

"I tried. I mean, I asked and I still might leave it, but I'd like to return it personally if I could. It looks ... personal. It's not a cell phone or wallet."

"So, you're waiting in the alley to ask questions of whoever comes out?"

"I don't think they'd want me sitting in the lobby."

The guy sucked down more smoke and stared at him. "Describe her."

"Tall. Taller than you. Skinny, but looked strong, in shape.

Curly brown hair. When I dropped her off the other night, she was wearing a wedding dress."

Did something flare in his eyes at the mention of the dress? It was hard to see in the dark shadows of the alley. The guy took his time answering, dropping the end of his cigarette and grinding it out under his foot. "I see nothing without a little green."

Max was ready for that. He stepped away from the wall and handed the guy a twenty.

"Still not sure I see anything."

"I'll find more if what you saw is worthwhile."

The money disappeared into the same inner pocket as the smokes.

"She doesn't work in the kitchen. I know that. Plus, anyone that looked like that would be out front somewhere."

Max waited for him to continue, but he didn't. "That's it?"

"All I got, but that cuts down your search of the hotel staff by about half."

The man kicked the milk carton aside and the door swung shut with a clang. Max returned to his car. As he drove to the next pickup, he realized the man had told him perhaps more than he wanted. The bride worked at the hotel and the man likely knew her. He hadn't followed up on the dress or even asked about it. Almost anyone would. It was a strange detail. Unless they'd seen it before. Or recognized the description. Or knew who he was asking about.

CHAPTER FOURTEEN

Max woke up sore. Why was the second day always worse? A boxing workout the morning after getting mugged in an alley probably hadn't been his best idea. Or following that up by sitting in a car for nine hours. After questioning the kitchen guy in the alley, he'd spent the rest of the night driving between restaurants, bars, various college campuses, and farther-flung suburbs. It was a typical night. No puke. Nothing memorable. He'd made money. He'd seen more of the city. If he hadn't been nursing some serious bruises, he'd have no complaints.

He groaned as he rolled out of bed. He looked at the bottle of aspirin on the bedside table, but decided he'd try to let a hot shower and some caffeine take the edge off before he continued the assault on his liver and kidneys. He walked down the hall to the kitchenette, filled the basket with Columbian dark roast, poured water into the canister, and flipped the switch. The pot began to burp and burble as he walked back to the bathroom.

In the bright fluorescents over the sink, the bruises across his back, shoulders, and ribs were taking on technicolor hues of yellow, purple, and black. They looked terrible, but he stretched an arm over his head, then rolled his neck. He winced but now that he was moving, he decided nothing hurt any worse than yesterday. He took that as an encouraging sign. He stood in the shower until it ran cold, then forced himself to stand still for another thirty seconds before getting out and toweling off.

He felt somewhat more human after his shower and two cups of coffee. He listened to the noon news headlines on the small secondhand radio he'd rescued from the building's trash room. It was dented and beat up but pulled a clear signal. Max didn't need more. The headlines detailed the upcoming city elections and the rise in violence in certain neighborhoods. Most of the grim incidents were up in the northeast, but a couple mentioned neighborhoods close to Max's apartment. Two pundits batted the question of the cause back and forth. One blamed rising drug trafficking from Mexico and Central America. The other took the domestic end and blamed decreased school and outreach funding with a side helping of prescription drug abuse. Max doubted the answer was as black and white as either man claimed, but that was the world everyone demanded now. Black and white. Right and wrong. Simple and easy. A sound bite. There was no room for confusion, uncertainty, or shades of gray. He snapped the radio off. He glanced at his gym bag near the door. The shower and coffee had revived him, but he thought he'd earned a day off. His stomach growled, ending the debate.

He walked across the street to The Skyline and found Ronnie Shelton sitting in one of the cracked leather banquettes finishing a hamburger and reading the latest edition of *The Philadelphia Inquirer*. Two guys in dusty coveralls with battered hard hats hanging off their belts sat at the counter. The rest of the place was empty.

"You mind some company?" Max asked.

Ronnie looked up. "Have a seat. A man my age doesn't have the luxury of declining company. Most of my friends are dead or already heard all my stories."

Nia brought over a cup of coffee and a water glass and raised an eyebrow at Max. He hadn't put his body through the wringer with Ronnie so he couldn't, in good conscience, harden up his arteries with a victory egg and scrapple sandwich. "Burger, cheddar cheese, fried onions." Not that his lunch choice was much healthier.

"Fries?" In for a penny, in for a pound.

"Why not?" He caught Ronnie's look over the top of the paper. "What? I'm not training for a shot at Joe Frazier."

He knew that would get the old man going.

"Frazier. Meat punching mope. He was lucky he fought the big oafs he did. Most of them were too slow to get out of the way. The man had power, no doubt, but so does an elephant. He lacked skill. He was a puncher, not a boxer. Half the time he surprised himself, and everyone else, when he did manage to hit something. You want to throw out a Philly guy, go with Hopkins. Now, that was a boxer. An artist in the ring. Bernard Hopkins. Undisputed champ in two divisions. Unified the titles. Did you know he defended his belt—"

"Twenty times." Max laughed. He liked the old man, but Ronnie was right, he had a limited selection of stories. Six weeks and Max was already getting some repeats. He sipped some water and flicked a finger against the headline. The newspaper's front page echoed the radio report he'd just heard. The paper's headline 'South Philly Gang Wars Threaten a Generation of Kids' covered a series of shootings over the previous week just a few blocks south in the Gray's Ferry neighborhood. A smaller story about the upcoming city council election and the candidate's response to the violence was sidebarred beside it.

Ronnie dropped the paper on the table and put a crooked finger on the headline. "That is old, old news."

Max pulled the paper around to his side of the table and scanned the first few paragraphs. It detailed a burst of shooting violence and retaliation traced back to a slight, or perceived slight, of someone's mother on Instagram.

Ronnie continued, "The latest round of killing is new, but the roots are about as old as me. I lived down there for a bit after I got out of the Army before I opened the gym. 'Round '75 or '76. I dodged more bullets walking down 27th than I ever did from the VC."

"What started it? Instagram wasn't exactly around in '76."

"That's the thing. No one knows anymore. Not the kids pulling the triggers today. I wasn't kidding when I said it was old news. It's mostly geography. You grew up on this block, you're taught to hate those that grew up on that block. When you lay it on the table like that, it sounds silly. And it is. So much time and energy and blood fronting for a rep or an image. If half those boys put as much effort into finding a job or going to school as they did into feeling pissed off, the whole thing would flame out in a few weeks."

Nia came back and set Max's plate down. "The problem," she said, "is that it's easier to find a gun down there than a job for most of those kids. Two miles from City Hall and no one wants to do anything. It's been going on so long that it's just become normal. You believe that? You out walking the dog or picking up your kid from school and ducking bullets is normal." She shook her head. "You grow up in Gray's Ferry as a young black male and the odds are you are going to wind up dead, locked up, or paralyzed before you can legally buy a drink. Think about that."

Nia was tough and uncompromising, but Max had always

found her a positive person underneath the hard shell. Standing next to the table now, she just sounded tired and resigned.

"That's bleak," Max said.

"I know, but that's what the weight of all that violence brings. That's the trauma, the mindset. I understand why kids want to carry guns down there. It might be their best way to stay safe. Police aren't helping. City Hall isn't helping. Community is under siege." She shook her head and walked back behind the counter.

"Neighborhoods around here are changing," Ronnie responded. "Not just Gray's Ferry. You got the hospital projects pushing over the river. You got other ethnicities, the Mexicans and Latinos, moving into Point Breeze."

"You make it sound like a bad thing," Max said.

Ronnie shrugged. "Didn't say it was good or bad. It's how cities change. It's evolution. It's an opportunity. And what does opportunity bring?"

"What?"

"Money. Or the smell of it. And in my experience, opportunity plus money often brings in violence."

"Reading that, it sounds like the violence is already here. So maybe this helps. Brings some attention to the situation."

Ronnie nodded. "Maybe it does. Maybe it also brings even more violence in the short term. Fuel to a flame."

It was close to two p.m. when he finished lunch and left The Skyline. He decided to walk off a few calories. The afternoon was bright and clear. Standing in a yellow square of sun on the cracked sidewalk, he felt warm and drowsy. Max knew it was a mirage. It was one of those days where the line between late summer and early fall was blurred. You'd be fine in short sleeves in the sun, but shivering in the shadows.

He thought about the alley attack again as he walked east on Christian Street through neighborhoods of brick walkups and mature trees, past the old stone and large spire of St. Charles Borromeo on 20th then turning onto 19th. He still couldn't figure it. Had to be random. Just bad luck. If he was honest, Max attracted bad luck and trouble. But what was the point? They had taken nothing. It made little sense.

The blocks became progressively more commercial as he walked north, more reflective glass, more advertisements. Cat's Cradle Books was near the corner of South Street and 19th. A narrow storefront with a single window and a simple sign reading 'Books' gave way to a narrow space inside crammed with tapered aisles and cluttered shelves. Hand-lettered signs tacked to shelves denoted different subjects. Most of the time, they got you in the general vicinity of what you might be looking for. Max had learned that shopping at the Cradle was part art, part scavenger hunt, part bobbing for apples. It smelled of decaying ink and moldering paper.

Max opened the door, squeezed past the stack of shipping boxes in the vestibule, and nodded to Chim, who was sitting on his high back stool behind the counter. Chim was the owner. He had wiry gray hair that usually held one or two pairs of bifocals. His nose and mouth were pinched in a perpetual frown and looked too small for his face. He wore a navy button-up cardigan sweater year-round, and Max had never seen him move from behind the front counter. Presumably, he must use the bathroom or stock the shelves at some point, but it had never happened while Max was in the store.

Max gave him a nod as he passed. The mysteries and thrillers were toward the back of the store, and he was surprised to hear Chim's gravelly voice call out after him. He'd never spoken to him before other than to pronounce what Max owed after tallying up his purchases on an old big-buttoned calculator. "Nothing new in mysteries and pulp, but we did get a good-looking box of '60s sci-fi last week if you read those."

"Thanks. I'll take a look."

And he did. He browsed through the mystery section and saw nothing particularly interesting. He moved over an aisle and picked through the golden-age science fiction. He preferred crime books, but he didn't sniff at sci-fi. He liked the later stuff, Asimov, Bradbury, and others that focused less on the gadget or science and more on the characters using it. He picked up a battered paperback copy of Alfred Bester's *The Demolished Man* and added Walter Miller's *A Canticle for Leibowitz.*

"Six seventy-five," Chim declared. Max paid and took a paper bookmark and his brown bag and walked back into the rapidly cooling October afternoon. He walked two blocks north on Pine Street and then turned east toward the water. He stopped in Fitler Park and sat on a bench next to the ram sculpture and read the first fifty pages of *The Demolished Man.* By four, the park had come alive with kids released from the nearby elementary school. They swarmed over and around the brick paths of the pocket park. Max smiled briefly at the noise, then took his books and weaved south and west, grabbing a takeout coffee at Rival Brothers, and sipping it as he walked the rest of the way back to his apartment.

He spent the last hour before packing his cooler and heading to the PPCS lot looking at photos and online galleries of artificial intelligence art, or AI art. This is what Lawrence's brother Eddie liked as payment for the hacks that Max sometimes required. Max often wondered if Eddie admired the art or the machine artist more? Did Eddie identify with the outward expression of how machines saw the world? Or was it the collaboration between the human programmer and the machine to create the art? Was that how Eddie saw himself? Was he working with machines to solve problems rather than using them as a tool? Did he believe the AI was creating the art for other AIs to appreciate or for humans? Maybe one day he would get to ask Eddie these questions. After an hour of browsing, he picked out a limited Tom White print to be shipped to Eddie's PO box.

CHAPTER FIFTEEN

Leonard climbed the stairs up to the fifth floor and was glad Aaron didn't live any higher. He never took the elevator in the Towers. Or most other places, if he could avoid it. The janky boxes were so old, the odds were high you'd get stuck just by the bad luck of a mechanical breakdown, but it was also too easy to get trapped and ambushed. He knew from experience. He smiled and thought about how they'd set up Long John "LJ" Christin when he and Deke were coming up and looking to make a mark. Deke had rigged the elevators and LJ had taken a short step down a long, empty shaft. One less competitor for the Towers.

He made it up the last flight and caught his breath before knocking on Aaron's door. He could smell the weed over the odor of fried food seeping under the door. He shook his head. They had business to take care of, and this mope couldn't even keep his head straight for a few hours. Aaron opened the door and all the smells wafted out even stronger. Len waved a hand in front of his face. Aaron was a few years younger than Len but bigger, wider through the shoulders and neck with a bullet-shaped head and an ugly smile. He wasn't in Deke's crew, not officially, but it wasn't for a lack of muscle or fortitude to pull the trigger. It was just nobody wanted him. Aaron was crazy and a killer and only served himself. Leonard was Deke's right hand and hammer and had the protection that came with that status, but even he wouldn't turn his back on Aaron. The man was a rabid dog and eventually he'd have to be put down, but for the moment he still had his uses in the neighborhood. No one fucked with the Towers, partly because of Deke, but mostly because everyone was afraid of Aaron. Maybe it was better he was baked, Len thought. It might be tough to keep a rabid dog on a leash.

He gave Leonard a chin nod and stepped back into the apartment. Len followed and closed the door. Inside, the smell of damp mold and hot garbage mixed with the sweet scent of the weed. He trailed Aaron down the hall, past a small kitchen with a peeling ceiling and crusted dishes piled in the sink. Trash was overflowing a dented steel can that looked as if Aaron had taken it off the street and repurposed it for home use.

The central room in the small apartment was both sweltering and oddly cold at the same time. Len glanced around. His old man had worked as a janitor and HVAC repairman before keeling over on the job, dead at thirty-two of a brain aneurysm. He would have been horrified with how inefficiently the Tower's heating and cooling worked. Len's father loved efficiency, maybe more than his wife and kid. He would spend hours bent over the hood of his car in the garage to tweak some gauge or gasket to run a little tighter. Or he'd have Len practice his jump shot over and over, adjusting his elbow placement or off-hand. That all changed after he died. Something broke in Len's mom. After that, it was about survival, not efficiency. He subconsciously rubbed at his forehead. Strange to think Len was almost the same age now as when his father passed.

Len knew that the housing authority left the heat on year-round, mostly out of laziness. He supposed some older residents didn't mind. They probably hadn't been warm since the nineties, but the ones not collecting Social Security needed to figure out a way to combat the heat, so they didn't cook in their sleep. Aaron's unit faced inward toward the courtyard and would never catch a breeze. He'd hung an old A/C unit in the window frame. It hung lopsided and wheezed out cool air and dripped onto the floor. A foot away, the steam chugged out from the radiator.

Aaron dropped his bulk into a large black leather couch that faced a 70-inch flat-screen TV. Both pieces of furniture dominated the tiny room. Two additional doors were on the left. Len knew from being in other units that they led to the bedroom and bathroom. He didn't consider himself a picky or fastidious man, but his mama had taught him some manners and held him to standards above a rutting farm animal. Given the state of the kitchen, he had no desire to see the inside of Aaron's bathroom. He also didn't want to stay here any longer than necessary, but Aaron had picked up the joint and appeared to be settling in. He flipped through channels with the remote.

Len perched on the opposite end of the couch. "You good with this?"

Aaron slowly turned his head. "You asking me if I'm capable? You think I'm going to punk out?"

Len suppressed the urge to shudder at the man's flat, shark eyes. He put his own eyes on the TV where Aaron had stopped it on a re-run of the old *Press Your Luck* game show. "Nope. Just asking. I know where he's going to be until nine is all. Better to take care of it before then."

"Then relax, we got time." It was 8:40 by the digital clock. "Besides, we got more business to discuss before we get to it."

"What business?" Len looked over at Aaron. He'd already paid the standard upfront half. "We had a deal. You got your money."

Aaron's eyes sparked to life and he smiled, and Len glimpsed the base cunning that had probably kept the man alive this long.

"This whole thing had me thinking I'm doing this on the cheap. I'm thinking I ought to raise my rates."

"Nah. We had a deal. You don't want to do it, that's fine, but you're not getting more out of us."

"Really? I wonder if I go down to Barrow Street and find Deke in that fancy new apartment he's got and ask him if he'd say the same thing."

Shit. The rabid dog was smarter than he looked. Or he was bluffing, but Len didn't want to take that chance. He couldn't have Aaron bumbling around on the street asking questions. Or going to Deke. Len realized he'd made a mistake. He should have done this on his own. But while he knew where the guy would be, he didn't know much else. He'd only get one crack at this, and he thought two guns would be the safer play. Now he realized the added complications weren't worth it. It was a lesson learned the hard way and a mistake he'd have to fix sooner rather than later.

"What are you thinking?"

"Extra thousand might do it."

Masks wouldn't make a difference to anyone who lived in the neighborhood. No one in the neighborhood was crazy enough to rat on Aaron. The masks weren't for them; they were for the cameras.

The boy left the rec center and walked down the sidewalk, head down, scrolling through his phone. Len couldn't see much under the dreads, but he assumed he also had earbuds in. That might make it easier depending on which way he turned at the intersection. Len had no qualms about shooting someone in the back if it made the job simpler.

"That him?"

They'd been sitting in the car on the corner for fifteen minutes. Aaron was not a patient man.

"Yeah, that's him."

They each rolled down the black cotton ski masks over their faces and stepped out of the car.

The kid turned left on South Dover and headed away from them. The two men followed, closing the gap. Len looked around. It was a residential block without many people. They crept closer, guns hanging down at their sides. The kid kept scrolling and walking.

Then a woman came out of a house holding a little girl's hand. The woman spotted the two of them and their guns and hurried the girl back inside, slamming the door. The noise made the kid look up. Some deep-seated survival instinct made him look over his shoulder. He saw them and took off running.

"Shit," Aaron said. Len didn't waste a breath just started chasing.

The kid skidded around the corner and hit Dickinson Street, a wider, busier street with more people out. He kept running and started screaming for help. Len kept going. He had no choice. He had one shot at this. He heard Aaron's heavy footsteps somewhere behind him. Definitely a mistake. You didn't pay Aaron to run. He put it out of his mind and focused on the kid. He was yelling, running, and looking backward. It was a miracle he hadn't tripped yet.

Two people came out of Chang's Chinese takeout. The kid abruptly grabbed the door and dodged inside. Len caught up, but the kid was pushing back against the door and screaming at the woman behind the counter to lower the metal security gate. That couldn't happen. He pushed hard against the door, but the kid had locked his legs against the wall and Len couldn't get enough purchase to make him budge.

Aaron finally arrived and put his shoulder into it, but two people pushing on the small door was awkward and they ended up fighting each other more than putting additional leverage on the door.

"Fuck this," Aaron said. He put his gun against the glass and pulling the trigger.

Len saw blood and heard screaming. Aaron had hit something. Then he heard sirens in the distance. He pushed the big man away. "We gotta go."

CHAPTER SIXTEEN

Max was working his way west on Lombard Street, back toward South Broad and the center of town, when Lawrence called. He pulled over into a spot next to a deserted park with a basketball court and a dog run. Would a dog like a park made entirely of concrete? Maybe city dogs didn't know any better? He swiped the phone to answer.

"Eddie got some information on that cell phone and credit card," Lawrence said.

"I thought you were just going to send the details to my phone?"

"I did, and then I heard nothing from you and decided you'd probably forgotten to check your email, so I thought I'd call and remind you. Plus, I missed the sound of your voice."

Max had just finished a job, picking up an elderly couple from Radicchio's Cafe on Wood, in the shadow of 676, and driving them less than a mile south into Society Hill to an eighteenth-century townhouse on a cobbled street. There had been an awkward moment after he'd pulled up in front of the address on the GPS when they all sat still and waited.

Max had a moment of panic where he thought they'd both died on the quick trip, but when he'd glanced in the mirror, he saw them both placidly waiting. It finally occurred to him they were expecting him to open their doors. Max did and then helped the wife up the two steps to the door. The husband handed him a dollar and tottered in behind her.

What would Lawrence have done when that couple waited in the backseat? Max decided he likely would have helped them with a smile and then figured out a way to hack into their bank accounts or buy their house out from under them.

"You're right, I haven't checked my email today."

"Or yesterday?"

"Okay, in a few days. I'm not a slave to technology."

"Ho! Don't want to be throwing that term around with your only black friend."

"You are not my only black friend."

"Uncle Ben's microwave rice doesn't count as a friend."

"Eddie is my friend."

"Touché. He says thank you for the print, by the way."

Max took the phone out of the dashboard mount and tapped the email app. Lawrence's message with two attachments was there between an email asking for an urgent political donation to a candidate Max had never heard of and a different email telling him that these prices couldn't be beaten for portable oxygen concentrators. He tapped Lawrence's email and then tapped the first attachment. It was a very large and very detailed map.

"What am I looking at?" he asked Lawrence.

"It's a plat map from the US General Land Office showing the cell phone towers and relays in the Philadelphia metro area. Eddie likes his data. A simple Rand McNally scan wouldn't do."

Max pinched and zoomed the screen and maneuvered the

map until he found the wedge of land between the Delaware and Schuylkill Rivers where the city proper was located. Eddie or Lawrence had marked up the map in a few locations.

"Okay, I'm looking at the city and some notations. What do they mean?"

"What do you know about cell phone triangulation?"

"It's a way to get your phone's location similar to GPS."

"Hey, score one for the man living in the '90s."

"Cell phones existed in the '90s."

"Good point. Triangulation with your phone uses multiple towers, usually three, to measure how long it takes your phone to ping back the tower. Measuring the delays can translate to distance and give a pretty good idea of where your phone is."

"Seems ... intrusive."

"Such a criminal mind. Its original intent was to help the 911 systems and first responders. It also allows carriers to figure out the best towers to route your call for the best service. But yes, it could also be exploited if you think the worst of humanity."

"I do."

"Me too, most of the time."

"So, what did Eddie find?"

"That she made all the calls from inside the city limits."

That disappointed Max. He had been hoping for more.

"But there's more. First, he had to do some searching to figure out which carrier the phone was using. He did that and then sorted through all the calls using the city towers to find this number as the originating or receiving number. One interesting note. There were no incoming calls in the historical logs, just outgoing, and only a few of them. But he pulled all the originating calls and looked at the towers and antennae they used and came up with an approximate location."

Max perked up. That was better. "How approximate?"

"About half a square mile or so. Look at the blue circle he drew on the map."

Max used his finger to move the map to the right toward the Delaware River until he found the circle. It covered Point Breeze and Newbold, two neighborhoods a mile and a half west of his apartment. He knew the spot. He occasionally walked that way to get to a bookstore on Passyunk. He traced the route with his eyes. Broad Street cut through the right edge of the circle. Point Breeze was an ethnically and culturally diverse neighborhood, perhaps most famous for a Keith Haring mural. Its neighbor to the east, Newbold, was gentrifying more quickly, bounded by Washington Avenue to the north and Wolf Street to the south.

"Still a large area, at least 10,000 people must live in that circle."

"Open the other attachment."

Max tapped the second attachment in the email and a single-page document opened. "What am I looking at?"

"We ran a credit check on the that Visa number."

"And got an address."

"Yup, can't get a credit card sent to a PO box."

He disconnected with Lawrence and continued on South Broad. He had an address for the bride. Now he had to figure out what to do with it. He glanced at the time on the dash. His next job was at the airport in forty-five minutes. He stopped at the intersection at Tasker and noticed a kid, no older than twelve, waving his arms. It was late, past eleven now. Maybe the kid was lost or needed help? Max pulled over and put his hazards on. The kid smiled and approached the car. Max lowered the window. The kid didn't say a word, just held out a cell phone. Max took it and glanced at the screen. There was an active call.

"Hello?"

"Hello, is this Mr. Lindell?"

That was the last name Max was currently using. "Yes."

"Good. I'm calling from the FCM. I understand you're an independent contractor with Philadelphia Private Car Service. If you want to keep driving in the city, pay us every week. Or we will kill you."

"What?" Max was so surprised, and the caller sounded so pleasant and genteel, that the words and implications just weren't sinking in.

"La Familia de la Calle Misericordia." The caller then repeated his previous statement verbatim. It almost sounded like a script.

"I already pay someone once a week to drive and I already have a boss." He disconnected the call and handed the phone back. The boy took it, stepped back onto the sidewalk, and then disappeared into the shadows.

The threat had to be related to the two men he'd seen exiting PPCS, the pair that had caused so much tension in the office. How had they singled him out? How had they found him? Was showing him that they could find him anywhere part of the message? He glanced at his mirrors, but nothing set off alarms. If they had someone following him, they were good or, the message delivered, they were now gone. He hadn't talked to Liam again or anyone else after that first encounter, and he realized now that he didn't know enough about the local turf and affiliations to decide how he should respond. He needed to change that. He needed information.

He pulled back into traffic and drove past the big community center and free library, then the Children's Hospital clinic and through two more intersections, Moore and Mifflin, before turning right on McKean. He thought about driving by the bride's address just to get a feel for the place but didn't think he had time. Then, before he hit 24th and headed west to the airport, Terry beeped him on the radio.

"Need you to come back to the house, Max."

Max frowned. He was good at reading people and voices. He had to be in his previous life. It helped keep him out of prison. Or, at least out of prison for far longer. Terry didn't sound right.

"What's up? I have to get out to the airport for a pickup in," he glanced at the clock again, "about thirty minutes."

"I got Marco to cover that one. He's on his way."

"What's going on?"

"Tell you when you get here."

Max pictured someone standing in the office or looking over his shoulder. He wondered briefly if it was the voice he'd just spoken to on the phone. But the man had quoted him a week. To squeeze him now was too quick an escalation for an extortion and protection racket. The FCM, this Familia de la Calle Misericordia, would come after Max first. That's what he hoped. He was counting on it. He didn't want to put any people at PPCS at risk for his choices.

Instead of crossing the Schuylkill and zipping down 95 to the airport, he signaled and turned back north on 24th. Five minutes later, he was circling the block, looking for idling or parked SUVs similar to the ones he'd seen before. He came up empty. He pulled into the parking lot and got his answer.

CHAPTER SEVENTEEN

They'd parked an older model silver Toyota Camry in the handicap spot by the door. The back of the car hung low, no shocks, or there was serious equipment in the trunk. The passenger side panel had a dent just below a cracked side mirror. Max parked in the numbered spot for his company car and walked toward the building's front door. He glanced in the Camry's driver's window on his way past. There was a portable radio unit pinned under the dash and a magnetic emergency light on the back seat. Fast-food wrappers and crushed coffee cups lay two inches thick on the floor.

No doubt about it. Cops.

The pair sat at one of the round tables with mismatched chairs in the center of the room. If anyone else had been there when they arrived, they were gone now. The room was empty. Terry was visible through the open door in dispatch. He pushed his rolling chair back when he heard the door and just shrugged an apology at Max. They each had a steaming paper cup of coffee in front of them. They must have been desperate. The best thing you could say about PPCS's coffee was that it was hot.

It was a man and a woman. The man was older. His black hair was shot through with thin streaks of gray and combed straight back from his forehead. His eyes were hooded and wary. Dark stubble covered his cheeks and jawline.

Max put the woman in her early thirties. She looked Scandinavian, with blonde hair that was almost white, tied back in a simple ponytail, and thin lips that turned down slightly at the edges. Like her partner, she showed the effects of what was likely a long day in a string of similar days. Wrinkles creased her black suit, but her eyes were bright. He wondered how new she was to the job.

They both stood as Max approached, the woman detective took the lead.

"Cormac Lindell?"

"That's right. Most people call me Max." That was the name on the current papers that Lawrence had set up for him. If they asked, he could produce a valid driver's license or passport with a very convincing amount of data to back it up. It had gotten him over the border twice. He didn't think it would be a problem with two city detectives. Not for an introductory interview.

"I'm Detective Axelson. This is my partner, Detective Diaz. Third District. Have a seat. We just have a few questions. Shouldn't take long."

They all sat. Diaz took a sip of coffee and didn't grimace. Tough bastard.

"Did you have a pickup on October 12th around four a.m.? Near Ellsworth?"

They already had that answer or he wouldn't be sitting here. Terry would have pulled the logs.

He took a moment as he pretended to think it over. "The twelfth? What day was that, Thursday?"

"Technically, it was Friday morning, but yes, you would have started your shift on Thursday, if that helps."

"Okay. Yes. I'm not sure of the exact time, but I picked up a fare outside the St. Cascia shrine on Ellsworth."

"Did they flag you down or was it scheduled?"

Again, this was a question he was sure they already had the answer to, so why were they asking? Were they trying to nail down his answers and timeline, or was it something else?

"It came through dispatch. Local regs prohibit us from picking up street fares. Only licensed taxis can do that. Terry called me. Our cars have transponders. I was the nearest available."

"Okay." Axelson was taking notes in a small handheld notebook as they talked. She flipped back a page now, read something, then continued, "Who was the fare?"

"I don't know."

"You don't know?"

"No, not her name. She never told me, and I didn't ask."

"Is that unusual?"

"A little. Typically, we have a contact name from dispatch or through the phone app they can use."

"But not this time?"

"No. Terry just said I'd know her when I saw her."

"What does that mean?"

Max shrugged. "You'd have to ask her."

"Fair enough. So, did you?"

"Did I what?"

"Know her when you saw her?"

"It was four a.m. She was the only one waiting at the pickup address. She seemed to be expecting the car."

"But you never confirmed her identity as the one that set up the reservation?"

"Not officially, I suppose. How could I without a name? But her destination matched the ride request, so I guess that's a sort of confirmation." But was that right? Max tried to think back. Had she given him the destination, or had he volunteered it?

"Huh. Okay," Axelson said and scribbled something in the notebook. "And what was the destination?"

"The Clyde Hotel."

"On Sansom Street by Rittenhouse Square?"

Max couldn't figure out what was going on but didn't think they were here for him. They wouldn't be this informal if it had anything to do with him or his past. They'd have the FBI with them along with a fugitive takedown team. No, right now, he was just a driver to them. A lead to squeeze for more information. But information about what?

"Yes. That's it. Listen, what's going on? Am I in trouble? This was just a random fare. One in a hundred I've done this month."

Diaz leaned over and whispered something to his partner. She nodded and gave a thin smile. Max had been questioned by cops before, too many times to count, and saw through this little ruse to make him nervous.

"We appreciate your patience. Just a couple more questions."

Max sat back and kept his posture loose. "Go ahead. Happy to help."

"Good. What did this woman—you said it was a woman, right?"

"Yes, definitely a woman."

"Okay, what did this woman look like?"

"Well, it was dark." He could play games, too. "She was tall. Taller than you, Detective. Five-nine or ten. Thin. Brown or black hair. Short. Curly."

Max noted that Axelson didn't write any of this down. More information they already had. "Anything unusual about her?"

"Unusual?"

"Anything that could help us identify her?"

Max pretended to think about it. He wasn't going to give up the dress, the box, her scars, or anything else about her physical description until he knew more himself. "No, I'm sorry. I don't think so. It was my last fare for the night. I was tired. I picked her up. Ten minutes later, I dropped her off at The Clyde. That was it. Is she all right? Did she do something?"

Axelson closed the notebook and slipped it into a pocket. The light in her eyes had faded. Now, she looked as tired and resigned as her partner. "We're not sure. There was an assault reported near that address. We got your car's plate, or the company's car, I guess, off a traffic cam. Not a lot of cars at that hour, so we're checking them out. That's what we do."

They all stood and did another round of handshakes, and then Axelson and Diaz left in their dented Camry.

When their taillights had disappeared up the street, Terry popped out of his office. "What was that all about?"

"I have no idea."

Not yet.

CHAPTER EIGHTEEN

Max woke on Sunday thinking about the cops' questions. And coffee. He dressed and walked across the street. The Skyline was busy. It did a brisk business on Sundays. Max read a discarded *Inquirer* while he waited for a counter spot to open up. The lead story was about another shooting. This one in Gray's Ferry, where the two gunmen had chased a kid into a Chinese takeout before opening fire. The kid was in intensive care but somehow survived. He thought back to his conversation with Ronnie and Nia the last time he'd been in. This would do little to change Nia's attitude. The local city council member, James Watts, provided a quote in the article, as did his challenger in the upcoming election, Jeannette Walters. Neither seemed to have any answers to the rising violence and seemed more intent on attacking each other. A seat opened, and he tossed the paper aside so he wouldn't lose the rest of his appetite.

He stood outside the diner, full of strong coffee and scrapple, buttoned his short coat, and pulled on a wool beanie. A thick blanket of afternoon clouds had pushed low and blotted out the morning sun. The cold, gray pallor matched the mood of the city. Most of the idle chatter at the counter had revolved around the takeout shooting and the low competence of the police in various parts of the city.

He tucked his chin low against the wind and set out toward the address that Eddie had grabbed from the bride's Visa card number. He carried his backpack with the box inside. It was Sunday afternoon. The Eagles were playing. He could follow the game in bits and pieces from car radios, retail stores, and various shouts and groans from apartments as he walked. If she worked a regular shift at the hotel, she might be home. He'd be surprised if she was watching the game, but if she was, he'd return the box and finally get some answers.

She wasn't home. No one was. Max should have known it wouldn't be that easy. Still, he felt disappointed. The address matched up with a block of brick apartments called Oxford Gardens. It was an extensive complex with separate three-story buildings taking up a full city block with a courtyard, empty pool, and management office in the center. Residents had chained six or seven cheap charcoal grills to the pool gate near a collection of picnic tables. The buildings themselves looked utilitarian and vaguely military. Each one was the same except for the numbered addresses on the red triangular awnings over their entrances. There was a basement apartment, no doubt called a garden-level, then two more stacked on top with narrow windows and identical air conditioners underneath.

Max walked around the complex until he found the building that matched Eddie's address. It was on the far side, facing away from the management office. The complex was busy. Cars pulled in and out at regular intervals. He could hear the football game clearly from one apartment window that was cracked open. A group of kids was playing basketball at a park across the street. Max walked across to the park and found a bench that gave him a view of the building's entrance. He wanted to get a feel for the place. People entered and exited, but no one who looked like the bride. It looked like a normal apartment building. A mix of middle-class families and singles. Nothing jumped out to Max as suspicious.

After a half-hour, he watched a blue Ford F-350 park and a woman walk toward the building's entrance. He stood, jogged across the street, and grabbed the door just before it latched closed. The woman had already disappeared through the next door. Max stood in a small vestibule. There was a noticeboard to the right with various announcements and flyers. To the right were a block of mailboxes, a table currently holding two Amazon packages, and a recycling bin filled with junk mail. No cameras. He'd noticed a couple mounted on the complex's security lights. He wondered if any of them worked or if they were just for show, like fake alarm system stickers, to ease residents' minds.

The building had sixteen units, and the mailboxes were arranged in two rows of eight. The name on the Visa account was J. Murrieta. Registered to apartment seven. He scanned the small white labels on each box. The Changs resided in apartment seven. None of the other labels were even close to Murrieta, J., or otherwise.

A tall man with graying hair under a tweed flat cap came through the door. He was holding a fuzzy white dog on a red leash.

"Excuse me," Max said. "Do you know the Changs?"

"Sure, Asian couple in seven, sort of look like twins. Both med students, I think. Or pharmacy. I can't remember. Something medical. Only talked to them a couple of times. Like this, picking up the mail."

"They lived here long?"

The man scratched his cheek "At least two years."

"How long have you lived here?"

He took a step closer. The dog wiggled in his arms and he set him down. "Why are you asking?"

"I'm looking for a J. Murrieta. That name sound familiar?"

"I moved here eleven years ago after my Doris died. No one by that name has ever lived here."

"These apartments stay pretty full, or do they sit when someone moves out?"

"They're mostly efficiency places, but they're clean and well-kept and the A/C works. They might sit for a few weeks, especially in the winter, but not for too long."

"Okay, thanks." Max thought he was getting the picture.

"I used to be a history teacher over at Furness. The only time I heard that name was Joaquin Murrieta, the famous Hispanic outlaw during the California Gold Rush. People say he was the inspiration for Zorro."

"Never heard of him."

"Few have, but it's a bloody story, he ended up beheaded, and it got the kids' attention. At least for one class."

He scooped the dog back up and walked through the inner door into the building.

Max looked at the mailbox. It wouldn't take anything more than a butter knife to slip it open. The bride had her Visa card delivered, maybe when she knew an apartment was vacant. Or maybe not. It wouldn't be hard to figure out when they delivered the mail and when the card was due to arrive and intercept it before the owner got to their box.

He grabbed a few discarded pieces off the top of the recycle pile and noted the various names and same address. Even if the owner got there first, they would likely assume it was for a previous resident and pitch it. She could walk in anytime and pick it up.

It was a dead end. Or mostly, a dead end.

It didn't get him right to her front door, but it was

another data point. He took out his phone and looked at the map Eddie had sent. The apartment building fell on the left side, but within the blue circle Eddie had drawn. She might take the precaution of a dead drop, but how far would she travel to get to it? Max didn't think it would be very far. She might be near enough to watch for the mail being delivered from her window. He looked out across the courtyard but saw no one looking back. But he felt she was close.

CHAPTER NINETEEN

Len sat on the stoop of the Titan house in a sweatshirt and jeans. The sky was a flat gray, the color of old weathered wood. He looked up the street. Empty. Business was slow. The city felt sluggish, like it was huddling up and preparing for winter. He should have brought his coat. He hated winter. Hated the way the cold seeped into his bones. His mom told him once she had family in the Carolinas. More than once, he'd thought about trying to find them and moving down there, but he never did. He was a city boy, hot or cold.

He was smoking a blunt with Barbie and thinking about his Aaron problem. They had split up after the shooting, but he had been texting Len, asking about his money. Len could still get what he wanted, but it was taking more time and effort than he expected. The shooting itself wasn't the problem. Once it was done, Len rarely thought about any of them again. It was everything else. He realized now he'd always relied on Deke for that in the past. Deke had never pulled the trigger except for that one time, but he'd always planned things out, maneuvered people into place. Len just had to walk in and do the thing. He just had to be the hammer. Deke handled the aftermath. He hadn't understood how much Deke had contributed to the plan until now. Len realized he should have spent a little more time thinking through all the angles. He definitely should have thought more about Aaron. That had been a mistake. The entire thing was wobbly, but it hadn't fallen over. Len could recover.

A green Lexus pulled up at the corner of Titan and Latona. Two blonde women sat in the front seat. He watched DeMarco lean down and put his arms on the car door and smile. One of them must be seriously good-looking for Marco to try for a number. Probably drove all the way in from the Main Line. That's a serious habit. Would you want to get involved with something like that? Okay, just a night might be fun, but that was it.

DeMarco tapped on the door, the car pulled away and around the corner. A kid came down the steps from the neatly painted rowhouse on the corner. Brick on top, red cinder blocks near the bottom. Various pots filled with flowers and shrubs surrounded the brick stoop. Deke always made sure the houses looked good. Less chance of attracting the wrong attention. Didn't fool anyone for long, but Deke insisted it made a difference. DeMarco told the kid something and he ran back inside. A different kid, but just as young, would get the order and run out the back. Malik was handling the money. No worries there. Malik was solid, though even one of the ten-year-old runners could probably take two blondes in a Lexus if they tried to cause trouble.

Barbie handed the joint back. "Where's Deke at?" He was a skinny guy with rotten teeth who liked to hang around the houses and pretend he was part of the crew. He had a tendency to talk too much, but he was mostly harmless and always had good weed. His actual name was Taylor. When he was fourteen, he'd gotten a big wraparound barbed-wire tattoo on his right bicep. He thought it would make him look tougher or change people's perceptions. Or something. Len wasn't totally sure why he'd done it. The only tangible change it made was that it earned him a new nickname: Barbie.

Len shrugged. "Don't keep his calendar. Probably out buying another building or some shit."

"Man is rolling in it. Just doing it up. Gonna own all of Gray's Ferry soon."

"Yeah." Len took a hit. He didn't want to talk about Deke. If you were on the outside, sure, it looked good. Money. Clothes. Good-looking women. But what about all the people you stepped on coming up? What about the people who helped boost you up? What about the people you have to leave behind? He was in no mood to talk about Deke.

He took a long hit on the joint and passed it back. Barbie caught the vibe and started talking about the Sixers. Would Embiid stay healthy this year? Could he and Simmons work on the same team? Len let the chatter fill his ears and worked his Aaron problem.

Killing someone is easy. Len knew that. Getting away with it is more complicated. He was sure no one would miss Aaron. His own mama might shed a tear or two, but she'd probably get over it before the next *Wheel of Fortune* episode. The man was a freak who would only bring more misery to the world. But Len needed to make sure he did it clean. He couldn't afford to have his mistake keep compounding.

He figured the lure of money would be enough to get Aaron someplace relatively secluded. He would be cautious but wouldn't be able to resist the greed. But what then? Just shoot him? That was probably the safest bet, but not foolproof. If he missed or only wounded him and Aaron got his hands on Len or had his own gun, it could end very badly for Len. He needed a better way. He wracked his brain thinking about ways to kill someone. The key with Aaron would be avoiding his gorilla arms. It had to be done from a safe distance. Poison? What did Len know about poison? Jack shit. What else? He couldn't farm this out to someone. He had no idea how to find a contract killer. He ran through more ideas, mostly from films he'd seen. He couldn't douse the guy in gasoline and light him on fire. Even Len thought that was absurd. He kept coming back to the gun. He didn't like it. Felt risky with a guy like Aaron, but it still might be the best option.

His eyes drifted to the buildings across the street, and he got an idea. He thought about it. It was risky, too. Part of it at least, but it might be worth a try. If it failed, he could still go with the gun.

"Huh?"

Barbie had said something.

"Here comes the boss."

Len looked down the street and saw Deke's black Cadillac CT6 gliding down the street with the familiar-looking bulk of Cherry behind the wheel. A moment later, he felt the car's big twin-turbo V8 humming in his chest. Cherry pulled to a stop next to DeMarco. The window came down and Len could just make out Deke's profile as he spoke to the kid. As he watched, he saw DeMarco stand a little straighter. Deke had that effect.

Len took a long last pull on the blunt and tossed the end into the flowerpot at the bottom of the steps. He stood, brushed his hands over his shirt and jeans, and walked toward the car. Cherry didn't get out. He'd hold the door for you if you were with Deke, otherwise you were on your own. Len walked around and opened the back passenger door and slid in next to his oldest friend. A stack of newspapers was on the seat. Len knew Deke had a thing about newspapers. He claimed it was the spotty internet service around Gray's Ferry that made him rely on the newsprint, but Len thought Deke just liked telling people he had a subscription to the Wall Street Journal.

The window slid back up and Cherry drove the rest of the way down Titan and turned right on 28th. They passed a construction site. A four-story building with a brick facade and vinyl siding. Len wondered if it was one of Deke's, he'd lost track but assumed most of the renovations or new construction in this area were down to him. Deke didn't look over or say anything, however, so maybe not.

Instead, he picked up one of the papers and tossed it in Len's lap. "Tell me you had nothing to do with this?"

Len glanced down. Given how it happened, he thought it would make the news, but he hadn't expected this. Most murders in the southeast barely made a ripple. Many didn't even make the news. But this one had. Something had snagged the public's consciousness. It was the lead story with a big headline to match. 'Gunmen Shoot Teen After Chasing Him In To Chinese Takeout.' Len wondered if it was the Chinese takeout part. Would it have been newsworthy if it had happened in a park or playground? He read the first paragraph:

The teen, identified by friends and neighbors as 15-year-old Draymond Cooper, ran into Green Dragon takeout restaurant at 25th and Tasker Streets just after nine p.m. Tuesday. According to witnesses, the teen shouted he was running away from two men who had been chasing him in the streets and was begging an employee to drop the security gate and not let the men inside.

He scanned the rest. There were a couple of quotes from people inside the restaurant when it happened. Did the quotes make it newsworthy? The story continued inside, but he tossed the paper back on the seat between them.

"Course not. Why would I be rolling around near 25th at nine p.m.? No reason to give Bishop or one of his boys an opp to take a shot at me. Draymond Cooper? Don't even know the kid."

"That's Scootch. The guy you talked to. Bishop's guy."

Len shrugged. "No picture. Only knew him as Scootch. You think Bishop did it because we were talking to him?"

Deke blew out a hard breath and looked out the window. "Who knows? It doesn't make any sense. We can wipe Bishop and his little crew off the map like rubbing a bug off the windshield. He can't afford to be shooting his guys."

"Could be a coincidence. Guys have been getting shot on either side of 27 for years. Scootch just ended up in the wrong place at the wrong time."

"Definitely the wrong time, but it doesn't sound like that old shit. This sounds … targeted. Either way, this story has put the spotlight back on the southeast for all the wrong reasons. The old reasons. It will not help us with the city council or getting the permits. Shit, I'm going to have to talk to Watts again. The longer this kid holds on and the story stays relevant, the more I'm going to have to beg."

Len tried to keep the surprise out of his voice. "He's alive?"

Deke didn't seem to notice. "Yeah, appears we can't even do murder right in Gray's Ferry. The kid is in the ICU. One shot clipped him in the head, one in the chest, but the others missed. Still doesn't look good for him, but it's going to string the story out for a few more days." Deke shuffled through the paper. "I should try to talk to his family. If he pulls through, we could try to position it as a comeback story. Miracle boy."

The last thing Len needed was Scootch to wake up and start talking.

CHAPTER TWENTY

L ater, before her memories became too difficult and dangerous to pick through, she would remember three things from her time with Tio Rafa.

First, was how to make beans.

Tio lived in a small house next to the barn. It represented Tio's longstanding status and service to the family. Occasionally, other temporary field hands arrived to help with the harvest or large repairs. If they didn't stay in town, they would sleep in the loft in the barn. The house was constructed of rough stone with an adobe clay tile roof. It was a much smaller version of the main house. Each morning, she knocked on the weathered wood of the front door and Tio Rafa would tell her to come in. Inside, the house comprised a single room. Tio's bed was against the wall, just inside the door, under the window to catch the occasional mountain breezes that swept down into their valley. A small stove and kitchen prep area were along the back wall. A table with two chairs sat in the middle and a small bathroom was walled off in the back corner. Two brightly woven rugs were nailed to the walls. A third rug lay on the floor between the bed and the table.

It all looked very cramped and shabby to her, and she had said as much the first day in the blunt way that children sometimes talk. Tio Rafa went still for a minute and then nodded. "I suppose it would to you," he said in his accented Spanish, so different from her own inflections. She never learned where he was from. She would insult his home, but never had the curiosity or manners to ask about his past. "But it is all I need."

In time, she would come to love that shabby room and would remember the bright fibers of the rug and the worn grooves of the wooden planks, long after the memories of her bedroom faded. Every morning with Tio was identical. Maybe that's why the memory of that tiny room had stuck for so long. She would knock. He would answer. She would enter and smell the cafe de olla. The clay pot would be simmering on the stove, and Tio Rafa would be sitting at the table sipping a cup of the strong brew. The smells of cinnamon, anise, and orange peel would fill the room.

He would sip from his cup and then ask, "How did you sleep?"

"Fine, Tio."

"Are you ready to start?"

"Yes, Tio."

"Good." He would take a long swallow and finish the coffee and then walk to the kitchen. He would rinse the mug and place it upside down on a wood cutting block. "But first we make the beans."

She had been confused that first morning. She thought her father had sent her to Tio Rafa to learn to fight. Or for exercise. Or punishment for spying in his office. She didn't know for sure. Her cheek was still tender, and her molars felt a little loose when she tried to chew. She did not expect to learn to cook.

"Do you know how?"

She did not. The housekeeper or her mother had always prepared the food, but she was embarrassed to admit her ignorance over something as simple as beans. "Yes, of course."

"Good." He took a cast iron pot from a hook and then opened an earthenware jar on the counter. "Make a pot of beans and then meet me outside."

She had thoroughly ruined a pound of beans that morning, over boiling them with too little water until a mushy black crust rimmed the pot. Tio Rafa had said nothing. Her cheeks had burned with embarrassment. She would have rather he hit her again. They ate nothing for lunch except cups of water and dry tortillas.

The second day started the same way, with the same question. This time, she responded, "No," without meeting his eyes. He nodded and then showed her how to pick through the beans to remove any dirt, rocks, or damaged beans, then to rinse them thoroughly before placing them in the pot. He then added half an onion, some cloves of garlic, and some epazote stems that were growing in a pot on the windowsill.

"You must pour in plenty of water, more than enough to cover all the beans. Let it come to a boil and then lower to a simmer."

After the pot was bubbling gently, they walked out to the stable and fed the horses and cleaned the stalls. They returned to the stove two hours later to check on the beans. Tio Rafa added more water to the pot.

"It is better to have too much water than too little. You can always find a use for broth." He scooped a bean out and held it in the palm of his hand. "You see how the bean's skin has curled up? Now you add the salt. Add it too early and it will toughen the beans, not flavor them. But be careful, it is always easier to add more salt than it is to take it away. Do you understand?"

"Yes, Tio."

They left the pot and returned to the chores. That afternoon they ate soft, buttery beans with their tortillas for lunch.

"The same water that softened these beans would harden an egg. Do you understand?"

"Yes, Tio." She answered quickly and surely because she understood. Boiling water would affect things differently depending on what was in the pot.

He looked at her for a long time and shook his head. "No, I don't think you do, not yet, not fully, but someday you will." A rebuke but said with a smile.

That was the second thing she learned, but Tio was right, it would take a long time for her to understand that it's what you are made of, not the circumstances that will ultimately dictate your response.

They worked hard each day. He never asked her to do anything that he didn't do. She became stronger and tougher. Her skin became brown from the sun. Her hands were calloused and tough. They never began the training until all the work was done. "There is no point in starting when you are fresh. You will never be rested and waiting for a fight. That is a luxury. You must understand how to attack and defend when you are tired. You must have the discipline to overcome the fatigue and not make a mistake that might get you hurt. Or worse."

He was patient and fair and always had a positive constructive comment. He was a very good teacher. She felt bad the day she cut him.

They were working with knives. Tio Rafa thought guns

were a crude weapon akin to a cudgel or hammer. "We will learn about them because even if they are ugly, they are effective, but I can teach you all you need to know about them in less than a week. Better to take the time to make *yourself* into a weapon than rely on a tool." So, they spent their time with knives and staffs and kicks and takedowns. She had asked him once what they were learning. Was it jujitsu? Or karate? He had just looked confused. "There is no name. It is just the Aztec way."

They spent the most time with knives and small blades. He never took it easy on her. He defeated her day after day, but he always stopped with the metal against her skin, never splitting it. She slowly improved until the day she feinted and lured him forward into a trap, then she sprung it closed and cut into his arm and shoulder. The knives were not dull sparring weapons. She honed the blades each day as her last chore. They were very sharp. She saw the blood leak through the cut in his work shirt. She could also see the surprised pain in his wrinkled face. She'd cut an old man. She froze.

Her sister darted forward in the stillness and cut him on the other arm.

That was the third thing she learned.

She and her sister looked very similar. Standing beside each other, separated by just a year in age, they could be mistaken for twins. They both were tall for their age and lithe with a mass of curling hair and dark eyes, but inside they were different. They were made of different things. She stopped. Her sister didn't. She'd drawn blood and taken a step back. Her sister had stepped forward.

CHAPTER TWENTY-ONE

Ash drove the ice cream truck. The music played. It was trench warfare and Ash was getting pushed back. It was the ninth day, and he'd been sober the whole time. It was his longest stretch in a decade. But he was slipping. On the seventh day, he'd bought a pint of Old Grand Dad and taken it back to his motel room. It sat on the chipped dresser top, a security blanket and a temptation. So far, he hadn't cracked it.

But how much longer could he do this? He felt himself coming apart. The bourbon bottle was the canary in the coal mine. If he wanted to parlay this ... opportunity, this week of sobriety, into something more permanent, maybe another shot with Maggie, he had to get out of this truck. The money was good, great even, way better than he'd get starting over almost anywhere else, but ultimately it would not save him. He had a small bankroll in his pocket. It would give him a cushion, but nothing more.

He drove and turned the problem over in his mind. Now that he wasn't sleeping rough next to their dumpster, could he get a job at McDonald's? He knew their product lineup and clean-up procedures. Or there was that guy, some sort of community volunteer, who came around once in a while and tried to talk to him. Most of the time, Ash was high and didn't understand. The words were inky blots that dripped out of the man's mouth, but he thought he was offering some kind of help. He should try to find him. Maybe that was the next step up the ladder.

He drove the truck for four hours each day inside the rough square of coordinates that the man provided. Ash had become adept at avoiding any spots where kids might gather. Occasionally, one or two would try to hail him down from the street, but he just kept his eyes distant and unfocused and continued driving. It made no sense to him. What was the point? Everyone in the neighborhood must have seen the truck by now, but no one was buying. They couldn't. The truck was empty. He tried to keep it simple. He fell back on his military training. He shut off his brain and followed orders. He drove the route. He didn't stop. He got paid. He slept indoors. He could do it. The longer he stayed off the drugs, the more his discipline came back.

But the music. What would the military call it? An operational environmental mission variable. They would give it an acronym. An OEMV. The music was going to break him. He looked at the small digital clock stuck with double-sided adhesive to the dashboard like a cyst. Only twenty more minutes until he could park it. After that, he'd only have to drown out the echoes of the godforsaken music in his head.

CHAPTER TWENTY-TWO

Being lucky takes hard work. Or sitting on your ass for hours watching the comings and goings of an upscale hotel. That's what Max thought then. Later, he'd wonder if she only let him glimpse her when she was good and ready. And it served her purpose.

It had been a week and he'd seen no sign of her. She hadn't called again. The late October days smelled like cool rain, wet leaves, and the muddy banks of the Schuylkill. Summer had slipped her collar and was long gone now. The forecast promised a true cold snap was coming, along with the first snow. He spent his off hours in cafes and coffee shops with a view of The Clyde. Or, he sat on a cold bench, moving every half-hour, and tried to read, with one eye on the entrance. He drank a lot of coffee and learned where all the public bathrooms were, but he never saw her. He finished *The Demolished Man* and moved on to Leibowitz. If he ever became a private eye, he thought he'd get a lot of reading done. Something to consider. He liked reading. His injuries had healed up. His back and ribs still looked like a demented quilt, but he had full range of motion back.

As office workers began spilling out onto the street and the evening rush hour started, he was feeling pretty good, more like his old self, and wondering if the box and the bride were like chasing Ahab's white whale. Was it better to just give up? Whatever had happened that night hadn't come back on her. Or if it did, he hadn't heard about it and likely never would. She didn't need help, and that meant he was just a nutty stalker weaving delusions in the air to justify his behavior. He stood and was looking for the closest trashcan to throw away yet another empty cup of coffee when she walked out the front door. She even gave Gabriel a brief wave.

He dropped the cup in the trash bin and pulled out his phone. She wasn't wearing the wedding dress, but he recognized the tangle of curly hair that almost surrounded her head like a halo. She was across the street but walking in his direction with two other women. He snapped a couple of photos with his phone, trying to zoom in without making it obvious. He glanced around, nervous, but phones had become ubiquitous attachments, like noses on a face. No one gave him a second glance. He probably looked more out-of-place reading a book than taking a photo on a busy street.

The women walked past. None of them looked in his direction. While they each had on a different light jacket, they all wore similar dark polyester pants and dark sneakers. It was a uniform, likely for a cleaning position if Max had to guess. The other two women appeared older than the bride. The trio turned east at the end of the block and walked side-by-side up the sidewalk toward Broad Street. There was both a bus stop and the Walnut-Locust subway station nearby. If all he wanted was to return the box and dismiss the whole affair, he just needed to catch up and hand it over. But if he wanted answers, it might be better to talk to her alone.

Max picked up his backpack, the wooden box inside, and

followed. It wasn't difficult, even with the end-of-day pedestrian congestion on the sidewalks. One of the women was wearing a mustard-colored wool cloche hat, and Max could stay well back and still keep an eye on the hat as it bobbed along in the crowd.

Bicyclists in the city are largely invisible. They are background noise like pigeons, taxicabs, or panhandlers. You see them, but you don't. They exist, but they don't. Your body learns to navigate around them without thinking. Max would not have noticed this biker coming either, but something was off. Something made his brain register this particular pigeon as significant. He looked closer. He was a large man riding an older bike. He was wearing a heavy parka, much too warm for the sunny afternoon, and no helmet. The bike had a bright blue aluminum frame, paint badly scraped, handlebar tape stained and peeling off on one side. The cassette, derailleur, and chain all badly needed oil. The bike was a loud, rusty eyesore. It looked like the rider had pulled it out of a dumpster.

The man also didn't appear to have very good bike handling skills. The bike wobbled left and right, dangerously close to onrushing traffic, as the man scanned the sidewalk. The man's eyes caught on him, and Max took a sideways step deeper into the crowd. The stream of people approached a crosswalk, and as the light turned, more people swarmed from the other side.

As Max watched, the man veered closer to the crowd in the intersection and slung a messenger bag off his back. He held it in one hand and the bike's handlebars with the other. He then windmilled the arm holding the pack in a giant circle, once, twice. More people were noticing now. He gathered more force and momentum with a third cycle, then turned tight abruptly against the merging, crossing crowds in the middle of the street and slammed the bag directly into the face of an unsuspecting businessman. The executive crumpled in a heap, taking a woman behind him and a man on his left with him. Max could see blood gushing from his nose and a cut over his eye. The woman scuttled back and screamed. People stopped to help. The man laid out in the street was stunned and confused and lashed out at the would-be Good Samaritans. He caught one guy on the jaw with a wild punch and that guy ended up on his ass. Then the traffic light changed and cars inched forward. Max was afraid they would just keep coming, it was Philly, but then they stopped. And started with their horns.

It was chaos.

That's when Max noticed the sudden, sharp pressure of a knife in his side.

"Just relax and drop the backpack." A male voice said in his ear. Max felt things slow down. He tried to turn his head to get a glimpse at his attacker but felt the pressure on his side increase. "Uh-uh." No one was paying them any attention. But that could work both ways.

"No problem. Just take it easy."

The blade was pressed low into his gut on the left side, almost even with his navel. Something about this whole thing was off, Max thought. Like the guy riding the bike, the guy holding the knife on him was an amateur. He was holding the knife too low and on the wrong side. The right upper side has the liver and the big veins from the rest of the body, the left upper side has the spleen and the big abdominal arteries. You want to do some damage, that's where you want the knife. This guy might clip the kidneys or intestines, but even most of those were higher than his current aim. Max still didn't want to get poked, but if he did, he thought he'd survive. But he didn't plan on adding any new piercings today.

He let out a slow breath and relaxed his shoulders. The backpack slid down into the crook of his right arm. He leaned forward and let the strap fall into his hand, and then he dropped the bag on the pavement. He was leaning over at the waist. The man relaxed a fraction. It was going according to plan from his perspective. The pressure from the knife eased slightly. Max whipped up and around from the waist like a spinning top, putting all the force and momentum he could get into his leading elbow.

He hadn't been able to see the guy, so his aim was off. The man was shorter than he expected and his elbow was too high. It glanced off the top of his head, not solidly into the temple as Max planned, but it stunned him enough and gave Max the room to correct his aim and connect with his trailing right fist behind the guy's ear. The guy stumbled back, his eyes blank, out on his feet. He took two steps sideways, one back, and then sat down in the middle of the street.

Max took a good look now. Small, dark-haired, dark-complected. He didn't recognize him. The confusion from the biker attack was clearing up. The injured parties were moving toward the sidewalk. Cars were inching around on one side. The crowd was dissipating.

He turned to pick up his bag. Didn't see it. He scanned the nearby ground. It was gone.

He looked up the street toward Broad. Didn't see the mustard-colored hat. The women were gone, too.

The two things didn't feel like a coincidence.

CHAPTER TWENTY-THREE

"There's a fine line between noble perseverance and insanity," Lawrence said.

"Don't you think this nudges me back toward nobility?" Max responded.

"It might make the situation a little less insane, but I'm not sure it does anything for you."

Max could hear the grin in his friend's reply, but he also knew that he and Eddie would try to help if they could. He'd just finished filling Lawrence in on his earlier chat with Detectives Axelson and Diaz. After a week of little progress on his own, Max hoped Eddie might poke around behind some firewalls and find out why the police were interested in finding the bride.

"I sensed something was off about this whole thing. The cops only confirmed it."

"They didn't confirm anything, and you still know nothing or you wouldn't be calling me."

"I'm really calling for Eddie."

Lawrence ignored that. Eddie could find the needle in the

informational haystack, but it was Lawrence who could see the bigger picture.

"Have you considered that you might have the wrong end of the stick?" He asked now. "That you might be aiding the bad guys, to put it in terms you can understand. You are just a name on their list, right now. If you keep popping up, you might edge yourself right into the frame for whatever this woman did."

"Yes, I've thought about it. And I realize she might not want or need any help, but I've also been jumped twice, whacked on the head, and had something stolen from me."

"Something that didn't even belong to you."

"Doesn't mean they can rob me and take it back."

"I thought you were a man of faith? What happened to turning the other cheek?"

"I never claimed to be a man of faith. I am a man who is always searching and questioning faith. I believe in a god, I'm just not sure it's the one you are quoting to me now. That nugget comes up multiple times in the Bible, but I don't think it means just be passive and let someone trample all over you. I don't think any god would want that. I think it's a call to suppress the urge for revenge that inevitably comes when someone slaps us in the face."

"Only God gets to do revenge."

"But I think helping someone who is hurting, or needs help, would be fine with God."

"And if helping hurt someone else?"

"I think God might be okay with self-defense."

After he hung up with Lawrence, who had promised to talk to Eddie, he walked across the street to the gym and found Ronnie with the young kid who was usually there when Max was working out. The kid appeared to live in the gym.

Knowing Ronnie, he really might. The man would do anything to help these kids. He approached the pair and waited off to one side. Ronnie was holding punching mitts and moving them around for the kid to target. The kid had fast hands. After a minute, the stopwatch around Ronnie's neck beeped.

"Hit the speed bag, Javon. Gotta talk to this guy for a minute."

The kid nodded and walked to the opposite corner where an old red-stitched bag hung from a hook.

"Kid has the look," Max said.

"We'll see," Ronnie said, but Max had been around the old man long enough to realize this was a serious compliment. He usually dealt in insults. "What do you want? Not a workout."

"No, not today. Remember the other day in the diner, we were talking about the shootings and other troubles in the neighborhood?"

"Sure. Murder, taxes, and the weather. Nothing much changes around here. What about it? You figure out a solution?"

"No. I wanted to ask what you know about the FCM?"

"That a gang?"

Max didn't want to tell Ronnie any more than he had to. He didn't want to put him even remotely in harm's way. "I think so. Mostly Latino. You ever get kids in here from them?"

Ronnie shook his head. "Once they're in the gangs, I rarely get them back. Never heard of FCM, but that's not too surprising. Gangs are like weeds around here. I wouldn't even call most gangs. They're just glorified clubs where a couple of guys got a blade or a crappy old gun. Why are you asking?"

"My boss at the car service is having some issues. Thought I'd ask around. See if they're legit or if they're all smoke and he can blow them off."

"I don't know anything, but I can put you in touch with someone who might." He walked over to the beat-up metal desk near the door. He pulled open the top drawer and rummaged around in a mess of papers before he pulled out a thin, creased business card and handed it to Max. "You should talk to Bunk. He's out there every day and could tell you something."

Max looked at the card. It was simple and white on thin stock. *Darius Mack, Community Activist* with a phone number. "Why Bunk?"

Ronnie smiled. "Just like your boy Joe Frazier, Darius had heavy hands. If he caught you with a right, it could knock you back six feet and make you forget your damn name."

"Let me guess, it didn't mean bunk because he couldn't move his feet?"

"That's right. But he had some talent. I'd say I regret I couldn't coach him up, but he's much better at his current work. The bigger shame would have been if he kept at it, got his head scrambled, and never got to do that instead."

Max waved the card. "And what does he do? Community activist is kind of vague."

"In the best possible way. Talk to him."

He thanked Ronnie and left him to his young protege. Javon had finished with the speed bag and moved on to skipping rope to stay loose. The rope was a blur, but the kid looked relaxed and confident. Maybe he had a chance.

Max took the stairs back down to the street. A woman was pacing back and forth in front of a bench, smoking a cigarette. She gave him a tight smile that didn't invite any conversation. Max was okay with that. He walked a few yards up the sidewalk and punched in the number from Darius

Mack's card. It rolled to voicemail. He left a message, included Ronnie's name, and hung up.

After a week of unrelenting clouds, afternoon sun dappled the city streets with honey-colored light. The occasional trees that persisted in the concrete jungle showed splashes of red, orange, and yellow. Max walked east across the blocks. He liked fall in the city. Always had. Winter and summer were harsh and obvious with blankets of snow or stifling heat. Spring was often unpredictable and too short. Autumn was a slow burn. It was a season that gave you time to prepare. The air was briskly comfortable but had an edge, like a cotton ball hiding a razor blade. It promised winter on the horizon, but not yet.

He walked along Christian Street and then turned south on 19th until he crossed Washington, the unofficial border of Philly's Point Breeze neighborhood. He paused next to a park with a newly painted basketball court next to a small plastic playset and sandbox for younger kids. There was no one using the park. Monday afternoon. Perhaps everyone was still in school. He pulled out his phone and looked at the plat map that Eddie had marked up based on the bride's phone calls. He stood at the top of the triangulated circle. He didn't expect to bump into her. That was too much to expect, though stranger things had happened. But he thought he'd ask around. See if anyone recognized her picture or where she might live. He couldn't think of anything else to do. If it worked? Great. If he came up empty, but word got back to her somehow? If she realized that bike messenger stunt hadn't put him off? He thought that might force her to make a move. He divided the circle into four quadrants and started walking.

CHAPTER TWENTY-FOUR

He wasn't familiar with Point Breeze, even though it was less than a mile from his apartment. He'd driven through it a few times, but he didn't get many pickups or drop-offs in this area. The neighborhood was going through an upheaval. Max thought back to what Ronnie had said in the diner about money and opportunity. There were construction sites and development lots every other block. Old traditional row homes were being razed or renovated, replaced with cookie-cutter condos that looked like someone's version of a city from a movie set. Coffee bars and gastropubs were side-by-side with autobody supply stores and dive bars.

It wasn't just the buildings. You could see it in the people walking the streets, too. It was a mixed crowd of bearded hipsters, Lululemon, Latinx, and a scattering of Blacks and other nationalities. He recognized it all. He'd watched it happen to sections of Boston. Gentrification had rolled in like a slow-motion wave, erasing families, histories, and communities for fake facades, good intentions, and repaved streets. He wondered what the neighborhood would look like in another five years? Would it be homogenized across the board until it resembled a bland real estate brochure? Anytown, USA? There were benefits to gentrification, lower crime and better property values, but did that outweigh the costs? Were revitalization and rent hikes progress or a poisoned pill?

He walked the streets, sometimes turning down a side residential street to cut over to a different commercial section. The neighborhood had an energy to it. The narrow side streets still showcased many original two- and three-story Philly row homes among the construction sites. Maybe they'd been gutted and updated inside, but the classic brick architecture and neighborly stoops were still on display from the street. The mixed-use buildings persisted, too. He found plenty of sidewalk level mom-and-pop businesses with apartments or living spaces on the upper floors. There were barbershops, laundromats, pizza places, hoagie shops, pharmacies, and corner stores.

Max stopped in the laundromats, pharmacies, and convenience stores. Even if you lived a solitary existence and tried to stay off the grid, you still needed to wash your clothes, brush your teeth, and buy milk occasionally.

He picked the best photo he'd snapped as she walked out of the hotel with the other women, a three-quarters profile that showed her distinctive curly hair and two scars running across her forehead. He showed it to each clerk or salesperson he came across. Most encounters didn't last longer than thirty seconds. The clerk would perk up, their eyes brightening at the prospect of something more interesting than scanning a candy bar and making change, but then the light would go out again when they glanced at the screen with no recognition.

. . .

He had worked his way through most of his second self-defined quadrant and was at the intersection of Mifflin and 17th Street when he found her in a laundromat. He'd stopped at the small corner grocers and shown the two Lebanese brothers behind the counter the photo but got no response beyond a shake of the head and a shrug. The constant noes were wearing him out. He decided the next block would be the last for today. He'd grab the bus and head back home for a quick shower and to pack his cooler before heading to work. He needed to think about Liam's situation. The bride wasn't his only problem.

He walked across the street. The incoming tide of gentrification hadn't yet reached this far south. The brick and stucco buildings were tired and wan. The vacant buildings stood empty or boarded up. The cars parked on the street a little older. The people on the sidewalks a little more bent over.

The first-floor laundromat had wire cages over the two street windows and featured dusty, sun-faded signs offering free dries. Like most of the coin-op places he'd been that day, it was self-service, but along with the free dries and seven-day-a-week schedule, it advertised a wash, dry, and fold drop-off service.

He pushed through the door. Two dryers were running, but the place appeared empty until a man popped his head out of an open doorway in the back. Noting Max's lack of laundry, the rest of his body followed his head.

"Can I help you?" he asked.

He didn't appear older than fifty but had a head full of gray hair that looked like he'd combed it with a blender. He was wearing a burgundy Temple University sweatshirt with holes in the elbows and around the neck. His corduroys had shiny patches at both knees and both black Reebok sneakers lacked shoelaces. He looked homeless, but Max got an incongruous whiff of floral dryer sheets as he approached.

"I'm looking for this woman. Have you seen her?" Max held out his phone, the picture primed and ready. It was a well-choreographed dance at this point.

"Why are you looking for her?"

This wasn't the first time someone had asked that question. The first time Max had tried to explain the real story, it came out sounding crazy even to his ears, so he'd settled on a simpler reply by now.

"Her family hasn't heard from her and they're worried. They asked me to help." A hint of authority, a hint of sympathy. Most people didn't take it further.

The man looked, glanced away, then looked back. Max was already shifting his weight to walk out, anticipating the 'no' when the man replied. "No, but I know Mrs. Lopez."

He pointed a finger at the woman walking next to the bride.

Five minutes later, Max had walked half a block north on 17th to a stubby block of seven row homes. There was a small autobody shop carved out of the first two units with living space up above. It looked oddly out of place in the residential mix, but Max figured capitalism would find a space in any crack. And it looked busy. He could hear the whirring noise of a tension wrench as he passed, and cars were jammed up in the little side alley waiting for service.

He checked the numbers and walked up the steps of the fourth unit. It shared a stoop with the neighboring unit, the doors right next to each other and first-floor windows mirroring each other. He knocked and heard shuffling steps. A moment later, the door opened. If he had any doubts that the man in the laundromat was mistaken, they disappeared in the face of the older woman who now stood blinking at him in the doorway. Over her right shoulder was an oak coatrack with a distinctive mustard-colored hat hanging from a hook.

She said nothing and didn't seem particularly surprised to find Max standing on her doorstep. She pushed open the screen door and said, "You might as well come in," as if she'd been waiting impatiently for him to arrive. She didn't wait, just turned and disappeared deeper into the house.

The house was narrow and cramped like you'd expect from looking at it from the outside, but Max got a sense of family and love just from the short trip down the hall, past a living room and dining room, and into the kitchen at the back of the house. Photos lined the walls in haphazard collages, small pieces of handmade art dotted shelves, and furniture filled the rooms that looked old, but well-used and comfortable. The house may be quiet now, but it clearly once held laughter and great joy. Maybe it still did on a different day. Max hoped so.

Mrs. Lopez stood at an electric stove, stirring a bubbling pot. There were two more simmering on different burners. The small space smelled of garlic, tomatoes, and cilantro. She placed the spoon down and turned to him. "Please, sit down."

Her familiarity unsettled him. He sat down in a padded chair at a square wooden table. She was short and stocky, a few inches over five feet, thick through the hips and legs but with a soft face and intelligent eyes. She bustled about the kitchen with practiced confidence. Max watched her take a bowl from a cabinet and fill it with rice, then scoop out two steaming ladles from one pot on the stove before placing it in front of him along with a spoon and napkin. She turned back to the fridge and added a beer.

"Eat first. You'll feel better. Just sofrito. In Mexico, we use habaneros. I hope you don't mind a little spice." She said it with a smile and a bit of a challenge. Until the steam and warm spices were wafting up to him, he hadn't realized how hungry he was.

"Thank you. It smells wonderful." And it did. He'd been eating at The Skyline and from out of his cooler for so long now he'd almost forgotten how good and comforting a real home-cooked meal could be. He nodded his thanks and ate. She smiled and turned back to the stove.

Eventually, when half the bowl was gone, and he could barely feel his lips from the peppers, he asked. "Do you always let strange men into your house without question, Mrs. Lopez?"

"Please, call me Lorena. And my time for strange men is long past." She paused and checked on another pot. "I met my Don when I was seventeen and we were married for forty-seven years, so I'm not sure I ever had the time or inclination for strange men."

"A lucky man."

"And I was a lucky woman. Were you ever married?"

"Yes." He tried to keep his face neutral, but some of the past pain must have seeped into his voice. She watched him for a moment, then turned back to the stove. He was relieved when she didn't ask any follow-ups.

"You'll have to forgive me," she waved a hand around, "I tend to cook when I'm nervous or anxious. My kids are all grown. Don is over at St. Dot's. I don't know who I think will eat all this, but I can't seem to stop. It helps me stay calm."

"Why are you nervous?"

A buzzer sounded, and she opened the oven and pulled out what looked like a roast pork loin and set it on a side-board to rest. She didn't answer his question but turned to face him and asked one of her own. "Why are you here?"

"I'm looking for ... the bride."

If she found that an unusual response, she didn't show it. Instead, she just nodded and said, "And why are you looking for her? What do you want?"

"The short answer to both questions is that I want to help."

"Do you want to save her?"

"No, she looked more than capable of handling herself."

Lorena nodded at that. "Then why?"

A good question and one he'd been asking himself a lot as he tried to track her down. "Because I'm here and I wasn't sure anyone else was willing to do it."

"I'm not sure that answers the question."

Max shrugged. "It's the best I can do. I spent a good portion of my life so far screwing up and screwing over other people. More often than not, it ended up hurting people. I'm trying to change. I can't go back and fix what I broke, but I can try to do better going forward."

"Making amends."

He held out his hands. "It's the best explanation, I can offer."

"Are you good at it?"

He smiled. Another excellent question. "I'm not sure I'm the best judge of that, but I do my best."

She thought about that and came to some sort of conclusion. "You asked why I'm nervous."

"Yes."

Just then there were the sounds of a lock rattling and then a door opening. Max heard heavy footsteps coming down the hall. He tensed.

Lorena continued, "I think you're right. We need help. Adelita is missing."

Gabriel stood in the doorway.

CHAPTER TWENTY-FIVE

"Adelita was the woman I dropped off? Wearing the wedding dress?" Max asked Gabriel. He wore faded black jeans that looked gray in the bright kitchen lights, with a green-and-blue plaid flannel shirt tucked in at the waist. Max was still adjusting to seeing him out of his hotel uniform. He sat opposite Max, and Lorena had placed a matching bowl of sofrito in front of him. She moved around them, checking pots, wiping counters, but also clearly still listening.

"Yes."

"Your memory has improved."

Max took some small comfort in the fact that Gabriel looked embarrassed.

"Yes, I'm sorry, but we've learned ... to be careful."

"Of what?"

He leaned back, perhaps relieved to move on to broader topics. "It might be faster to list the things we aren't afraid of, but in your case: strangers, white men, unknown motives, stubborn behavior." He gave a small smile at the last one.

"Why not just admit that she worked there and have her

come down and get the box? It would have been over in thirty seconds."

Gabriel looked up and away, catching Lorena's eye over Max's shoulder. "You're right. That might have been a better way to handle it, but again, we didn't know who you were or what you wanted."

"I'm just a driver."

"But we had no way of knowing that and no way of really checking at four in the morning. We felt it was better to be cautious. Ade has a certain way she likes doing things." He shrugged as if that was an actual answer.

Max noted how Gabriel kept using 'we,' but he was tired of the runaround. "She's paranoid, you mean? Why?"

"It's not paranoia if it's real."

Max pushed his empty bowl away and put up his hands. "Look, you said you wanted my help, but all you're giving me are cryptic answers."

"I'm sorry. Adelita's story is not mine to tell. She can tell you if she chooses, but we do need your help."

"How?"

"Adelita is missing," Gabriel said.

"Why me? I'm not lying. I really am just a driver."

"You've already answered that," Lorena said. "Because you're here and you want to help." She walked behind Gabriel and placed a hand on his shoulder. "And you might be a driver, but you are not just a driver. Just a driver would not have kept pursuing it like you did."

Something about the way she said it made Max pause. "It was you guys that jumped me in the alley and then stole the box with the biker. Right?"

This time, Gabriel wasn't as embarrassed as before. "We were trying to help. You must remember that. We didn't want to hurt you, not badly, but dissuade you. These are bad people."

"Why not go to the police? They could bring a lot more resources than I ever could."

They looked at each other, then Gabriel said, "Any police involvement could get complicated."

It took a moment for the penny to drop. "She's here illegally."

"Yes. But not by choice. She was brought here."

"Illegally."

"Yes."

"Are you both illegals?"

"No, we are both citizens. I was born here, and Lorena has been a citizen since she immigrated with her husband in the seventies, though I sometimes wonder if that matters much anymore."

"How is she working at the hotel if she's here illegally?"

Gabriel gave him a glance as if he couldn't be that naïve. "It happens all the time. She is hardly the only one without proper papers working in the city. The documents are good enough. The hotel is happy not to ask too many questions and the people are happy to work. Much of the economy works this way. Much more than anyone in power wants to admit."

Max agreed but could see Gabriel warming to the topic and didn't want to get sidetracked. "What is she doing now?" he asked. "Why was she bleeding and wearing a wedding dress the other night?"

"She's looking for someone. Her sister."

"Her sister's also missing?"

"Her sister ..." Gabriel trailed off and Lorena picked up the thread. "Her sister, Soledad, was also kidnapped and brought here, to the United States, not Philadelphia, at the same time as Ade. Eventually, Ade escaped. Her sister found a different way to cope."

"Drugs?"

"Yes, drugs and a taste for violence," Gabriel continued.

"But you know where Soledad is?"

"Not exactly. We know she's involved with the Familia de la Calle Misericordia. Do you know them?"

"FCM? The gang?"

"Yes. I'm not sure they would call themselves that but, yes, it's essentially what they are. Bad men."

"And she can't convince Soledad to leave?"

"It's not that simple. Do you know any addicts?"

Max had known plenty in his life, in prison, in Essex, and back in Boston. "Sure."

"The gang is her source. Does any junkie give up a steady connect?"

"No, not willingly."

"Exactly. She also has other valuable skills. Have you ever heard of La Hoja?" Max shook his head. "It means the blade. Ade and her sister are very good with knives." He paused and seemed to be searching for the right words. "They learned at an early age. The FCM is trying to expand and flex its muscles in and around Point Breeze. Having someone like Sol on your side is very helpful. She's fearless with her knives, and the stories that circulate on the street about La Hoja only make her bigger and scarier. A folktale to help others fall in line. She doesn't want to leave, and the FCM doesn't want to let her go."

"But Ade is determined to save her sister?"

"Yes."

That was a sentiment Max knew well. His brother Danny had swum in the same pool as Sol. Drugs. Violence. Crime. Would Sol also come to a violent end? Now Max understood why the look on Ade's face that night in the back of the car looked so familiar. He'd seen it in the mirror countless times. It was willful determination in the face of insurmountable odds. It was a soldier going over the wall into a hail of machine gunfire. It was taking the next step regardless of the consequences.

"Sometimes family is a terrible burden," he said.

Max pushed open the bedroom door but didn't step in, just stood in the doorway. It was a simple square, small, but comfortable. A single bed with a blue comforter and matching pillow sat in the center of the room between two windows. A wooden end table sat to the right. A gold-plated lamp with a square shade and a tissue box sat on top. A closet was to the left. A slim upright chest of drawers that matched the nightstand was to the left of the door. An overhead fan had been installed in the center of the ceiling. That was it. No pictures. No trinkets. Nothing personal on display.

"How long did she stay here?" he asked.

Lorena stood on the top step. "About six months."

"Did it always look like this?"

Lorena moved closer and peered into the room. "Like what?"

"Empty."

"Yes, she has little."

Max went in and opened the top drawer of the dresser. Nothing inside. He pulled open the next two drawers. Same result. "Clothes?"

"She hung a few things in the closet, but she mostly kept things in a black duffel under the bed."

Max knelt and lifted the white bed skirt. Nothing under the bed but a few dust bunnies. He got back to his feet, ignoring the flare of pain from his side, and opened the closet door. It was full, with a few loose hangers on the right side of the rod.

"Yours?"

"Yes, I keep my spring and summer clothes here."

He closed the closet and moved to the nightstand. He expected the drawer to be empty like the rest, but it wasn't. There was a book inside, a novel in Spanish. The cover was in pale blue and showed a Western vista. He didn't recognize the title or author. He flipped through the pages but found nothing. Not even a bookmark.

Adelita had lived here for six months and hadn't left a mark. He felt a pang of sadness at a life lived so shallowly, then he wondered how much different this room was from his own place just a few miles away. He had a few more books, true, and some clothes in drawers, a radio, and a coffee machine, but would anyone walk in and be able to know anything about him? So how deeply was he living?

Gabriel had retreated downstairs, maybe for more sofrito, or to explore the other bubbling pots, but Lorena still stood in the doorway.

"You last saw her two days ago?" Max asked.

"That's right. We finished our shift and came back here. We ate dinner and watched some television. She went out for a bit, a couple of hours, she did that sometimes, said she was going for a walk. She came back around ten. We were both in bed by eleven. When I knocked to wake her up for work, she was gone."

"Did you ask where she went on her walks?"

"Yes, but she said nowhere. She just walked. No particular destination."

"Safe to walk around here at night?"

"Depends on the block. I told her that, but she didn't seem concerned."

"What's she like?"

"What do you mean?"

"You lived in the same house, shared the same space, how would you describe her?"

"She was una fantasma, a ghost. She was quiet, polite, and

pleasant, but you never really saw her. You could never tell what she was thinking or feeling."

"Why? Was she hiding things? Afraid of something?"

"I don't know. I am not family. I do not come from that part of Mexico. Gabriel knows more of her story, though I don't think even he knows all of it. It broke something inside of her. She is damaged."

"From the trafficking? From getting across?"

"Maybe." She shrugged and looked away.

Hiding her past like she was hiding now. Max thought about the cage in his chest where he kept parts of himself hidden and locked up with a heavy chain. And the secrets he kept about why he did it. Was Ade hiding things from herself or keeping those things locked up because it was safer that way?

"Do you have any idea where she might be? She can't be on the streets. Friends? Other family?" Max asked.

"No, we've called the other people from the hotel. The ones she was friendly with at work, but they haven't seen her."

"And she wants to find her sister?"

"Yes, I know that for certain. Ade wants to rescue her."

But did Sol really want to be rescued?

CHAPTER TWENTY-SIX

H e was sitting in a small bus stop enclosure three blocks from Lorena's house and trying not to think about whether the dark pile in the corner was dog or human feces when his phone rang.

"This is Max."

"This is Darius Mack. You left me a voice message." The voice was a deep baritone.

"Yes, thanks for calling me back, Mr. Mack—"

"Nobody but the little ones call me mister. Make it Darius."

"Okay, Darius. Ronnie Shelton said you might be able to help me out. He said you know the surrounding neighborhood pretty well. I was wondering if I might buy you a cup of coffee and pick your brain for a few minutes."

"What are you looking to learn?" The deep voice now carried an edge of wariness. Max knew trust was paramount in a job like Darius's, and being seen as a snitch could erode any chance he had at success.

"I was looking for some information on FCM?" He stopped and let the question hang.

When Darius answered, his voice sounded a little more relaxed. "I know a little about them. Not as much as the workings of Deacon Jones's crew in Gray's Ferry, but some. Where do you want to meet up? I'll tell you what I know."

Twenty minutes later, Max pulled open the door to Charlie's Sandwich Shop just north of Point Breeze on the corner of Wharton and 21st. It was a small, simple shop with a counter and register at the back underneath a menu board and four tables set up in the remaining space upfront. Darius Mack was the only customer, sitting at the table closest to the window. Even if the place had been full, Max would have guessed the guy was Mack. He dwarfed the table and, while he'd probably spread out a bit with age, he still resembled the heavyweight that Ronnie had trained. His shaved head glistened under the shop's overhead lights. His shoulders looked like bowling balls and his hands were the size of cinderblocks. The six-inch sub he was holding looked like a breadstick in his hand.

"Max?" he said between bites.

"Yeah."

He kicked the chair opposite him out a bit. "Have a seat, and please excuse my manners. This sandwich is too good to interrupt." He took another bite and chewed, then continued, "People will always think the cheesesteak is the food that represents Philly, and maybe for some it is, or maybe the cheesesteak people just have better marketing. For my money, the roast pork sandwich is our signature sub. Look at this. Fall apart, shaved pork shoulder, provolone cheese, and broccoli rabe on an Italian roll." He took another huge bite to accentuate his point. "And don't overlook the roll. The roll can make or break any sandwich." He looked down at the sesame roll in his hand. "This one is very good. Gotta ask where they get 'em." He took two more bites, finishing his sandwich, wiped his hands, and pushed his basket to the side.

With the sandwich gone, he now had Mack's full attention for the first time since walking in. "So, you know Ronnie Shelton? You go to his gym?"

"Yeah, I get over there a few times a week. Stay in shape." Max replied.

The big man studied him. "Pfft. You don't look like a boxer, but you might be a fighter."

"Played hockey for a bit."

"That it?"

"All that's worth mentioning." They sized each other up some more before Max continued, "What about you? You still go to Ronnie's? You look like you can still handle yourself."

"Now you're just being polite. What did he tell you? That I was slower than an elephant?"

Max couldn't hide his smile. "He also said you were about as powerful as one, too."

"Ah, that man drove me crazy but, I'll admit he wasn't wrong. These days I eat too many of these sandwiches to even think about getting in the ring. I go over there, but it's mostly to chat with Ronnie and check on the kids."

"What exactly do you do, Darius? A community activist is kind of a vague job title."

"True, true. I remember standing in Staples getting those cards made up and trying to figure out the answer to that exact question. The lady at the counter listened to my story and told me I was a community activist. So, that's what I did. Sounded good and the lack of specificity helps. I wear many hats. I go around to different schools and tell my story. I try to deter kids from joining the gang life. I don't sugarcoat it. Nobody wins going down that road. I tell them about getting arrested, being in jail, getting stabbed. I tell 'em the real deal.

Some kids hear the truth in it, for a few it makes a difference."

"Does Philly have a gang problem?"

"Sure. Just about every major city in the US struggles with gang violence in some form. Philly doesn't make the big headlines because we're not dealing with the nationally known gangs like the Bloods, Crips, or Latin Kings. Philadelphia is home to more loosely organized gangs. Hell, I wouldn't even classify ninety percent of them as gangs. Most are just sort of cliques. But they are just as bad. They probably account for half the crime in the city—random violence, muggings, street theft, drug dealing." He was getting worked up now, ticking them off on his fingers. "What really bothers me is I see them all recruiting younger and younger—elementary and middle schoolers as well as teenagers. And social media is making it even easier. Now, the youngsters are organizing themselves and they are just as or more violent because they want to prove themselves to the older guys. It's an ugly cycle. We gotta find a way to break it."

"Boxing?"

"That's one tool, yeah. Put that aggression into the ring, but you gotta get the kid to the gym first and then you gotta get him to come back." He leaned back and took a breath. "But you didn't track me down to listen to my life's story."

"No, but it restores some of my waning faith in humanity. What do you know about FCM?"

"La Familia? Unlike some of the other ankle biting riff-raff, I have no problem calling FCM a gang."

"They based out of Point Breeze?"

"No, they started farther east, closer to the water. The CM in their name is for Mercy Street. Calle Misericordia. I sometimes wonder if they picked it as some kind of joke. They bring no mercy, only misery."

"They still there?"

"Sure, they've got a place there, a clubhouse of sorts, but they're expanding west so I'm not surprised you heard they were in Point Breeze. Their leader, a guy named Jorge Campos, has aspirations. He looks at all these little ragtag groups and sees a wide-open playing field."

"Where's he from? Mexico? He's not tied to the cartels?"

"I don't know where he's from. If they get big enough, the cartels would be interested. They probably get their drugs supplied by one of the cartels, but the FCM has their hands in a lot of criminal pies if I understand correctly, not just narcotics."

That rang true with the shakedown call he'd received and what he'd seen from the two guys at the PPCS building. "So, it's what? A bunch of dudes from Latin America organized by this Jorge guy?"

"That's how it starts. Guys get here and can't find the American dream. No job, no place to live, no food. FCM helps them out in exchange for some labor. Here, the labor is mostly strongarming, beating, dealing, and stealing. Those welcome gifts come with hefty interest payments. It goes from there. Campos has it down to an art form. He slickly lays it all out. You'd think you were signing up for Amway. He's also a paranoid fucker. You asked about a headquarters earlier? There is one, but you'll rarely find him there. He stays on the move and works out of his car. His office is this big, steel-plated black Mercedes." He seemed to have blown himself out with all the talking and leaned back. The chair gave off a dangerous-sounding crack. "Why are you so interested?"

Max didn't see a reason to lie and told him about his phone call and the incident at PPCS. He didn't mention the bride.

"That tracks with what I've been hearing," Darius replied.

"Is FCM responsible for all the violence over in Gray's Ferry?"

"I don't think so. There's a long-running beef between some cliques over there, but that shooting of the kid in the takeout restaurant was disturbing on many levels. Didn't sound like Deke. Deke Jones has quietly ruled that area for a long time, and it's been mostly peaceful. Not perfect, nowhere near it, but quieter than the eighties and nineties when crack was tearing the place up. But, he's getting older and, from what I've been seeing and hearing, making a show of going more legit. He's smart. Got his hands in a lot of pies. Real estate and shit."

"Is that good or bad for the neighborhood?"

"When has real estate ever been good for the hood?"

CHAPTER TWENTY-SEVEN

Len watched as Aaron exited the front door, walked across the parking lot, and got into a blue Ford Ranger pickup. Even rabid dogs had to pay the bills. You can get paid for murder-for-hire but you can't exactly report it on your W-2. And it wasn't a full-time job. Aaron wasn't in Deke's crew, he didn't sell drugs; he paid for all that fast-food and premium cable by moving bags at the airport for Southwest. Len had called up the airport, got routed around, but eventually landed with a shift manager.

"I need the work schedule for Aaron Cranmer."

"Who's this? We don't give out employee information over the phone."

"Listen, don't jerk me around. This is Lieutenant Smith. We need to serve Mr. Cranmer with some papers. Now, we can get all hot and bothered and come in heavy, really mess up your workplace looking for him, or you can give us the information and we can handle it quietly."

There was a pause, and then keys shuffling. "Cranmer, you said?"

"Yeah."

"His next shift is on Friday morning. Eighty-thirty. Listen, what are the papers for? Is it a felony warrant?"

"Sorry, we don't give that information out over the phone."

He hung up with a little pep in his step. That was some Deke-level shit he'd just pulled.

He followed Aaron through the streets of Gray's Ferry. Traffic was heavy but provided plenty of cover. He stayed well back. They drove across the bridge, south on 95 for a few miles, and then Aaron pulled off one exit before the airport. Len was more cautious now, but Aaron never slowed. He pulled into the employee parking lot off Bartram Avenue and, five minutes later, Len watched Aaron board the employee shuttle that ran from the lots to the terminals. Through the wide windows, he saw Aaron walk to the back and sit alone. As the bus chugged out in a haze of diesel, Len made a U-turn across the double yellow and headed back to the Towers.

The stairwell reeked of urine, shit, nicotine, and body odor. Len didn't find it comforting, but he did find it familiar. For most of his life, he'd called a Housing Authority complex his home. They all stank alike. He climbed the five flights and tried to breathe through his mouth. A door banged shut somewhere higher up, but he saw no one. On five, the smell improved slightly, or was just covered up by grease and cooking oil. No one was in the hallway, but people were home and awake. He heard two different televisions blaring behind two closed doors and a woman having a one-sided argument about a leaking toilet behind another.

He took a Chick-fil-A gift card out of his wallet. If anyone appeared, he'd step back and pretend to be waiting for Aaron to open the door. A door slammed again on a different floor and he flinched. He wiped one hand then the other on his jeans and re-gripped the card. Chasing Scootch through the streets barely made him sweat but doing this had his pulse racing. Go figure.

They built everything in the Towers cheap, including the locks on the doors. Len held the card at an angle just above the knob and wedged the flexible plastic between the frame and the door. He had plenty of practice. Len's mother had tried to lock him out of the house more than once over the years. He pushed the card in as far as it would go and then moved it back and forth between the doorknob and the frame. He put his shoulder against the door to add more pressure. He worked the card a little more and then it slipped under the angled end of the slant latch. He turned the knob and quickly ducked inside.

He stood still for a moment. He didn't expect anyone else inside, but you never knew. He waited and listened. He could see the edge of the microwave from where he stood. He waited until the pale green numbers on the clock changed. Heard nothing. Felt nothing. No vibrations. He hurried down the hall and double-checked the bathroom and bedroom. Both empty. He relaxed a fraction.

Nothing in the apartment appeared to have changed since his last visit. He stood in front of the air conditioner unit in the window. He turned the dial to off, unplugged it, tugged it out of the window, and set it on the floor. It was an old unit and had been used hard and never serviced. Not even to wipe down or rinse the air filter. The state of it would have horrified his old man. It was already leaking and likely corroded inside. A puddle of dirty, rusty water was warping the linoleum under the window. He doubted the unit running in the bedroom would be any different. He believed both would serve his purpose perfectly.

He took the screwdriver he'd brought from his pocket and unfastened the front plate and set it aside. Air conditioner units were simple machines. As he looked down at the exposed blower, compressor, coils, and filters, it brought all the jobs he'd gone out on with his father rushing back. There was a sudden tightness in his chest and his breath caught in his throat. He pushed past the feeling, no time to get weepy, and looked for the lines going to the compressor. As he suspected, both were corroding because of the leaking water and the constant running to compete with the heat in the room. He took out his pocketknife and used the tip to puncture several small holes in the larger freon coil. He forced himself to take his time and make the punctures small and near the most corroded areas. He doubted anyone would look closely, if at all, but if someone did, he needed it to look convincing.

He left the cover off but plugged the unit back in and turned it on. He let it run for a few minutes. Soon, he saw the telltale bubbles forming around the pinholes in the freon coil. His old man used to call them champagne leaks because of all the tiny bubbles. He turned the unit off. He didn't know how long it would take, but he was sure freon was hazardous and highly poisonous. He didn't want to be breathing it in himself. He put the panel back on and put the unit back in the window.

The bedroom was in the same state of disgusting disrepair as the rest of the apartment. Black silk sheets covered the unmade king-sized bed that dominated the room. A strip of unopened condoms lay across a chipped nightstand along with a lamp and a partially burned candle. He wasn't sure how Aaron used the closet. The bed took up all the space. Len looked around. Clothes scattered the floor. Maybe he didn't.

Len had just enough room between the mattress and wall to edge around to the window. He pulled the unit out and carried it out to the living room, so he'd have room to work. He repeated the same process and replaced the unit in the bedroom and turned it on. He switched on the first unit and then quickly double-checked the room. He'd left wet footprints in-between the bedroom and sofa. He quickly looked in the kitchen for some paper towels but couldn't find any. He grabbed a stack of thin takeout napkins from the counter and wiped up his footprints.

He stuffed the wad of soggy paper in his pocket and went to the door. He listened again. Was it his imagination or was he a little dizzy? He pressed an ear to the door. The woman had stopped screaming about the toilet, but the noise of the televisions was still there. Steve Harvey was shouting on *Family Feud*. Was that a headache? No way it worked that fast, right? He pulled the door open, jogged to the stairwell, and ran all the way down.

He lowered all the windows and ran the car up close to a hundred, stupidly fast, inviting a cop to pull him over and yank him out of the car by his armpits, but he didn't care. The smell, real or imaginary, had spooked him. It felt like death running a finger up his spine. If he slowed down or turned around, he'd find himself trapped. So, he floored it. He flew over the Walt Whitman bridge into Jersey, flashing over the water and past other cars, the wind screaming in his ears and his mouth wide open.

Eventually, he slowed to the speed limit and then slower, almost coasting to a stop in the right-hand lane. He took the next exit. He turned randomly and pulled into a roadside pizza joint. The parking lot was empty save for one other car. It was barely past 10:30, but he walked inside and ordered two plain slices and a large Coke. If it surprised the round man in the stained apron to have a customer this early, he didn't show it. He put the slices through the oven to warm them, shoveled them onto a plate, and filled a paper cup with soda. Len paid and returned to his car. He ate both slices without tasting them, barely noticing the vague discomfort as the cheese burned the roof of his mouth.

The fat and sugar steadied him and washed out the chemical taste that had been clinging to his tongue since leaving Aaron's apartment. He started the car, but before he headed back to the city, he leaned over and opened the glove compartment. There were four cheap plastic phones inside along with the registration, owner's manual, and a small flashlight. He couldn't remember how the flashlight had ended up in there. He grabbed one phone. Deke bought them by the case. There was always a need for a clean phone. Seemed like the more legit they got, the more phones they used, Len thought.

He powered it up and dialed the number he'd memorized. A voice answered.

Len was careful. He knew cell phones were basically just unsecured radios. "This is your friend from across town."

There was a pause. "Yes?"

"Is the man there?"

Another pause and then another voice, but the same question. "Yes?"

"Are we still good?"

"Yes, we will hold up our end of the deal. Will you?"

"Yes, I'm still in. What about——," he'd almost let the other man's name slip out, "our mutual friend?"

"Everything is still in place. Is there a problem?"

"No. I just wanted to check. When?"

"We'll be in touch soon."

Len disconnected and then broke the phone and SIM card into pieces. He dropped them out the window as he drove back across the Delaware River and into the city. He had one more thing to take care of and then it would be his city.

Part of it, at least.

He sat on a rough-cut block of stone near a Halal food cart and tried not to gag. The air smelled strongly of spices and burnt lamb but had an excellent view of the Jefferson Hospital emergency room entrance. He watched people flow in and out and thought about his problem. Len knew he couldn't just walk in and ask for Scootch's room. That would be a one-way trip. He needed a way to make it in and back out again. He sat there for almost an hour with the stink of the meat in his nostrils and the tinny foreign music the guy was playing from a portable radio echoing in his ears until the solution walked right past him. He smiled. So simple it would be perfect camouflage.

He stopped first in a Starbucks and found a discarded newspaper. Even a week later, the story hadn't faded from the front page. Not completely. It had gone below the fold, but it was still taking up healthy real estate in the front section. It was the kid. It had touched a collective nerve. People were attached, invested somehow, in the outcome. He skimmed the story. Still in a coma but doctors were now more hopeful. They were going to be disappointed.

Two doors down from the Halal cart, he stopped in at the florist. He saw the woman behind the counter flinch slightly and hesitate when he walked in. Len was used to that reaction outside the neighborhood and let it roll off him.

"I'd like to buy some flowers. Tall ones."

Her smile came back.

Ten minutes later, he walked through the automatic sliding doors of the ER and approached the information desk holding two large, tall displays of flowers. To Len, they smelled only slightly better than the food truck, but they did take the focus off his face.

"Can I help you?"

Not that this old biddy would recognize him. He had the sense that she was the type who might struggle to differentiate between brothers.

"Delivery for Draymond Cooper's room."

"One moment." She pecked some keys in front of her. "Room 1216. Elevators are to the left."

He rode up juggling the flowers. He didn't know flowers, but the scent was strong, and his eyes itched. The elevator opened directly on a small lobby and a nurses' station. A man in a rumpled sweatsuit was asleep, sprawled across two chairs in a corner. The nurses' station was empty. He walked past and, after a false start, found the correct hallway.

The flower scent was cloying, but it was better than the shit and antiseptic smell of the hospital hallway. He passed a nurse and doctor hurrying in the opposite direction. Neither paid any attention to him. It was quiet. The lights were low. It felt like a church. Or a morgue. The soft beeps and inaudible murmurs were making him nervous. There was that caress of a finger on his spine again. Death was close. He needed to get this done.

He followed the numbers and walked past 1216. The small window set into the door showed only dark shadows inside. There was an unoccupied metal folding chair outside the door. Maybe Scootch had a guard initially, but after a couple of days, and no immediate retaliation, the Philly PD had pulled it? Too cheap to keep paying for overtime? Or maybe the guard was still around, but the guy guzzled coffee to stay awake guarding a comatose patient and was off relieving himself in the bathroom.

He reached the end of the corridor and ducked into the stairwell. He put the flowers down and shook out his arms and shoulders and settled his nerves. He didn't expect a struggle, not if the kid was still in a coma, but there would be monitoring machines that would react. He had to get in and out. He took out a pair of gloves from his pocket and pulled them on. In and out. Strong and quick.

He picked up the flowers and walked back up the hallway. The chair was still empty.

CHAPTER TWENTY-EIGHT

She no longer knew for sure when she was awake or asleep. The membrane between reality and dreams had become soft and permeable. She lay in the dark now, hot and sweaty, and relived that final afternoon. Must be dreaming now, she thought vaguely. Or hallucinating. She rarely remembered it with any clarity anymore. For a long time, it was all she could see when she shut her eyes, but the drugs eventually helped with that. The drugs and more damage piled on top. It was an ugly and crude type of therapy, but it was effective. She couldn't remember the last time that day had floated up in her memory.

It was a Sunday. They had returned from mass an hour earlier, and she and her sister were helping their mother prepare lunch. Their father had stayed behind to talk to a group of men on the church steps. He had waved them on. The sisters were slicing radishes, onions, and limes to top the pork pozole soup that was bubbling gently on the stove. Her mother was humming the closing hymn softly to herself. The sisters were whispering about Javier and Miguel Angel and Ade's approaching quinceanera celebration.

They both heard their father come through the front door and then his boots running along the tiled entryway. They looked at each other, both frowning, and then he was in the kitchen. He was sweating. Dirt smudged his cheeks. His shirt was dark with sweat under his light cotton suit.

"Mannie? What is it? What's happened? Are you okay?" When faced with the unknown, their mother fought back with questions.

"Marco is dead."

Their mother's hands flew to her face, now ghostly pale, and she sagged against the counter. "What? How... " The questions died as fast as they had come. The sisters knew that name, had heard it occasionally when their parents talked. He was their father's boss. He was the big boss. The sisters didn't know exactly what their father did. But they suspected. Or could guess. They had seen the box. They had seen how townspeople looked at their father. They knew this was bad, even without their mother's reaction.

Their father walked around the island to the stove and gripped their mother by the shoulders. "Take the girls to Tio. He will know what to do." Her eyes were glassy. She shook her head duly from side to side. He shook her, hard, and some life came back into her features.

"Yes, I'll find Tio," she said.

Their father nodded and walked into his office. He returned with a bag and handed it to their mother, then disappeared upstairs. It was the last time either of them would see their father.

They ran down to Tio's small house, but it was empty. Her mother looked on the verge of panic again.

"The barn. He likes to ride on Sundays," Ade said, and they backed out of the house and walked the short distance to the barn. She was right. He was there, just back from a ride, unsaddling and brushing down Cancion. She would wonder later what would have happened if he'd not been in the barn. If he hadn't returned in time. Her life would likely have been shorter, but would that have been better?

"Marco is dead," their mother said.

Tio looked at her and took in the news, then nodded. His expression didn't change. He threw the saddle back on the horse, who bristled. "Saddle up another horse. You two will share," he said.

"Where are you taking them?"

He stood in front of her, very close, and took her hand. He was more gentle than their father. "Mannie knew this day would come. He hoped it would be further down the road when the girls were grown and gone, but we don't always get what we wish for. He took precautions. The girls will be all right. I will take them to some friends who will get them to safety."

They could hear shouting in the distance now but getting closer. The smell of smoke carried on the wind.

"Hurry," Tio prodded, and they finished saddling the horses. Tio looked at the shelves and began stuffing supplies into the saddlebags. He then paused and looked around, consulting some mental list, and then he nodded. "Hug your mother, girls, you might not see each other for some time," he said.

They all embraced and stayed that way. She remembered the fear now overtaking the confusion as Tio pulled her gently away and nudged her toward the horse.

"Time to go."

They rode the horses out of the barn and onto the trails behind the house that led up into the mountains. Ade had the reins and kept them close behind Tio. She gripped her older sister's waist, then turned and looked back and watched their mother until she was a small black speck that blended into the landscape.

They rode north, picking their way through the mountains first and then the arid, steep-sided arroyos. They did not talk much. What was there to say? They rode, they ate, and they slept. Near the end of the third day, they met up with a pair of men outside a small village. They were leaning against a dusty, rust-coated Nissan Versa. Their father's friends. Tio seemed relieved. He dismounted and raised a hand, leading the horses closer.

The taller of the two pushed off the car and shot Tio. He fell, and the horse stumbled to a stop over his body.

The man pointed the gun at the girls. They had no chance to fight.

In her father's business, friendship and deals were based on power, fear, and money. Their father might have made arrangements and paid in advance, but he no longer had the power or the fear. The only reason the girls weren't shot and left in the desert was because they were worth more alive than dead. The men took them across the border and received a nice fee in exchange for delivering them to a trafficker in Texas, then Louisiana. Her sister would tell her all this later. Long, hard lessons learned in their new country.

CHAPTER TWENTY-NINE

By the time Max had finished talking with Darius, the sun was slinking behind the Center City skyscrapers and the October shadows had teeth. He glanced at his watch. It was almost five. There were no set hours for PPCS. If you needed time off, you asked. If they needed you at a specific time, they'd ask, otherwise you showed up roughly when expected. It was a loose system, but there was enough overlap and redundancy that it worked.

He was going to be a little later than normal. He pulled out his phone. No messages from Terry or Carlee for specific pickups, so it shouldn't be a problem. Still, he jogged across the next intersection and picked up his pace. Twenty minutes later, he made it back to his apartment. He quickly changed clothes, then packed a hasty dinner in the cooler and added a couple of sodas from the nearly empty fridge before leaving again.

The streets gradually emptied as he walked into the industrial neighborhood around PPCS and closer to the highway. Even in the growing darkness, the electric-blue building glowed like a beacon. He smiled. Better to be notorious than boring, Liam liked to say. The home of PPCS was straight ahead, but Max cut left, walking parallel on the next block. He didn't know what made him do it, he'd seen nothing suspicious, but he'd learned to trust his instincts. It had been a week since the threatening phone call. His grace period was up. He walked the surrounding blocks. The normal nine-to-five workday was over. Most places were closed, but a few places remained open. There was a light on in the office of the nearby salvage yard and Max could see someone in the window on the phone. Two guys were talking in front of the rent-a-wreck place on the opposite block, but neither of them paid him any mind as he passed. He spiraled in closer. A man was locking the door to the roofing supply business two storefronts up. Max waved and the guy gave him an absent nod. He entered through the open security gate. Maybe he was being paranoid.

Maybe not.

He sensed the change in energy immediately. There were too many people around. Too many lights. Too much chatter. It should have been calm and quiet. A few extra voices or bodies during the shift change. It wasn't. It felt like the aftermath of a bar fight that had spilled into the street. Or a traffic accident that everyone walked away from but could have been much worse. Scattered groups of twos and threes stood outside the open garage bay doors. Everyone was nervous and jumpy. A torque wrench whined nearby. He frowned.

He approached the closest group, three guys, all drivers. He knew one guy's name was Ignacio, Iggy for short. He didn't recognize the other two. He'd spent twenty minutes one night during a changeover debating the merits of the

Canadians and Bruins forwards with Iggy. It wasn't a conversation he expected from a guy named Iggy in the middle of Philly, but that's what made life interesting.

"What's going on, Iggy?"

"No se, Max. It was over when I got here, but Liam is inside," he pointed at the garage, "with Terry. Most of the cars are all fucked."

"What do you mean fucked?"

"Someone slashed the tires. Keyed, scratched up the paint jobs, too."

That explained the torque wrench. He walked past Iggy and entered the garage. All three lifts held PPCS cars. Max could see Rodrigo moving around the one on the far left. No one was around the other two. It appeared Rodrigo was the only one working. Max walked closer to the sedan in the middle and looked at the rear tire. He ran a hand over it. It looked fine. He moved to the front. A deep gash slit the sidewall. Not an accident. It was the mark of a very large, very sharp knife.

He walked to the front of the garage and found Liam sitting in a metal folding chair with a bag of ice balanced on his head and another covering his right hand. There was a vacant expression in his eyes that Max didn't like.

"Liam?"

No response.

"Liam," Max said again and knelt in his eyeline. Still nothing.

Terry came out of the connecting door to the office carrying more bags of ice and a bottle of Jameson. He checked Liam, the bags of ice, then sat down in the empty chair next to him. He dropped one bag on the floor between them and held the other bag against the red welt growing under his eye.

"Was it the same two guys?" Max asked.

"Were you here the last time? I can't remember."

"I ran into them in the parking lot as they were leaving."

"Yeah, same two. Scary fuckers, right? Not much to look at but gave off, I don't know, a vibe that hurting you was just part of the job. The fun part. Here, do me a favor, unscrew the top." He held out the bottle of whiskey. Max unscrewed the top and handed it back. Terry took a long swallow while he held the ice against his face. The alcohol wouldn't wash away the memory. Max knew that for a fact, he'd tried, but it could help with the pain. Temporarily.

When Terry came up for air, Max asked, "What did they want?"

Terry put the bottle down and wiped a hand across his mouth. He adjusted the ice slightly and winced. "What do you think? You look like you've been around the block. You don't exactly seem surprised. What do guys like that always want?"

"How much?"

"I don't know." Terry glanced over at Liam. The man hadn't moved since Max walked in. He might not have blinked. The ice melted, and he looked at something only he could see. "He wouldn't tell me. Just said he handled it before, he could handle it again."

"Told me the same thing."

"Stubborn feckin' gobshite." Terry reached down for the bottle. Max needed some details before the whiskey fully soaked his brain.

"What happened?"

"They came in just like last time. Didn't talk to anyone, just continued upstairs. A minute later, they came back down and started puncturing tires and scraping up the paint. Liam came flying down the stairs and they took him apart. I mean, he might have had a chance forty years ago, but not now. They were almost laughing as they did it. Liam was down after two punches, but they didn't stop. Stepped on his hand. Kicked him up and down. I tried to break it up and they tagged me, too."

"No one else jumped in?"

"No, and I don't blame them. What's in it for them? They got no stake in this. I should probably be thankful they didn't kill us."

Not yet, Max thought. This was an escalation, but still polite. "He hasn't said anything since?"

"No. I got him in here and got the ice on him. Got Rodrigo to stay and start on the cars."

Max looked over his shoulder. He could see the looping white grooves through the paint job on the hood. It was a minor inconvenience. It would take a day or two to fix the fleet, but it wouldn't put them out of business. They could have torched the cars, but there was no extortion money in a bankrupt business.

"We need to get him to a hospital to get checked out. At the very least, he has a concussion. You too, probably. Did they just mess up the fleet cars? Is your car drivable?"

"Yes, we can take my car," he stood and carefully dug his keys out of his pocket and handed them to Max. "But I'm bringing the bottle. Call it anesthesia." Max could see the whiskey was having an effect, but he didn't argue. Not after what Terry risked helping his friend, even if all it did was get him bloody.

"Did anyone call Fiona yet?"

"No."

"Okay, let's get him to the hospital first." Max didn't relish that conversation.

He gently took Liam under the arm and pulled him up. Liam didn't resist. It surprised Max how light the man was.

"C'mon, Liam," he said, "going to take you over to Jefferson. Have you checked out. That all right?"

Max moved toward the bay doors, but this time Liam didn't follow. Max turned back. Liam was looking directly at him now. "They asked about you."

CHAPTER THIRTY

Max drove angry. He stamped the gas pedal and the engine of Terry's old Impala shuddered and tried to keep up as he sped between the blocks along Broad Street. Then he slammed the brakes at the red lights, itchy and impatient to go again. It wasn't late and people were out on the streets and shot him wary looks as they crossed the street in front of the car. He ignored them. He fidgeted, not sure what to do with his hands. He put the windows down, then back up. He switched radio stations, mashing the button on the dash. On green, he pressed the gas pedal harder. He knew it was childish and dangerous but he couldn't stop. He needed the outlet.

After another three blocks, he wrestled it under control. He flexed his fingers on the wheel and forced the fury down and locked it back up. For now. It would be useful, he knew, but not yet.

He turned off Broad onto Snyder and then Mercy Street. Calle Misericordia. His pulse had dropped back to normal. He was clear-eyed and focused. The windows were up. The radio was off. Mercy Street was an old side street a block off

the main commercial strip on the east side of South Philly.
Time and development had chopped it up into pieces. It
started and stopped, interrupted by wider, newer thorough-
fares, city parks, and dead ends. The portion off Snyder was a
tight street with single-side parking and low, brick residential
boxes broken up by the occasional beige clapboard siding or
dirty yellow stucco. Max cruised all the streets twice before
parking in the driveway of a dark house within sight of La
Champincita Grocers.

The store sat on a corner and wrapped around to front
both streets and take up most of the irregular block. It was
the only commercial business on this part of the street unless
you counted the house directly opposite with a large purple
cross glowing in the front window. That place might sell
something, too, but currently appeared empty. La Champincita advertised 24/7 service. Its overhanging awning advertised soda, vegetables, cigarettes, fruit, meat, coffee, ice
cream, and an ATM available inside. The green awning was
ripped and dirty. A picture of half a hoagie sandwich was just
visible on one torn end. They must have been good sandwiches or free because the place was doing a brisk business.
Max counted a dozen cars pull through the back lot in the ten
minutes he watched. Two people had gone inside and come
back out carrying brown plastic bags. The rest never left their
cars.

He walked past the store on the opposite sidewalk for a
closer look. Dust and old ads covered the long windows and
blocked his view inside. He kept walking and watched a new
car pull slowly into the lot. A man stepped out of the shadows
and leaned down to the window. Max could see he wore the
same long braided belt as the two guys who had visited PPCS.

He had the right place. He thought of Liam in the hospital bed and that anger pressed against its cage.

Fiona had been calmer than he'd expected when he'd made the call. There was just a sharp intake of breath and then a slow exhale as if she'd been waiting to let it out. Maybe Liam had told her something or maybe after nearly fifty years of marriage, you don't need to say anything at all. She was dry-eyed and stoic when she pushed through the curtain of the small ER treatment bay and saw her husband hooked up to the machines. Max had left her, with Terry passed out in the visitor's chair.

He returned his attention to the small lot that ran behind the grocers. A privacy screen weaved into the eight-foot fence shielded it from view. It was a strange nod to discretion for what was essentially an open-air, drive-through drug market. You'd enter from Mercy, place your order and pay, drive around to the exit on 4th, the perpendicular street, grab your order and then take a quick left, and after two traffic lights be right back on the highway. Five more minutes and you were over the Walt Whitman and into Jersey or heading north for the Main Line suburbs. Quick and efficient, and Max had to admit it was a pretty slick set up.

At the end of the block, Max crossed the street and doubled back on the near side of the street. He walked past the entrance and could feel the man's eyes flick over him. Max kept walking and entered the store. Upright coolers of drinks and refrigerated items ran along the back and side walls. Three low aisles in the middle had dry goods and a hotbox with congealed pizza and shriveled hotdogs as an end cap. A register, lotto machines, cigarettes, and impulse buys were stacked upfront. Fisheye mirrors were mounted in two corners to help the clerk monitor the stock. No sign of the hoagies.

A bored-looking attendant with greasy hair sat on a stool

behind the counter watching a small television. He didn't look up or offer a greeting when Max entered. One other person, a teenage boy wearing oversized headphones and a backpack, was inside, studying the selection of ice cream pints through the frosted window. There was a door marked 'Private' next to the coolers in the back. Max walked the aisles and waited for the kid to make his choice. He took his time, pulling multiple containers out and then putting them back. Max found himself oddly intrigued by what he would select. Eventually, he chose one and headed for the register. Max took a bottle of iced tea from the cooler and checked the mirrors. As the clerk bagged the ice cream and took the kid's money, Max slipped through the private door.

"Luis, that you?" a voice asked.

The back room was larger than Max expected. There were floor-to-ceiling shelves, lined with sundry items to restock the store. A bathroom was built into the near corner. A small, handheld fire extinguisher was clipped to the wall next to the door. Max took it and walked down the aisle toward the sound of the voice.

"Who the fuck are you?"

The man sat behind a desk covered in papers with a laptop off to one side. A 9mm Smith and Wesson sat next to the laptop. Max glanced around. His fingers were tingling, itching for a fight, but the first rule was to always have an exit. He could retreat through the store the way he'd come in. The clerk might not even notice. There was also a door over the guy's shoulder to the left that presumably led out to the parking lot. He'd be pinched between the two ends of the drug drive-through. He was sure both men would be armed. Not good, but he had options at least.

"My name is Max."

He was older than the guy manning the fence outside. Higher up the food chain. That was good for Max's purpose. He had thick shoulders and an inflated chest. He'd spent a lot of time with a weight rack. Probably in prison. Tattoos covered his forearms and biceps. He stood. He wore a braided belt around his waist.

"And?"

"I'm looking for Jorge."

"No Jorge here."

"Then I want to talk to you." Max kept his voice low and steady.

"I doubt it. I think you made a mistake."

"I don't think so. I got a phone call and Jorge was asking for me."

"He called you?" There was a little nervousness in his voice now.

"Yes, he wanted to discuss your extortion business."

"I don't know what you're talking about."

"Better to just be honest."

"Are you listening? I don't know what you're talking about. I run a corner store."

"Really? You or the FCM? I wouldn't find anything interesting in those papers or on that laptop?"

"I think that would be a dumb thing to try." His hand inched toward the gun.

Max ignored it. "I wouldn't find anything about Philly Private Car Service or me?"

"I don't know that business or what you're talking about."

"I think you're lying."

"You think I care?" Now he picked up the gun but held it at his side. "I think you should beat it if you want to get out of here in one piece."

"Philly Private Car already has protection."

"What?" He smiled. He was a big guy. With a gun. He was confident.

"Back off. You don't want a war with us."

He could see the confusion mixing with the anger. Max watched the veins pop in the guy's neck. It had probably been a while since someone talked to him like he was a stupid child. Max knew it wouldn't take much to push him over the edge.

"You've got to be kidding me. Get lost, guy, before you get hurt."

Max almost smiled. He wanted a fight. Wanted to feel something crack and break. Wanted to let loose some of the frustration of the past week. He unlocked the cage.

He was confident, too. "Your call."

He thought about what he was going to do. Visualized it in his mind. Then he moved.

He took a step forward with his left foot and swung his right arm back, not far, he didn't want a long windup; what he'd lose in velocity, he'd make up in surprise. He brought his arm forward, using his momentum to offset the short backswing, and launched the glass bottle of iced tea. His aim wasn't perfect, but it was good enough. The man flinched and turned. The bottle hit the side of his head with a solid thunk. He stumbled back, stunned. Max kept coming, brought up the fire extinguisher and fired the noxious chemicals into the man's face, then took two more steps and swung the extinguisher with both hands in a downward chop. This time, his aim was a little better and the butt end hit the man behind the ear with a sharp crack. He dropped the gun but somehow remained on his feet. He raised an arm, his eyes swimming, his fingers groping the empty air. Max swung again, this time hitting the man's elbow, bending it the wrong way with a satisfying crunch. The man gave a strangled cry and sat down on the floor. Max kicked the gun away and dragged the man clear of the chemical cloud by his collar. He whimpered on the floor, clutching his broken arm. Max searched the desk and grabbed a black marker.

He slapped the guy on the cheek until his eyes stopped swiveling and found Max's face.

"We've got a message for Jorge and the FCM," Max said.

"What's the message," the man hissed through his teeth.

"You."

Max stood and kicked him twice in the side of the head. The man flopped over on the floor and stayed still. Max bent down with the marker.

CHAPTER THIRTY-ONE

Max took two minutes and flipped through the ledger and papers scattered across the desk. He couldn't make any sense of the ledger. They wrote the entries in some sort of code, but he took it anyway. Even if he never decoded it, taking it would be an inconvenience. A finger in their eye. He scooped up most of the loose papers, too. The man on the floor moaned but remained unconscious. Max nudged the mouse for the laptop. It was password protected. He didn't even try to crack it, not standing there, but added it to his pile.

As he searched, he came across two cans of white spray paint in a drawer. He paused. He'd been inside the store for less than five minutes, but it felt like five hours. Eventually, one of the two guys outside would check-in. He had to go. He grabbed a can of paint and doubled down on his message in case the unconscious guy was too subtle. He wrote in large letters that dripped off the unfinished concrete wall. That should be enough.

He picked up the bottle of iced tea from the floor. It hadn't broken, and he exited the way he'd come in. The clerk didn't look like he'd moved. If it surprised him to see Max come through the door, he didn't show it. Perhaps he was used to guys coming and going, taking what they wanted, and had learned it was better not to ask questions.

He tucked the papers inside the front cover of the ledger and dumped it, along with the laptop, on the passenger seat. He drove Terry's car back to the hospital with the windows down. He was hot and jittery from the adrenaline of the fight and let the cold air wash over him. It calmed him. His hands stopped shaking on the wheel. He locked it all away again deep in his chest. He wasn't sure what he had accomplished, but there would be a comeback. The FCM would have to retaliate. That would be a start.

And then Max would end it.

He parked in the garage on 10th Street opposite the hospital's main entrance. He took the laptop and ledger and walked across the street. He'd left Liam, Terry, and Fiona in the ER earlier in the night, but they'd moved since. He made his way to the information desk and gave Liam's name to an older woman in a pink cardigan with reading glasses hanging from a chain around her neck. She slipped the glasses on and looked at her screen.

"He's been admitted. Room 612, but I'm afraid visiting hours are over except for direct family."

"I'm his son."

The lie came easily, like they had all his life, but he felt less bad about this one than he had about many of the others. He wondered if they would require ID, but she didn't ask, only nodded. He likely looked too frazzled, or too tired, or too crazy to bother.

"Okay. In that case, follow the blue line and take the elevators around the corner," she pointed off to her left, "and get off at the sixth floor and follow signs for Neurology."

Five minutes later, he was standing in a darkened room looking down at a sedated Liam. Terry looked only marginally better sprawled out in a different chair with a white cotton bandage around his head. Fiona was in another chair. She was awake. Max inclined his head to the door. She let go of Liam's hand and followed Max out into the hall.

"What did he tell you?" Max asked.

She was shaking her head before he finished. "Nothing. I didn't know about the previous visit. But that shouldn't surprise you. You've seen how it works there. He's a man of his generation. Fifty years of marriage hasn't changed that. We're partners, but I still have to fight tooth and nail to get him to tell me anything about the business that he thinks he can handle. He really only lets me do the things he doesn't want to do."

"He's lucky. Those are just scrapes and bruises. It's going to get worse."

She looked back into the room. He wasn't telling her anything she hadn't already figured out. "What do you think we should do?"

"Sell out and move someplace warm. Why bother with these guys now? You aren't the first business they're muscling in on. If we ask around, I'm sure we'll hear similar stories from your neighbors. Why fight the current?"

She shook her head again. "He won't do it. He'll see it as surrender. As giving up. Throwing away everything he's worked for his entire life."

"It's not throwing it away if you get a fair price."

"He won't see it that way. It won't be his decision."

"The harder you worked, the harder it is to give up."

"Exactly."

"What did the doctors say?"

"A concussion. Some broken fingers. They want to observe him for at least a day and make sure nothing internal is bleeding."

Max thought they'd be safe enough in the hospital. He wasn't so sure after that. She seemed to read his mind. "Then we go back to work. This isn't the first time this has happened, Max. We're older, but it appears the rules haven't changed. We won't get caught by surprise again."

Max wasn't confident that would be enough.

The hospital's chapel was at the end of the hall and as he passed it on the way back to the elevators, he pushed open the door. It was a small rectangle of a room with dim lighting and a stained-glass window on one wall. There was a simple wood table at the front with two white candles. A foldable screen, hand-painted with a tree in different seasons, was behind the table. There were three rows of benches split down the center with an aisle. It was quiet and, unlike the bleach and antiseptic that pervaded the hospital corridor, smelled pleasantly of burnt wood and pine needles.

Max stood in the aisle looking at the tree and wondering what had pulled him inside. The door opened behind him and a woman entered wearing a pink and white robe, almost like a graduation gown, with a long multicolored stole around her neck. She looked almost as surprised as Max to find anyone else there.

"Sorry," he automatically said.

"Please don't be. This space is for everyone at all times. I just wasn't expecting anyone in here so late."

"I wasn't expecting to be in here."

She smiled. "Not the first time I've heard that."

She looked at him as if waiting for him to say something, and Max realized he did have a question.

"How do we know who to help?"

"A simple question without a simple answer. Are you a Christian?"

"Raised that way."

"Then you might remember that the Bible reminds us over and over again of the comfort and peace that come from being known and loved by God. He knows us and loves us more than we do ourselves, which is good because I think we often find it difficult to recognize our own needs."

"So, trust in God?"

"In the mystery of God's wisdom. What we think we need and what we actually need are not always the same thing."

"You can't always get what you want, huh?"

She smiled. "Mick and Keith were prophets."

"Even if there is a God, and He loves me and is watching me, I still have free will, right?"

"Of course."

"That's what I'm afraid of. I'm afraid that rather than helping, I'm enabling."

"Enabling yourself or enabling someone else?"

"Maybe both."

"If you are worried about someone else, rest assured that no one likes to see someone suffer, but preventing suffering is often not wise."

"There needs to be accountability."

"Yes, both for that person and for ourselves. We all need to feel the consequences."

"What if trying to help is just an excuse for enabling parts of myself?"

"That might be more difficult to answer. You must examine your own heart. Do you enjoy the feeling that providing help brings?"

"I don't know."

"Don't know or don't want to find out?"

"I'm working on it. I know that all injustice and pain make me angry."

"God is real and just, but evil is also real and has influence in the world. Your outrage at suffering only proves that there is goodness in the world. That faith in a higher power, call it what you want, has a home. So perhaps you have your answer already."

CHAPTER THIRTY-TWO

The car rocked on its struts as Cherry climbed out of the driver's seat with an agility that belied his size and opened the rear door. Councilman Watts slid in next to Deke. This time, Deke made sure Watts came to him. Len sat in the front seat to make room for the impromptu meeting.

"Deke."

"Councilman. Any updates on the kid?"

"He's still in the ICU, still in a medically induced coma. Doctors are hopeful. He's held on this long but still no way to tell yet which way it's going to go."

"I want to reiterate that we had nothing to do with this. Nothing." Deke said, slapping the seat to punctuate his point.

"You know that doesn't matter, Deke. It's all optics. You're the de facto mayor of Gray's Ferry and this doesn't look good for you. People have little use for facts anymore. You could prove beyond a doubt that you were tapdancing on center court at the Spectrum when it was all going down and not everyone would believe it."

"What can we do?"

"Pray."

"That's it? That's all you got?"

"For now. Pray the kid pulls through. Pray he's not a drooling vegetable they wheel out in front of the cameras. Pray he wakes up and can tell a good story. And maybe we can figure something out that gets you in the clear and back on track."

Len looked at Deke and could see the frustration ripple across his face. Deke hated nothing more than feeling helpless. He'd worked most of his life to put himself in a position to never feel powerless, and now, when the brass ring was so close, he found himself at the mercy of the fickle whims of medical science and a kid's will to live.

Len knew the feeling. His fate hung on the same strand. At the hospital, as Len had moved toward the kid's door with the flowers, the cop had come around the corner. Len wasn't sure if he was security or Philly PD, but it didn't matter. Either one was more than capable of calling in reinforcements. Len shuffled stepped back into the center of the hallway. The guy had been looking down at his phone and didn't notice. They passed each other without a word.

"Does the family need anything?" Deke asked now.

"No, what you've sent already is good for now."

"All right. Hit me up if you hear anything." Deke nodded and Cherry got out again and opened the door. Len watched Watts cross the short distance to his waiting car. Youngblood was leaning against the side of the car, watching them, and smoking. He stubbed the cigarette out as Watts approached, fired off a brief salute toward Deke's car before following his boss into the back of the car.

.   .   .

Youngblood waited until they were around the corner and out of sight before he leaned in and got in Watts's personal space. This annoyed Watts, and Youngblood only deployed it on certain occasions, but he had to make sure the message came through loud and clear. "You told him?"

"I told him. He wasn't happy."

"Of course he wasn't happy, but this kid getting shot can help us."

Watts raised an eyebrow. "Don't let any hot mics catch you saying that, Michael."

"You know what I mean. We didn't want this to happen. We wouldn't have wished for it to happen. We're not monsters, but we can make it work for us. Make it work for your constituents."

"Since when do you care about them?"

"Fine. Make it work for you. Deke has too much leverage. Too much power over you right now. If this kid dies, it could give us the room to take a little back. I do not want to owe a man like Deacon Jones any more favors."

"Favors won't be worth a damn if we don't get re-elected. I can handle Deke if he delivers the votes."

"Be careful what you wish for. He is not some punk that rose to the top of the local drug pile. He's as devious and smart as—"

"A politician."

Youngblood sat back in his seat. "Maybe."

"That's good. You have vast experience dealing with politicians."

Youngblood looked out the window at the passing city. "I'm working on it."

Cherry drove them out of the shadows of Route 76, to the rec center on Morris and 26th. It was an old post-World War II brick building that was crumbling in places but still had echoes of its past grandeur. Tonight, it was hosting a town hall event where voters could pose questions to Watts and Jeannette Walters, his challenger for the council seat. A small crowd was massing on the sidewalk and queuing to go inside.

"Pull over here, Cherry," Deke said.

Cherry guided the car smoothly to the curb half a block short of the entrance next to a fenced-in blacktop area that might have held a basketball court at one time but now held six large, raised container gardens. This late in the year, there were splotches of green, but the plots were mostly filled with yellowed or brown stalks waiting to be dug up or turned over.

Len moved to open his door and felt a hand on his shoulder. "Why don't you sit this one out," Deke said and climbed out before waiting for a response. Len felt the blood rush to his cheeks and glanced over at Cherry, but the big man's face was a placid mask as he stared out the windshield. Len felt both angry and relieved at the same time. These political events were the thing he loathed most in Deke's new world, but, as much as he hated to admit it, being shouldered aside also burned him up. He watched Deke shake hands and greet people as he moved through the crowd and up the steps toward the doors.

Councilman Watts's car pulled up a few minutes later and, as he watched the councilman exit the car, Len was struck by the thought that Watts and Deke didn't look much different as they both smiled and glad-handed their way through the locals. Len noticed Youngblood go around and slip in a side entrance. He didn't see Jeannette Walters arrive. Maybe she was already inside. Or maybe she was the type who liked to arrive late. Or slip in the back. Len wondered what was better for a politician. He knew what was better for a gangster.

He and Cherry sat in the car in silence, watching the street. After Watts was inside, the crowd on the sidewalk dissipated, either walking away to Carr's Bar around the corner or heading inside for the debate. Soon there was nothing to look at and the strange, tranquil zen of Cherry started to weird Len out and make him antsy.

"Fuck this," Len said and reached for the door handle.

"You seen Aaron around?" Cherry's deep baritone was like a thunder crack after the quiet.

Len's mind raced. Why was Cherry asking about Aaron? He fought to keep his voice neutral. "Cramner?"

"Yeah."

"No, I try to stay clear of that psycho. Why?"

Cherry shrugged, the action rippling down the folds of his body. "Deke was asking me."

"Why does he care about Aaron? In his new world, you'd think he'd want to keep the Aarons of the world far, far away."

Cherry shrugged again. "Not a lot of people cold enough to shoot that boy down in the street like that."

"And Deke thinks Aaron might be one?"

"That man doesn't run hot or cold. He feels nothing. Shooting that boy would be the same as swatting a fly."

"Huh. Hadn't thought of that."

"We ain't paid to think."

Len looked at him. It was full dark now. The streetlights lit the car's interior with a dull yellow light. Cherry kept his eyes straight ahead, tracking the small movements on the street. A man crossed north on 26th. A woman ducked out the side door of the rec center to sneak a smoke. A feral cat ran through a hole in the fence, chasing a mouse into the garden dirt. Cherry missed nothing. Len felt something worm through his gut.

"Well, I haven't seen him in a while."

"No one has."

The car fell silent again.

"I'm gonna get some air," Len said, and this time he made it out of the car.

He walked to the end of the block, away from the rec center, and turned onto Morris. He walked along the fence line, past the dying container gardens. A large community swimming pool sat behind the center. It was massive. Ten lanes across, sloping from a shallow to a deep end that disappeared in the darkness. It was empty now. The faded white tile glowed slightly in the glimmer of the security lights mounted on the fence posts. Len heard kids laughing and smelled smoke from somewhere inside the fence. He kept walking. It wasn't late, but the temperature had dropped in the last few days and the sidewalks were empty. He saw lights and people in some first-floor windows as he walked past. Something or someone rattled a metal trashcan in an alley. He kept going. This was his turf. He had nothing to fear. Not from anyone on these streets.

He passed Uncle Tony's pizza shop on the corner and caught a whiff of grease and cheese that had leached out the door. It should have made him hungry but didn't. His stomach cramped instead. Scootch, Deke, now Aaron. It was messing him up. He needed to find a way to end it.

Halfway down the next block, he turned into a courtyard made by the four surrounding apartment buildings. These were Deke's buildings. He bought the lot and renovated the buildings last year. New bricks, new landscaping, same drugs. He recognized Barbie's skinny arms and legs sitting with two other guys on a couple of benches off in one corner.

"Hey, Len," Barbie said. They tapped fists and Barbie made room on the bench. Len didn't recognize the other two.

He suddenly felt old. They were both at least five years younger than Len and that might as well be a different generation in this business.

"I thought you were with Deke tonight at the rally," Barbie said.

"I am," Len nodded back in the direction he'd come, "they're all inside now."

One guy stood suddenly and hustled off toward a jittery man who stood across the street near a fire hydrant.

"Didn't want you inside, huh? Gotta keep the business and the gangster separate."

Len looked at him but Barbie wasn't being mean, just saying what was on his mind. Probably saying what everyone else in the crew was thinking. Len would always look shaggy and out of place next to Deke. Even if he dressed up in a shirt and tie, he would always be Deke's gangster. His hammer. An unpleasant reminder of the past.

"Nah, not that. I just can't sit still and listen to people talk about bullshit that's never gonna change. I'd rather be out here. Politics ain't my thing."

That last part was definitely true.

"I hear it's gonna be all our thing soon," the guy at the other end of the bench said. He had a round moon face with light skin and dark eyes.

"What's that?" Len said, sitting a little taller and putting some bass in his voice. It was one thing for him to think a certain way about Deke, but a whole other thing for it to come out of the mouth of babes.

The guy didn't seem fazed. "The way things are going, I expect I'll be handing out buttons and campaign stickers soon."

"What's your name?"

The guy finally seemed to tune into the potential minefield he'd walked into. "Wallace."

"You gotta problem with how Deke's doing things?"

Wallace shrugged. "Nah, course not. It's fine, long as it pays."

Len didn't disagree with the guy, but he couldn't say that. Not now. Backing up Deke was a reflex. He had to toe the line. He gave Wallace a stare until the kid stood and walked off and joined the other guy dealing near the gate.

"Sorry 'bout that. Young 'uns got no respect these days," Barbie said.

"Forget it. Just talk."

"You say so."

"What? It's not."

"Maybe. But, you know, I like to ramble, get around the neighborhood a bit. I've been hearing it more and more."

"Shit about Deke?"

"Not that bold, but whispers."

"People think Deke's gone soft?"

"People see that things are changing. Makes them uncomfortable."

"Yeah, well, comfort kills ambition, too." He stood. "Tell Wallace to remember that."

He left Barbie on the bench and retraced his steps back to the car. Someone had opened the old rec center windows in a likely futile attempt to let in some fresh air, and Len could hear the shouting as he passed. The town hall was getting testy. He kept going. He knew all the shouting in the world would not bring any change to Gray's Ferry. It might raze some lots and bring in new construction, but all of that would only be building on top of old bones.

The car hadn't moved. Len could see Cherry's big, square head through the back windshield. It didn't look like he'd moved an inch. Not paid to think, my ass, Len thought as he walked to the passenger door. He had the sudden intuition that Cherry's job was a lot different than what it appeared.

He was a sponge. A giant fucking sponge. Always around, always quiet. He sat there and soaked up the details that people let slip when they thought he was just the driver. If they even noticed him at all.

The debate was over. Youngblood stood at Watt's elbow as he gave a few wrap-up quotes to a clutch of local reporters. Youngblood kept one ear on his candidate but was thinking about the next moves. Walters had likely won on policy, but debates weren't scored rationally. She had not gotten under Watts's skin as she had in the past. Most observers would call it a draw, and that meant a win for Watts. He hadn't ducked any questions and if his answers sometimes rambled, they did so in a charming aww-shucks kind of way that didn't hurt his image. Watts's strength was not debating strategies and guidelines. He was a sweeping sermon guy, a glad-hander, a big ideas guy. He worked the rope lines, kissed babies, and pressed the flesh. Overall, Youngblood thought, tonight Watts did a good job.

He passed Walters's campaign manager, an uptight political newcomer named Nera, and could see on her face that she realized her candidate hadn't done what was necessary. He gave her a curt nod and continued past. He found a door and pushed outside. He was behind the building next to a decaying basketball court missing both rims. A large, drained pool sat farther back. Youngblood could hear but not see some kids laughing in that direction. After a moment, he saw the red spot of a cigarette or joint flare in the night. If he couldn't see them, they couldn't see him, but why take the chance. Youngblood was a cautious man. He quietly stepped around the corner and took out his phone.

Youngblood had the sense that things were stabilizing. That it was all going to be a blip. In two or four years, no one would even remember Watts's close call with Walters in winning his re-election. His finger hovered over an unnamed contact number. But Youngblood was a cautious man. Why leave something to chance when you didn't have to. He tapped the number and put the phone to his ear.

CHAPTER THIRTY-THREE

Max left the hospital and walked four blocks west on Walnut to Broad, but the grate was down over the subway entrance. It was past one o'clock in the morning, and the subway was done for the night. Late for some, but not Max. After driving for PPCS for six weeks, his body now belonged to the night. He gave the grate a shake and then kept walking. He crossed Broad and continued down Walnut. He wasn't the only one out. The city slowed down but never quite stopped. People were out. The activity and noise varied by the block as he walked. He cut through the old concrete and the even older trees of Rittenhouse Square and came out on 19th Street where it crossed South, the unofficial boundary of South Philly. He turned west again on Kater. It was residential and mostly quiet. The two-story brick row homes were stacked up like dominoes along the narrow street and almost indistinguishable from each other except for the colors of their front doors.

Two low-slung cars with bright neon lights highlighting their side panels raced past him at the next intersection. He thought briefly about the FCM, but the odds of them stumbling across him were infinitesimal. They had a name and his place of employment, but little else. If they got into Fiona's files or forced her to give them more information, the address on file would only lead to a PO box. He would avoid that until this was over.

He kept walking until he hit the eight-foot brick wall on Bainbridge that surrounded the old naval property. He turned south and zigzagged through the streets until he made it home. Ronnie's gym was dark. He made a quick circuit of his block to satisfy the paranoid part of his brain. He saw nothing. No one leaning in doorways. No one sitting in parked cars. He walked around to the back entrance, off the resident parking lot, and used his key to get inside.

His body was tired, but his brain was awake. He flipped through the papers and the coded ledger again. FCM was selling a lot of something, likely a panoply of drugs, but nothing in the papers directly spelled it out. There were a couple of initials and phone numbers on a page in the front. Those might come in handy. The rest remained gibberish. He tossed the book on the coffee table.

He read *Canticle* for a little while in bed but found his thoughts drifting back to the hospital chapel and what the minister had said. He couldn't square the idea that helping the bride could be a bad thing. Not all bad, at least. But what did he know? Only what Lorena and Gabriel had told him. Maybe he was hoping she needed help because it gave him an excuse to unleash that dark part of himself. Maybe he was making it worse for her by getting involved? Could helping someone also hurt them? Was this less about the bride and more about him? Was he getting closer or further away from redemption? There were no answers or divine inspiration before he fell asleep.

. . .

Lawrence called at four a.m. and Max woke with a start. He knocked the splayed book off his chest. The bedside light was on and the phone was vibrating across the nightstand.

"Hello?"

"I thought you were a creature of the night now?"

"Even creatures of the night get days off."

"You never take a day off. What happened?"

Max realized it was sometimes nice having people in your life that knew you. He told Lawrence what he'd learned at Lorena's house and about FCM from Darius and then about Liam being in the hospital.

"And what did you do?"

"Why do you think I did anything?"

"Roland Verns."

"It's not my problem that kid couldn't spell."

"But he could still kick your ass."

"One time. Everyone laughed at him every time they saw that tattoo. It wasn't just me."

Lawrence laughed now, remembering the bully from their juvie days. "He was an idiot, but you still shouldn't have provoked him. That's why I'm sure you did something. Your blood gets up and you react."

"Someone has to."

"So, what did you do?"

"I might have paid them a visit and asked some questions."

"Get any answers?"

"Not sure yet." He told him about the ledger. "You want to take a look?"

"Maybe. If it doesn't help now, it could be useful down the road."

"You're like a squirrel saving up for winter."

"Forget gold or silver, information is the most valuable commodity."

"I don't doubt that you could squeeze a profit out of a rock, Lawrence."

"Let's talk about your bride. Eddie found some information and, I gotta say, you sure have a knack for picking them, Max."

"What's that mean?"

"I think I know what might have brought those detectives to your door."

At that moment, there was an actual knock at his door. It wasn't a tentative, are you home, I know it's late knock. It was a fist on the door knock. Max knew that type of knock. He slid out of bed and glanced out the window. There was a dented silver Camry parked at the curb. "Speak of the devil."

"What?"

"Lawrence? How fast can you get to Philly?"

CHAPTER THIRTY-FOUR

They left him in the interview room for three hours. They hadn't arrested him and hadn't taken his personal possessions. They hadn't cuffed his hands to the metal ring on the table. He still had his watch and imagined the city outside as night turned to dawn and dawn turned to full daylight. It wasn't the first time he'd been placed in a room like this. He sat. He waited. He thought about putting his head on the table and taking a nap, but wasn't tired and wasn't keen to have his skin in contact with the table either. Cigarette burns dotted the surface. Past occupants had etched names, graffiti, and messages into the laminate. Most of the messages were not polite to the police.

Axelson came in at one point and apologized for the delay with a bogus excuse and an offer of a cup of coffee. He declined. Making him wait was a tactic. Waiting was a skill that Max had long mastered. Bank jobs and robberies happened fast, but the planning was slow. Three hours was a blink of an eye. In the past, he'd sat still and waited five, six, seven hours to get a three-second glimpse of a door opening or to watch the specific timing of a certain truck arriving.

Eventually, Axelson came back into the room. She was carrying a brown paper bag. Diaz trailed behind her and leaned against the back wall. Axelson sat across the table from Max and placed the bag by her feet. They looked to be reprising their same roles from last time. Eager, cooperative good cop and quiet, older bad cop. They both looked more or less like they had the last time he'd seen them at PPCS: stressed, tired, anxious, frustrated, and edgy. And trying to hide it all. Diaz had dark circles etched under his eyes, his gray skin matched his wrinkled gray suit. Axelson looked marginally better than her partner. Maybe she'd stopped to splash water on her face. Or maybe she was the tougher of the two.

She pulled a notebook and pen out of her jacket pocket and placed them on the table. She followed that with a small digital voice recorder. She glanced up at Max, a question in her eyes. He nodded and she pressed the red button. Max watched a counter begin on the small LCD screen. Axelson read out the date and gave her name and Diaz's name before turning to Max.

"Can you state your name for the record, please?"

"Cormac Lindell."

"People call you Max?"

"Some do, yes."

"Your date of birth?"

"January 21, 1982."

Neither of which was true, but they matched up with his current identification and would be what the detectives expected.

"And your home address?"

"2391 Montrose Street."

"Across from the mill building?"

"Yes."

"Bit of a dive, isn't it?"

He looked at her. What was the point of that question? "It works for me."

"Phone number where we can reach you?"

He recited his current cell phone number. The one he used for work.

"You sure you don't want that coffee?"

"I'm okay."

"All right. Cormac Max Lindell. Is that your real name?"

That shot a little electric current through his chest. He kept his voice steady. "Yes."

"You have dual citizenship?"

"Yes, Canadian and US."

"I've been to Niagara Falls once. Never really been to Canada proper."

Max tried not to roll his eyes. Waiting was one thing. Enduring pointless questions was another. "What's the deal, Detective? You've kept me here long enough. Let's get this done. What do you want to know? Ask your questions."

She smiled slightly, like she'd scored a point. "I am, Max. What I want is to learn more about you. Fiona O'Brian says you've only been working for PPCS for a couple of months. Where were you before that?"

"Here and there. I was traveling. I was actually up in Canada before coming down here. Canada proper. Prince Edward Island."

Axelson jotted something in her notepad. "And now you're here in Philly."

"Yes. I'd been here as a kid. Liked it, thought I'd come back and try it as an adult."

"And?"

"And it's fine so far."

"And you've been working at the car service the whole time."

"Yeah, I've been in town for about two months, had the job at PPCS for about six weeks."

"I heard the owner was in the hospital."

"Yes, he had an accident in the garage."

Was that what this was all about? Was this about his little back room retaliation on FCM?

But Axelson pivoted away. Maybe she was trying to keep him off balance.

"I want to ask you again about that supposed late-night pickup outside the shrine."

"Supposed?"

"Yeah, funny thing. We can't confirm anything about it. No name, burner phone number, dead-end credit card number."

"I dropped her off at The Clyde Hotel."

"So you said. No one there confirms this woman's presence. So far, she's only a figment of your imagination."

He could show them the photos he'd taken on the street outside The Clyde, but what would that prove? To them, it would be a random woman, as good as a stock photo.

"You think I made her up? Why would I do that?"

Axelson didn't answer that, but she gave that smile again and Max had a feeling he'd stepped right where she wanted him to. "Good question." She reached down into the paper bag and pulled out the wooden box and placed it on the table. It was inside a plastic evidence bag but otherwise looked the same as the last time he'd seen it. "Recognize this?"

He suddenly understood he might be in a more precarious position than he first realized and wondered about calling a stop to this and asking for a lawyer. But he was also curious how Axelson and Diaz had ended up with the box. Learning a little more information now might be worth the risk.

"It's a piece of property that the woman left behind in my car."

"The mystery woman? The potentially imaginary woman?"

"Yes."

"Funny that her prints don't show up on this strange little box. Yours don't either."

Max was now very happy he'd taken the precaution of wiping the box down before putting it in his backpack that day to return it. Lawrence could provide him a new ID and a new backstory, but he couldn't change his fingerprints. If he were ever formally arrested and printed and they put those prints through the system, it would set off alarm bells. A lot of them.

Max shrugged. "I found it in the back of my car. Not sure what else I can tell you."

She leaned back over and pulled a file out of the bag, then removed three sheets of paper from the file. Three photos. She spread them out on the table. Two headshots, both young men with short-cropped hair, vaguely similar, maybe brothers or relatives. Max didn't recognize either one but realized this is likely what Lawrence had been calling about. The third photo was likely from a traffic camera or public surveillance camera. It was taken from an acute angle and was slightly out of focus and grainy. Still, it wasn't hard to discern the participants. Max stood over the man in the street just after knocking him unconscious with an elbow.

Axelson let him look before she added a fourth photo. It was a harshly lit overhead photo of four severed fingers lined up next to a ruler.

He realized he should keep his mouth shut but couldn't help himself. He pointed to the fingers. "What is that?"

"That is what was in the box. But I think you already knew that."

"I think I want a lawyer."

.   .   .

Erica Childs looked nothing like the woman who'd been drunk and comatose in the back of his car. Had it only been a few weeks? She wore a soft, cream-colored blouse under a navy suit jacket with a matching pencil skirt. She wore small gold stud earrings, and a hint of makeup with hair that was still slightly damp and dark at the ends. Fifty minutes after he'd called, using her business card that he'd stuffed in his wallet at the end of that shift, she swept into the drab interview room with blustery confidence and the scent of light floral perfume.

"I'll need a few minutes with my client," she said and turned to Max, dismissing Axelson and Diaz with barely a glance. She took Axelson's vacated seat and waited. The detectives left. They'd played this game before, too. Childs waited a couple of beats after the door closed and then slumped slightly in her seat.

"What the hell is this?"

Her breath was the only thing that he thought hinted at her problem. It was minty, too minty, as if she was self-conscious about her breath. He wondered if she'd hit the point where she needed a morning slug in her coffee to get her motor running.

"I'm new to the city and, well," he waved a hand around the room as if that answered her question, "I'm in a bit of a situation here."

"I'm a corporate tax attorney."

That answered one of his questions but didn't change the basics parameters of his problem. He had to get out of here and he had to do it fast. He could have hired his own attorney or had Lawrence help, but all of that would have taken time. Hours, maybe days. He didn't know the exact statutes in Philadelphia but, if Axelson and Diaz thought he was guilty of butchering more than one person, he was pretty sure they could hold him for a good long time without arresting him and starting the clock on an arraignment. If they got to that point, Max was cooked.

"Look, I don't need you long-term. You happen to be the only attorney I know in this city. I need you to help get me out of here now, as fast as possible. After that, you won't hear from me again."

"What's stopping me from simply walking out of here?"

"Nothing. Or maybe the same thing that got me to drive from Merion over to Cheltenham to make sure you made it home safe. You're a decent person."

Her cheeks flushed at the mention of that night. "You bet your one phone call on that?"

"Yes. I believe most people want to be good. That they are decent."

She stared at him for a long moment, then leaned over, just like Axelson, and took something out of her bag. She placed a leather folio on the table and pulled out a silver pen. "All right, tell me what happened."

He took a breath. He wasn't out of the woods yet, but it was the first step. Before he could open his mouth, she held up a hand. "Wait, let's start with an easy one. What's your name?"

He almost laughed.

Max kept his mouth shut and let Childs make their arguments.

"You have no actual probable cause."

Axelson nudged the box, which was back on the table in its plastic bag. "We have the box."

"Which isn't my client's property."

"He admits it was in his possession."

"It was in the car that he drives for employment. Does he also own the people and their possessions that get in his car?"

"We cannot find the person he claims left it in his car," Axelson retorted.

"That's not our problem. Just because you haven't located her doesn't mean she doesn't exist. Try harder, Detective. That's your job."

It continued like that for two hours. Max had the sense that Axelson was resigned to letting him go after an hour but kept bickering with Childs to drag it out as long as possible. The photos and box weren't enough. It was all circumstantial and not indicative that Max had done anything wrong. He walked out of the Third District police station a little before noon, blinking in the white October sun.

"Thank you," he said to Childs.

"You're welcome. I sort of enjoyed it, to be honest. A little different from my usual beat." They shook hands. She had a firm grip. He liked that. "Call me. You have my number." Max watched her walk away and thought about those open-ended last two sentences. She was attractive and smart, but also full of her own demons. He watched her walk down the stone steps and turn left onto 11th Street. He breathed in the air. It felt clean and cold in his chest after the hours of body odor, stale coffee, and floor wax of the police station.

Five minutes later, Erica Childs was the least of his concerns.

CHAPTER THIRTY-FIVE

It takes between five and six hours to get from Boston to Philly if you don't get bogged down in construction or get unlucky with traffic accidents. Lawrence thought about flying. There would probably be a six a.m. flight out of Logan that could get him there quickly, but he didn't want his name on any paperwork. He took a big Escalade, hell on gas miles but better comfort for his lanky frame, that he leased through a couple of shell companies and would never get a sniff of his name or address. After hanging up with Max, he made one stop at an apartment building he owned to get some supplies out of a basement storage locker and then hit 95 headed south. He set the cruise control to seventy-five, passed Hartford two hours later, stopped for gas once and a bathroom after crossing the George Washington Bridge in New Jersey. After that, he kept driving until he was on the Delaware Expressway. He wound his way around City Hall and south onto Broad Street and the City of Brotherly Love a little after 10:30 in the morning.

He'd done some business in Philly in the past but had not spent any extended time in the city. It had been all work, never pleasure. Away from the tourist claptrap, it looked like a town he might enjoy. He might consider crashing with Max for a few days after this was over. If that was possible. Which was not a given. When Max got in trouble, he left a path of destruction in his wake like Sherman marching to Atlanta. That was part of the reason Lawrence picked up the phone when he called. Lawrence liked the action. He needed it almost as much as his friend. He spent most of his life trying to appear quiet and conservative. He tried to do everything not to attract attention. That's really what Max should be doing now, but he seemed incapable of it. The man had every reason to be quiet and stay on the sidelines, but he didn't. Or couldn't. He stuck his foot out. He put his nose in it. He pushed back. It was what Lawrence liked most about him. Plus, wreaking havoc could be a lot of fun.

He'd made the drive in under six hours. He pulled off Broad Street onto a smaller side street and got out to stretch. His mouth tasted like wallpaper glue. He bought two bottles of water at a corner store and then tried Max's phone. It rolled over to voicemail immediately. Max wasn't great with his phone, but if he could answer this time, he probably would have, which meant that he couldn't, which likely meant he was still being held by the detectives that had come to his door. Cops never did question anyone quickly. He needed to find out where the detectives had taken Max.

Only one person could help with that. He tapped a different contact and let it ring. This phone had no voicemail. A sleepy voice eventually answered.

"What?" Any time before three or four in the afternoon was the middle of the night for Eddie.

"Wake up, sleepyhead. I need you to do some quick research for me."

. . .

The Third District police station was a two-story concrete building that looked like it came off the Brutalist architecture assembly line in the sixties. They had replaced the entrance on the corner with panels of glass and a colorful mural to soften it and add some modern touches. Lawrence wasn't sold on the result, but his hesitancy might have been a bias against the police.

The station was in a residential area and fronted a wide avenue bisected by trolley tracks. Eddie had quickly found Detective Diaz's home precinct and hung up on Lawrence. The Third District was a short drive south down Broad Street and a left on Wharton. He found a street spot for the Escalade that provided an unobstructed view of the station. He could see down the main drag as far as the maintenance building next door, and the smaller side street that led into the surrounding blocks.

Lawrence sat in the Escalade with the windows cracked and watched. He sipped the second water and ate a granola bar. He decided he'd watch until noon before he took more direct action. He didn't want his face or his name on any official record, even to ask the old sergeant that he'd bet was sitting at the front desk. His preference was always to stay in the background. People rarely noticed what wasn't right in front of them. He'd carved out a good living for himself by slipping in and out of the seams of life.

Max emerged from the precinct with a woman a little before noon. He watched them talk briefly and shake. The woman walked down the street to a black Audi sedan. Max remained on the top step with his head tilted back. A man happy to have escaped a very small box. Lawrence reached for the door handle so he could step out and wave to his friend when that primitive survival sense lit up. He realized he wasn't the only one watching and waiting for Max.

The car, a navy Nissan Altima, drove past Lawrence. He

could almost reach out and touch the passenger door. It drove slowly. Too slowly. The driver might have been looking for parking, but Lawrence could see he was focused on the front of the station. As Lawrence watched, the man raised a hand out the window. A signal. Lawrence shifted his gaze and immediately picked out three more men spread out on the sidewalk in front of the precinct.

Max descended the front steps and walked down Wharton toward Broad, likely heading for a bus or a subway stop. Or maybe still enjoying the sensation of fresh air. Lawrence opened the door and received a harsh horn blast from a car coming up the narrow side street.

"Max!" he shouted, but it was a busy street and an old trolley car was rumbling into view.

Lawrence saw how it would happen and knew he was too far away to be any help. He had to give the crew credit for having the brass-plated balls to snatch a guy within spitting distance of a cop shop. They timed it right, too. Not their first rodeo. Two approached from the back. One from the front. The car inched along. The guy in front was looking down at his phone, or pretending to, and stumbled into Max. Max stopped. That's all it took. The two coming from the back closed up. One took an elbow, the other took his neck, and together they steered Max off the curb and into the idling car. Lawrence hadn't even seen a weapon, and he'd been looking. It was all done in less than five seconds. Right out in public. Quiet and discreet. These guys wouldn't lose their cool easily. That was good to know for what Lawrence would need to do next.

Max was half awake and half a step slow. It cost him.

The cool air revived him briefly on the station steps as he said goodbye to Erica, but the midday sun on his face also made him drowsy. The long, stressful hours in the interview room had taken a toll. So did thinking about the fingers again. But it was over. He decided he wouldn't go back in that box if he could help it. Even if it meant running. For now, he wanted to get back to his apartment, grab some sleep, and wait for Lawrence. With some rest and a clear head, they could regroup and figure out the next best move.

He set off toward Broad. The SEPTA trolley wouldn't get him home. He needed a bus. His stomach rumbled, and he glanced across the street at the luncheonette. Eat when you have the chance was his rule, but he was afraid if he sat down in a booth now he'd pass out before the food arrived. He also wanted to put some space between him and the cops. That lunch counter was too close. He kept walking. He'd grab something at The Skyline. If he passed out, Nia would only have to carry him across the street. She was thin, almost slight, Sherrod's cooking didn't stick to her ribs, but he'd seen her carry six fully loaded plates at the same time. She could probably haul him out of the diner one-handed. He smiled at the thought and bumped shoulders with a man going the other direction. Max turned to apologize and stared at two guys standing uncomfortably close, both holding small guns discreetly at their sides. The guy he'd bumped into had moved off the sidewalk and opened the door to an idling car. Max knew getting in the car was a bad idea, but so was getting shot in the street. Live to see the next minute was another of his rules. He let them guide him into the back seat. The gun guys bracketed him on each side. The other guy climbed in the front. The driver accelerated into traffic. No words were spoken. No muss, no fuss. A normal weekday morning kidnapping.

Max looked around the car. It was quiet. No radio. No squeaks or rattles. No idle chatter. Two of the guys were younger, mid-twenties, and two appeared to be about Max's age. The younger ones wore the braided FCM belts and had the same empty eyes as the pair he'd seen outside PPCS. Someone had ratted him out.

"Mind if a buckle my seatbelt?" Max asked.

No one responded.

Eventually, the guy in the passenger seat half-turned and shrugged. "If you think it will make a difference."

Max slowly reached up, took the seatbelt, and clicked it into place. He sat back and kept his hands in his lap. If anything was going to happen, he needed these guys to relax at least a fraction. The two guys in the back still had their guns out, but they weren't pointing at Max. Not exactly. He'd already dismissed trying anything in the current situation. Even if he disarmed one of them and got one gun, it was suicide. The other guy would simply press the gun to his head or his chest and shoot him. He had to assume the guys in front were armed, as well. No point. Live to see the next minute.

Max watched the city slide past the window and tried to pick out their destination and form a plan. Any plan. They drove east, before turning south. Traffic was heavy. There was a planned march today to protest the police response to the recent shootings in city neighborhoods. They had cordoned streets off and the typically bad city traffic was getting worse. Max didn't mind. He wasn't in a rush to get wherever they were going. The driver said something in Spanish. The passenger shrugged as if to say 'what can you do?' but didn't respond. The driver took them farther east, on smaller, less populated roads, and they eventually broke free of the bottleneck. Max watched the taller midtown buildings fall away as they drove closer to the water. They turned south on Christopher Columbus, past commercial plazas with Ikea and Best Buy, and deeper into the few remaining acres of the working marine port in the city.

"Hay un camión negro siguiéndonos," the driver said.

There's a black truck following us. Max had picked up some Spanish over the years with different heist crews. It was important to know if your partners were going to screw you.

"Estas seguro?"

Are you sure?

"No."

The driver slowed and then randomly sped up, raced past the few remaining cars on the road, before he slowed way down again.

They all waited.

"Se ha ido ahora."

No longer there.

The guy in the passenger seat tapped his phone and held it to his ear.

"Dos minutos."

Two minutes.

Max watched everyone's shoulder drop a fraction. No need to stress. Almost there.

Suddenly Max was upside down and trying not to bite his tongue in half.

CHAPTER THIRTY-SIX

L awrence followed the Altima, keeping four or five cars between them on the city streets when he could, and tried to think of a plan. Nothing came to mind. He was in an unfamiliar city on unfamiliar streets. He decided he had two options. Stay close and wait for serendipity to give him an opening or use brute force to make his own luck. He followed the kidnappers through congested downtown streets before emerging on the edge of the city on more open roads. They crossed under 95 and turned south. They passed rehabbed commercial blocks near the water and entered a more industrial area. He could see the Delaware River off to his left, the city of Camden, and the Jersey waterfront sitting on the opposite shore. A dividing line between Pennsylvania and New Jersey somewhere in the middle of the river.

They passed huge, old brick fortresses topped with stagnant smokestacks. Rumbled over long-abandoned railroad tracks, then rolled by newer, low corrugated steel warehouses. The area quickly became less populated with cars and filled with trucks hauling shipping containers. Whatever the desti-

nation, it was likely coming up soon. They were running out
of road. Lawrence decided in this case patience and
serendipity would not be a virtue. He needed to act.

He brought up the Escalade's GPS and zoomed out. He
quickly studied the area and surrounding roads. By heading
into the port area, they had cut down his options but not
eliminated them. He took the next left and a quick right to
get on a parallel service road. It was smaller and narrower and
in rougher shape, probably the original road to the docks
before they put the larger boulevard in, but it was empty of
traffic. Lawrence put the accelerator to the floor. The big
SUV paused, gathered itself, and then leaped forward. He
shot another glance at the map. He passed the first cross
street and kept the speed high until he saw the cut in the
road for the second cross street. He braked, got the speed
under control, the last thing he could afford was to roll the
truck, and made the turn.

The space between the two parallel roads had narrowed
further. The cross street was barely a block long, less than
two hundred yards. A blue and gray painted office building sat
on the right. An older, larger, brick building loomed over the
road from the left. They provided cover for Lawrence and the
Escalade but also blocked his view. He raced up close to the
corner. There was no traffic light, only a two-way stop at the
crossroad. They would have the right of way. He inched up to
the mouth of the intersection until he could see left and
right. Clear on the left, all the way to the next bend in the
road. Good, he hadn't missed them. The right was clear, too,
then a car traveling slowly, very slowly, came into view.

What were they doing? Did they get a flat? Some other
car trouble? Were they going to try something right here?
Shoot Max and dump his body on the side of the road? That
made little sense. The area was less populated but hardly
deserted. And why drive all this way to do that? Easier to

stage it like a gang drive-by back near the police station. No, it came to him. They were looking for a tail. They must have gotten suspicious or paranoid. As he watched, the car sped up. The road remained empty in both directions. Lawrence put his window down so he could hear the Altima's approach and backed up the Escalade so he wouldn't be visible to the other car until they were committed to the intersection. He double-checked that his seatbelt was buckled.

He couldn't afford to miss. He had to time it right. If he whiffed, there would be no second chance. He visualized what he wanted to do. Ideally, he'd clip the back rear panel like a police PIT maneuver and force the Nissan into a fishtail. The authorities gave it a fancy acronym, but it was a tactical ramming. Take the bad guys out of commission without killing them and limit the damage to your vehicle.

He kept his left foot on the brake and pushed down on the gas. The engine revved up and he could feel the big V8 push against its restraint. He watched. He listened. He waited. He pressed down further on the gas. The RPMs crept higher.

The Nissan's engine drew closer. He inched up on the brake. The Escalade rolled forward. Then he didn't need to listen, he saw it. The Nissan cleared the edge of the low warehouse and was in full view. Lawrence picked his foot up off the brake and slammed the gas pedal down the rest of the way. The Escalade shot forward.

He was too quick.

He hit the Nissan right in the center, on the I-beam between the front and rear seats.

A Nissan Altima was a solid sedan, but it was no match for a speeding Escalade reinforced with a front grille guard.

The car went airborne and flipped half a dozen times. Max

lost count after two. His first instinct was to grab for one of the guns, before the roof airbag punched him in the neck. Bright starbursts popped in his eyes, and he forgot about the gun. Metal shrieked. Glass shattered. Something sliced into his scalp. A sharp pain dug into his shoulder.

The world abruptly stopped spinning. He was upside down.

Something was burning.

Someone was screaming.

He saw feet walking toward the car.

Lawrence exited the SUV. He paused, a hand on the side mirror, and let the nausea pass. The airbags had deployed and did their job. Other than the passing nausea and a touch of vertigo, Lawrence was okay. He looked down at himself and took a quick inventory. He spit. No blood. He moved his tongue around and shook out his arms and legs. A couple of teeth felt a little loose and his hands shook from the adrenaline, but there were no broken bones.

When the horizon settled back into a straight line, he got moving. The crash had been more demolition derby than tactical ramming. He hoped Max wasn't hurt too badly. He opened the back door and pulled a Ruger GP100 from the canvas bag of supplies he'd brought. Lawrence did his best to avoid guns, but when he needed one, he liked the old school Dirty Harry look. It was reliable and the .357 packed serious firepower, but it mostly looked intimidating and scary as hell. Just pulling it out usually got the job done. He tucked it into his waistband and shut the door.

He patted the truck's side panel affectionately. The engine hissed and ticked. The grille bar was bent and the impact had scratched the hood, but otherwise, the truck was in remarkably good shape after the violence of the collision. As long as nothing was leaking underneath, he didn't think it would be a problem to get it going again. They'd need to dump it eventually, but it would get them clear of this scene. First, he needed Max.

Lawrence jogged across the empty road. The Nissan was in much worse shape. The car was upside down. It had skidded up on the sidewalk and left deep grooves through a small strip of grass that surrounded the office building on the far side of the intersection. He could see faces glancing out the windows. He glanced up and down the road. Still no other traffic. But he knew he couldn't count on that for much longer. Even during an off-hour, any road leading to an active port would get cars and trucks, and people inside the surrounding buildings had undoubtedly heard the crash. Someone would call the cops.

Lawrence approached the last few feet slowly. He smelled gas and oil. He took a knee and looked through the shattered windows. Four guys inside. No one was moving. The driver's seat was empty. Lawrence looked around. The driver had been ejected, and he lay twisted unnaturally around a nearby telephone pole. No need to check on him. He tried the rear door and pulled it halfway open. Max was in the middle and hanging by his seatbelt, Lawrence felt some relief at seeing that, eyes closed, one arm twisted behind him, a line of blood dripping off his chin. The other two lacked seatbelts and had paid a heavy price. One had a deep gash that creased the side of his head and split his skull. Lawrence saw splinters of white and gray through the blood. He didn't want to know exactly what he was looking at it. The second guy looked to be alive. He was unconscious but breathing shallowly. The front seat passenger mewled, his eyes rolling in their sockets. Lawrence could see a bone sticking out from his lower leg.

"Max?" Lawrence gently pushed his arm. "You in there? Max?"

He heard a car stop somewhere behind him. Doors opened and closed.

Was that a siren in the distance? This was taking too long. They needed to be long gone before any cops showed up. He reached in and unlatched the belt. Max flopped down across the front seat. His eyes fluttered open. They were soft and unfocused before locking in on Lawrence.

He managed a weak smile.

"Sorry, I couldn't think of anything more creative on short notice," Lawrence said.

"Thanks," Max whispered. He held out a hand. Lawrence gripped it and started to pull Max out of the car. Max's eyes flicked to something over Lawrence's shoulder.

Lawrence turned and the younger one shot him.

CHAPTER THIRTY-SEVEN

Ash's cell phone rang. The one that the man had provided. It took him a moment to realize what it was. It hadn't rung before and the high-pitched chirping wasn't familiar.

"Hello?"

The man was speaking quietly, almost whispering. "I need you to go to the corner of 29th and Tasker and pick a guy up."

"A guy?"

"He'll have more information for you."

"Wha—"

But he'd already hung up.

A guy? Ash thought. A strange request, but this entire job was strange. And he was in too deep to question it now. He turned left on Reed and started working his way back to 29th. Maybe the new guy would have some ideas about stopping the music.

The intersection of 29th and Tasker was residential. There

was a park on one corner with a fenced-in section of bright green artificial grass. Ash saw five or six dogs running around while their owners mingled near a set of benches. A few glanced over at the truck as he pulled it to the curb. Across from the park was a low, nondescript, tan building. A red square sign spotted with holes that might have once displayed the Coke logo hung off the side under blocky, rusting text that said: The Store. Ash couldn't figure out what the place sold or if it was still even open. The other corners were older post-WW2 row homes whose facades were in various states of disrepair.

There was no one waiting, but Ash spotted a guy walking purposefully through the park toward the truck and the exit on the corner. He was short with wide shoulders and a thick neck. He wore a light black Adidas windbreaker over dark jeans with lighter streaks across the thighs. He carried a rolled-up paper grocery bag in one hand. Ash met his eyes through the windshield and raised a hand. The man didn't respond in any way. He kept walking, cut across the street, pulled open the sliding passenger side door, and climbed in.

"I'm Ash."

The guy still didn't respond. He set the paper bag on the floor, glanced around, taking in Ash behind the wheel like any other feature of the truck, and eventually said, "Drive."

No names. Okay. Ash looked at the guy. "Where?" Up close, he looked to be in his late twenties. He had light, almost honey-colored eyes. Old acne scars flecked his cheeks. A thick keloid scar was visible on his neck and disappeared into the windbreaker.

He pointed. "Head down Tasker. I'll tell you when to turn."

Ash checked the mirrors, waited for a car to pass through the intersection, then pulled the truck back onto the road and headed west on Tasker.

The man was looking out the window, studying the people in the dog enclosure as they drove past. Once they were through the next intersection and picked up a little speed, he sat back.

"Can you turn that music off?" he asked.

Ash almost laughed but said, "No," and kept his eyes on the road.

The guy looked over at him, checking if Ash was messing with him. Ash talked when he was nervous and this guy's vibe made him nervous, so he explained. "The music is always on when the truck is moving. I can't turn it down or turn it off. It's the way the truck is wired."

The man must have decided Ash was telling the truth. He muttered something under his breath and then returned to staring out the window. They reached the end of Tasker.

"Go right, head north."

Ash turned, and they drove north for ten minutes, skirting the edge of Gray's Ferry on 33rd before turning right again onto Gray's Ferry Avenue and heading out of the neighborhood into the old naval base area and the tangle of construction that was going to be the new medical buildings. The guy started giving him directions on surface streets. Ash recognized some of the streets. He'd driven the truck through this neighborhood on his rounds but lost track of where he was exactly. Occasionally, he could spot the Schuylkill River off to the left.

The man guided Ash to a short, stubby road dominated by an old brick warehouse on the left. The sign out front listed various small businesses. A similar building faced it on the right side, but this one had been converted into apartments or condos. A fifties-style silver diner sat at the far end.

"Pull over here." There was two-hour street parking and Ash navigated the truck into a double spot almost directly opposite the warehouse entrance.

"Now what?"

The guy studied the sign, apparently found what he was looking for, and sat back. "We wait."

"And then?"

The man reached down into the shopping bag at his feet. He tossed something on Ash's lap. Ash didn't know what it was at first and flinched. The man laughed. Ash picked up the rubber mask. It was a clown mask. The kind that completely covered your head. There was a flare of red hair around the crown and matching lurid red lips around long, jagged teeth.

"And then we kidnap a guy."

"Whoa, what?" Ash held the mask by its floppy ears, sure he'd misheard.

"We grab a guy. A kid, really. Get him in the truck. Don't worry, you're the driver. I'm the muscle. You've been driving around for what, a week? No one is going to give this heap a second look. We find a quiet spot, we roll up, I grab him, get him in the back and we're done."

"Done?"

"True, there's a couple of more steps, but the hard part would be over."

"Hard part?"

The man glanced over at Ash. "You stuck on repeat?"

Ash tossed the mask to the floor like it was suddenly on fire. "Hell no. I signed up to drive a truck. That's it. This fuckin' music hasn't made me so crazy that I think it's okay to kidnap a kid."

"Chill. Nothing is going to happen to the kid. He's simply leverage. We're going to stash him away for a bit and then we'll let him go."

"We? You're not listening. I am not doing this."

This time, the man didn't smirk. He reached into the paper bag again and pulled out a gun. Ash recognized it. A Sig Sauer M18. It was the most common handgun in the US

Army. He recognized it, but it looked strange and wrong inside the ice cream truck. "The man thought you might get cold feet." The guy put the gun on the truck's dash and held out a small plastic baggie. Ash recognized this too. "He thought this might help."

And it would help. Ash knew that. People who had never taken the drug had no idea. It was almost impossible, Ash knew, he'd tried many times, with both addicts and in rehab circles, to explain the warm, bubbling rush of euphoria when the heroin hit your brain and the dopamine kicked in.

He dropped his head. So, this was the price for ten days of normality. The balloon payment due on his fresh start. It was all a mirage. Too good to be true. Was he tucked up next to the McDonald's dumpster right now? Was this one long final dopamine dream as his body finally gave in to death? No. It wasn't a dream. It was a visceral nightmare. Worse than going cold turkey. Worse than any DTs. He had to help kidnap a kid or this guy would beat him senseless or put a bullet in his head. Not a lot of choices.

It took a monumental effort not to reach out and snatch the bag greedily from the guy's outstretched hand. The man looked at him, smiling again, almost like he was teasing a dog. He shook the bag lightly. "On the house," he said and tossed it in Ash's lap. Ash's hands started to shake and saliva flooded his mouth as he stared at the three small blue balloons knotted inside the baggie. He fought back. He really did. But he could feel his fragile discipline crack.

Ash was worried as they made their fifth circuit around the block. Even if the truck was largely invisible, you eventually noticed the gnat flying around your head. Finally, a tall, skinny kid exited the warehouse front doors wearing a backpack, sweats, and a hoodie. He was dipping his head, listening to something on his headphones.

"That's him." The man looked up and down the street. "Wait until he's past the diner, in that empty space, then pull up in front." He picked up the gun and pulled his mask, a matching clown only with a blue fringe of hair, down over his face. "Don't forget your mask."

Ash picked his mask up off the floor and held it. Putting it on was like releasing the safety catch on Pandora's box. So far, it had been theoretical. They hadn't done anything. He dipped a pinkie in the open balloon he'd stashed in the cup holder and snorted a bump of the heroin. He'd done a small toot earlier to keep his nerve. Now he needed to reinforce it or ride the hit past it. He pulled the mask down.

Ash wondered how they were going to do this in broad daylight on a street and get away with it. But they had. Ash waited until the kid was clear of the diner. As they drove by, Ash could see it must be only a breakfast and lunch place. It was closed. He timed it so the kid was on the sidewalk in the middle of the empty lot and pulled up alongside. The kid's headphones must have been jacked up high. He didn't notice anything until Ash steered the truck next to the curb, and he finally glanced over. He looked puzzled for a moment before he shook his head and waved Ash off. He wasn't interested in ice cream. He kept walking, but the man came up behind him and snapped a handcuff around one wrist. The kid swung around, surprised, and stared down the barrel of the Sig. His eyes went wide. The man snapped the other handcuff closed and pulled him into the back of the truck. It had all happened fast. Ash used the mirrors to check the street. Empty. Normal. Nothing had changed, except now Ash was a kidnapper.

There was a thump from the back. "Go," the man said.

The kid kicked against the walls of the empty coolers in the back. Ash took that as a good sign. The kid was alive.

Two minutes later, they were six blocks away and the second bump of heroin fully lit up Ash's brain. He didn't think about the kid again for a couple of hours. By then, it was too late.

CHAPTER THIRTY-EIGHT

The pain was patient. Max floated in the dark. He heard voices. He opened his eyes, and the pain pounced like a jackal on carrion. His bones ached. His chest felt like someone had used it for a trampoline. A spot on his scalp above his ear pulsed with his heartbeat. He shut his eyes. He wanted to go back into the peaceful dark. There was a sharp sting on his face. A slap.

"Open your eyes," someone said.

Another slap. Still, the darkness was better. If he could slip back into the dark, the slaps wouldn't matter.

"Open your eyes or I'll shoot him again."

Max opened his eyes. They'd bound him to a chair with baling wire. Lawrence sat, also tied up, in a chair next to him. His chin slumped against his chest. The gunshot wound bled from his shoulder. Max watched until he saw Lawrence's chest rise. He was still alive.

"That's better."

Max looked up at the speaker. He wore the same clothes as the first time Max had seen him outside PPCS. Stiff jeans, white T-shirt, rope belt. This time, there was also a light blue button-down shirt over top. Maybe a concession to the cooler weather? The jagged scar was still visible across his throat above his shirt collar. Max looked past him. There were three other men in the room. Each one held a gun.

He took in the rest. It was better than thinking about the pain. The room was a simple square, twelve feet by twelve feet, with a poured cement floor and cinderblock walls. A pair of incandescent bulbs hung at intervals from the ceiling, otherwise the room was empty except for the men and the chairs and the baling wire. It smelled of wet concrete, mildew, and a sourness Max couldn't place. He could see through the open door into a larger room with hulking, rusting equipment.

"You going to stay with me? I don't want to have to put another hole in your friend."

Max said nothing. His throat was dry and his tongue was stuck to his teeth. His bones popped and sizzled. He tried to focus.

"Good," the man continued as if Max had answered. He took out a cell phone, tapped a button, and held it to his ear. "He's awake," he said. He listened for a long time. "Okay. Yes. Okay." He put the phone away and thought for a moment then he took it out again, tapped and swiped, before he put it back in his pocket. "Julio, give me your phone." He held out his hand.

One man stepped forward and looked at him in surprise. "What?"

"Your phone. I need it."

Julio handed it over. The first guy took it, swiped, and then nodded as if satisfied. "Okay, here's what's going to happen. We're going to let you go." He held up Julio's phone. There was a photo on the screen. It was a black and white still from a security camera. It was low quality, but Max could still recognize Adelita. The bride. Max tried not to react.

"You'll start paying your debt to us by finding this woman and bringing her to us."

"Who is it?" His voice came out a hoarse whisper. His throat was coated in razor blades.

"Doesn't matter. Just find her."

"How?"

"Doesn't matter. You had no trouble finding La Champincita Grocers the other night. If you find her and bring her here, that little indiscretion will be forgotten. More importantly, to you, we'll let your friend here go too."

"When?"

"As long as your friend here can stay alive." The guy kicked the leg of the chair and Lawrence made a soft gurgling noise in his throat but didn't wake. "That's your clock. You get this woman to us and we'll swap. One for one. Is it a deal?"

Max nodded.

"Good."

They cut him loose. He stood slowly and rubbed his wrists where the wire had cut into his flesh. The man handed him Julio's phone. "I took the password off. There's one number left plus the photo. Call when you have her." He held out a set of keys. "We brought your friend's car with us. It's a little banged up but usable."

Max took the keys and walked toward the door. He could feel an itch between his shoulder blades as he walked across the larger space to the door. Outside, the sun was low, but it was still light. He hadn't been unconscious for too long. There were three cars lined up outside. Two identical black Chevy Suburbans with the smoked window glass he'd seen at PPCS parked next to a black Escalade with New York plates. Someone had used baling wire to tie the Escalade's grille bar to the bumper to hold it in place.

Max unlocked the doors and climbed in carefully. There

was a half-empty bottle of water in the passenger footwell. He leaned over and grabbed it, grimacing against the pain. He was a walking bruise. He finished the water and could have drunk two more bottles. He had no plan, but he needed space to think and he needed some powerful painkillers if he was going to do anything besides groan. He started the SUV and drove off.

They had taken him to an old, abandoned warehouse deep in the docks. They must have been close when Lawrence rammed them. Max remembered a phone call. Dos minutos. It explained how they reacted so quickly.

Efficient one-way blocks set up for truck traffic divided the port area into easy-to-navigate squares. Two turns from the warehouse and Max was back on the outlet road heading north. He passed the intersection. Other than the grooves in the dirt and some scattered safety glass, it looked like nothing had happened. A fast and coordinated response like that took either a lot of speed or a lot of influence. Or a bit of both. He needed to think about that.

He merged back onto Christopher Columbus Boulevard toward the city when a head suddenly appeared in the rearview mirror. He jerked the wheel to the right in surprise and hit the brakes.

"Easy. I'm not ready to die yet."

The bride climbed into the passenger seat.

CHAPTER THIRTY-NINE

Christopher Columbus Boulevard was a major north-south thoroughfare through the city that ran parallel to Route 95 south of the Ben Franklin Bridge. It was once the primary route connecting the docks and piers along the Delaware River when Philadelphia was still a major shipping destination. It had fallen into disrepair and disuse in the last half of the twentieth century as industrial jobs jumped overseas and the interstate funneled traffic away. The area was making a comeback through tourist attractions like Penn's Landing and an aquarium and big-box shopping stores. But revitalization was slow. There were still many spots crumbling into the nearby river.

Max pulled the Escalade off the main drag and onto a small service road that ran in front of a hulking, white facade with crumbling cornices and broken lattice. A listing chain link fence surrounded the building. He stopped the car next to a faded orange construction sign.

He took a deep breath. Or tried to. His chest protested. Not a good sign when it hurt just to breathe. He glanced out the window at the old pier. It looked like the collision between a train station and a cathedral. A proud building slowly being chipped and pecked away by time, the salted air, and indifference. He wondered if some developer was smart enough to use the bones or stupid enough to raze it. Whatever was cheapest and most expedient, he guessed. Another piece of history bulldozed.

He lowered his window and let the river breeze fill the car. Ade seemed content to wait.

"Lorena and Gabriel are worried about you," he finally said.

She looked at him, and he watched a shadow cross her face. "Yes. I am worried about them, as well. It is why I hid. I know they want to help. I know they would help, but it worried me that I might put them in more danger."

"How?"

She looked away and didn't answer. "What did they tell you?"

"They said you were looking for your sister."

"Sol."

Max didn't know if that was a statement, a question, or a plea. He said nothing.

She turned her face to the window and the gray ribbon of the river. "Sol needs help. Sometimes I'm afraid that I'm too late. I dream that I find her again and she's already gone."

"Gabriel said little, he said it was your story, but he mentioned the FCM?"

"Sí. Yes. They have her. I know that. They use her. I know that. We are circling each other. Hunting each other. But I cannot find her. I cannot get close enough to save her."

"Are you sure she wants help?" It was the same question he'd been asking himself about Ade.

"That is the wrong question, I think. I am her sister. Her only family. Sol is ... troubled. I am not sure she knows what she wants."

"But you think you can help."

She shifted in the seat and turned to face him now. "Yes." No hesitation and Max saw the commitment in her eyes. She would keep going until she couldn't.

"But you need help." Not a question.

"Yes." Committed, but not entirely stupid. She wasn't on a suicide mission. Not yet.

"Lorena said you've stayed with her for almost six months. You looked that whole time?"

"Yes."

"And haven't found her?" Philadelphia was a large metropolitan area, but not that big.

"I saw her twice. The second time she was not in good shape. But still, I moved slowly. I wanted to get her out, to help her, but I also wanted us to have a life afterward. I wanted to slip in, save her, and slip back out before they realized what had happened, who had done it. Maybe I was too slow, too cautious. I tried to be discreet, at least at the start."

Max thought of the fingers in the box and the detective's questions. "You're no longer being discreet?"

"No. I am afraid for Sol. Time is running out. It will make no difference if I save only the husk of my sister. This is also why I left Lorena's house. I didn't want to bring any violence back to her door."

"What have you been doing? What were you doing the night I picked you up?"

"I've been asking questions, same as always, but more directly. That night I was at a costume party that I'd found out about. I knew many of the younger FCM members would be there. It was at a large house. It was dark inside. The people were mostly drunk. It was loud. I got two guys alone. Men are very stupid most of the time. I asked my questions. No one heard their screams."

"Why the fingers?"

She gave him a cold smile. "Something I learned from my father."

"Did you get answers?"

"Only Tuco." She waved a hand back in the warehouse's direction. "I was following Tuco. He is one of Campos's top men. Campos is the boss, but more of a ghost. A rumor. A boogeyman. He is always on the move, difficult to pin down. I have only seen him once. Tuco is easier. He is always around. He is visible. I thought he might know where my sister is."

"And Tuco was at the warehouse now?"

"Yes."

"He has," Max moved a hand near his neck, "a scar?"

"Yes, that is him."

"Okay. I don't know much about Tuco, Campos, or FCM. At first, I was only looking for you. Then I was trying to help my boss. FCM is trying to muscle in on his business. I talked to a community guy who gave me a little background, but I feel like you are 200 pages ahead of me in this book."

She waved a hand again. "The FCM is a gang. A baby gang compared to the cartels in my country, but it is powerful in its little pond. It has many soldiers and even more eyes and ears. Its influence is growing. The rest of the details do not matter. Not right now. They have my sister and now they have your friend."

"Did Tuco tell you anything?"

"I didn't have time to ask. I was at the warehouse, inside and ready to move, when he got a phone call. They were expecting someone. A few minutes later they all rushed out."

"Because we never made it. The crash."

"Yes. I did not follow. My car was too far away. But, lucky for me, they brought you right back."

"And you still want to ask your questions?"

"Yes."

"When?"

"We should go now."

"Now?"

"Yes."

Max looked at her. She stared back. She looked almost as tired as him, but she also looked determined and competent. And, he realized, she was right. No one would expect Max to return now. He'd limped out the door less than fifteen minutes ago. He needed medical attention. He needed to find the woman. That would all take time. They would be relaxed. Maybe careless.

"You're right. Surprise might be our best option. Plus, they might decide to move him. Better to go before that happens. I know at least three of the guys had guns. What do we have?"

She smiled. "Your friend helped us with that. Look." She got out and opened the rear door. Max followed. He watched as she reached over and used two hands to lift a large black bag from the third row of seats. There was the clunk of steel, aluminum, and plastic rearranging themselves in the bag. She unzipped it and stepped back.

"Lawrence does nothing halfway," Max said.

He sifted through the contents. Two shotguns, one cut down and shorter than the other. Four handguns, all similar, black matte polymer. Two lethal-looking folding knives, also black, plus boxes of bullets, shells for the shotguns, and a couple of lightweight Kevlar vests. It was a small armory. It looked like Lawrence had raided a SWAT team supply store. There were also half a dozen small canisters that looked like little one-pound weights with a tab at the end. He held one up.

"Grenade?" That seemed like overkill even for Lawrence.

Her brow furrowed. "I do not know the English word. They make a lot of noise and smoke but don't hurt you."

"Ah, flashbang." Those might come in handy.

Max wasn't a gun nut. He knew the basics and that was enough. A gun was a tool, one he tried to avoid on the jobs he planned in the past, but he wasn't stupid, either. It could be a very effective tool. The guys he brought in usually had a gun preference, and he was happy to go along if the choices didn't get in the way.

He picked up a handgun from the bag and examined it. It looked new and smelled like plastic and oil. Taurus was stamped on the barrel. He found the slide release and safety up near the thumb. He released the slide. Empty. He found a box of 9mm bullets, loaded the magazine, slid it back in and engaged the safety.

Max looked at her and nodded at the bag. "You ready?" he asked.

She nodded and pulled a silver revolver from the back of her pants. She picked up another bag he hadn't noticed on the floor and removed a slim, short object about three feet long.

"What's that?"

She slid a hand over it, moving a cover above a small round hilt. Max caught sight of a sliver of steel.

"A sword?"

Max thought about the fingers in the box.

"A wakizashi. Americans love guns and explosions," she nodded toward the bag. "This is quieter, and I know how to use it." She climbed into the passenger seat. "Let's go. I'll show you."

CHAPTER FORTY

They drove straight back to the warehouse but didn't go straight in. Ade provided directions to where she'd parked her vehicle, a beat-up anonymous gray Honda Civic, across the street in the lot for an old eight-story brick warehouse that had escaped the wrecking ball and now had a second life as a self-storage company. Max put the Escalade in a spot toward the back, not entirely visible from the FCM warehouse across the street.

"This safe?" Max asked.

"Hiding in plain sight. C'mon, follow me." She strode off across the parking lot toward the storage company's front door. Max noticed she left the sword behind, so this was still surveillance, not stabbing.

Inside, the first floor was a public space. A small square with a sales counter to the right with a bored clerk clicking through screens on an old desktop. Stacks of brown cardboard boxes in various sizes were stacked on a wire shelf next to the counter along with packing tape, hangers, bags of Styrofoam peanuts, and blue furniture blankets. There was a large freight elevator with wide doors directly opposite the counter. A unisex bathroom was in the far right corner. The small space smelled liked adhesives and decomposing corrugated cardboard. A fire door was immediately to the left inside the entry door with stairs going up.

The clerk looked up from his screen with mild interest, but Ade didn't break stride. She waved and pushed through the door for the stairs. The stairs doubled back on each other and halfway between each floor there was a tall, slim window that faced the street. Ade stopped between the fourth and fifth floors and motioned for Max to look. The window gave a view of the north and east sides of the building across the street. He watched a man smoke a cigarette near the door. Max couldn't pick out his features from this far away but could see a blue shirt and the red slash of a belt at his waist. He was too tall to be Tuco.

"Who's that?" Max asked.

"I don't know." She shrugged. "I only know Tuco and Campos. The rest of them are nothing. Just men in the way." Max wondered about the casual way she said it and everything that must have happened to bring her to that point. Just men in the way. Maybe he'd ask her someday, but now wasn't the right time. He returned his attention to the window. The man finished his smoke and ground it out but remained outside near the door. He was standing guard or waiting for something.

"Only one truck. There were two when I left," Max said. "Tuco might be gone."

"Maybe. They could have moved it."

They waited in silence. No one entered the stairwell. The man leaned against the wall across the street. Ten minutes later, a small hatchback with a metallic pizza sign on the roof drove up and dropped off two boxes and a white bag. The man took them and disappeared inside.

"Dinner," Max said.

"Yes, we should go soon. The food will distract them."

"Let's check the back first. If there's no truck, we can assume there is at least one less person inside."

"Okay."

They descended the stairs, past the clerk, and back to Lawrence's SUV and his mobile arsenal.

Max picked up one of the stun grenades from the bag.

"Fast and loud?"

Ade moved her gun from the back to the front of her pants, covering it with her shirt, then grabbed her bag and slung it across her back. The handle of the wakizashi sword protruded above her left shoulder. She tapped it with her right hand. "Fast and quiet."

He tossed the grenade back in the bag. A wave of exhaustion rolled over him thinking about the next fifteen minutes. A drumbeat pounded in his head. The weight pressed down on his chest. Each joint ached. He gave himself a five-count. He thought about Liam in the hospital and Lawrence bleeding across the street. No time for sleep. No time for rest. He pushed his feelings aside. He pulled the slide back on the pistol and cycled a round into the chamber.

No time for pity.

The warehouse stood at the intersection of two now unused piers. They worked their way around near the waterside and found a loose section of fencing to peel back. The rear of the warehouse was a collection of old output ducts and pipes and a square of rusting coils Max couldn't identify, maybe a defunct generator. No one had moved the Suburban around back. But there was another door.

It was still daylight, but dusk was gathering. Car and truck traffic was picking up along the access road as people left work and overnight shipments hit the road. It would be simpler, and less risky, going in the back.

"You don't think ..." Max said.

Ade crept up and tugged the handle. She shook her head. There were no windows on the first floor and the ones on the higher floors, even if they could get to them, were big plate glass windows. No simple sash to jimmy. They could knock out a few panes, but it would cause a racket.

"So we go in the front," Max said. "Quiet or loud, we're going to need to be fast. Shots might not be uncommon around here, but someone will call it in."

She nodded. They stayed close to the side of the warehouse. No lower windows to get in, but also no way to see out. They moved up to the front corner. Max peeked around. No one out front. He ducked back. Pulled the gun out and flipped off the safety.

"Any ideas on getting in?"

"We wait," Ade said.

"Why?"

"The man we saw before, the smoking man, he will need another after he eats. He will come outside again. We take him and we take his keys. That leaves only two inside."

"That's a good idea. Makes sense, but how? It's thirty or forty feet from this corner to the door. That's a long time to be exposed."

"What did they tell you I looked like?"

"What?"

"They told you to find me, right? How?"

He pulled out Julio's phone with his free hand and showed her the photo. She studied it, then pulled her hair back and tied it up on top of her head. She rubbed her face until there was some color in her cheeks, and unbuttoned one too many buttons on her shirt.

"Does it look like me now?"

Max looked back and forth between the phone and her face. And tried not to glance at her chest. "A little. Can't change the scar."

She lifted a hand and let it drop back. A shadow drifted across her face. "No, you cannot hide that." She straightened and set her shoulders. "But I only need a moment."

They waited. Eight minutes later, they heard the squeal of the door hinges. Max peeked one eye around the corner. Blue shirt, red belt. It was the same man. Smoking will kill you. Ade moved around him and was out in the open before he could react. There was nothing he could do except watch.

She covered ten feet before the guy spotted her. She didn't break stride. She said something that Max couldn't hear. The guy looked confused, a half-smile on his face. She covered another ten feet. Max saw her arm start to rise. Something clicked for the man. He dropped the smile. He tossed the cigarette away and reached behind him.

Too late. Ade's arm gripped the sword's handle and pulled it free. The man's expression changed from anger to fear. She moved fast and Max remembered the attack in the alley. He'd never seen her and had barely heard her. She whipped the blade down, striking the man diagonally across the shoulder and following through across his chest to his hip. She did it with little effort. It almost looked as if she were dancing. The man's face changed again from fear to confusion. The blade must have been very sharp and cut very deep. So deep he didn't realize it yet. So deep he thought she'd missed.

He smiled at her and tried to bring his gun hand up. Nothing happened. She hadn't missed. His arm dangled. He looked down. His face now showed disbelief. Ade pivoted, placed a second hand on the sword's grip, and reversed her movement. Now she pierced instead of sliced. The blade disappeared into the man's stomach. He staggered back, skewered on the end of the short sword. Blood cascaded from his wounds as his body finally caught up to Ade's strikes. She kicked the man in the chest and freed her weapon. He took two steps backward, fell, and died with a last look of surprise on his face.

The entire thing from Ade striding around the corner to her putting the sword through his spine had taken less than ten seconds. Max was still trying to take it all in when he saw the door swing open again. The attack had carried Ade past the door. Her back was to the door. Max moved, pulled his gun, but he was still too far away to help. The hinges crunched. The door opened fully and blocked his view. He heard a male voice, then the sounds of scuffling feet moving across grit and sand. A grunt. A gasp. And the door swung closed again.

Ade stood over a second man. A cigarette and a lighter still gripped in his hand.

"Didn't you want to ask them questions about your sister?"

She spit on the ground. "I've asked guys like them before. They do not have any answers. They are like cattle. They are dull and stupid and prodded in the direction they are told. Asking them questions is a waste of time. Besides," she walked over to the remaining Suburban, parked near the warehouse door, and used the sword to puncture the front tire. "I think we might have a problem." She nodded back toward the door.

It took Max a moment to spot it. There was a small square piece of black plastic, the size of a credit card, mounted over the door, partially recessed in some cracked bricks. A cheap but effective security camera. It wouldn't provide great resolution or give a 180-degree view, but it would spot someone trying to come in the front door.

"If they have a camera, why did the second guy walk right into you?"

"Just because it's there doesn't mean someone's watching."

"But the longer we wait out here, the better the chance someone checks."

"Exactly."

He searched the less bloody man's pockets and came up with a single key.

"Ready?" he asked. She nodded.

They moved through the door fast and low. And quiet.

CHAPTER FORTY-ONE

Max expected to get shot. Anyone who was monitoring the security feed could easily set up an ambush and pick them off as they came through the door. They'd be the proverbial fish in the barrel. But there was nothing. No shot. No footsteps. No sound at all except the distant noise of passing traffic and the murmuring of roosting pigeons in the rafters. Maybe they really were cattle.

The interior of the warehouse was a large, open rectangle broken up at regular intervals by rusting support beams. The floor was old, slightly uneven paving stones now scattered with bird shit, tufts of feathers, and bits of trash or discarded equipment. An old hoist and pulley system with a thick rusting chain and hook block dangled from the high ceiling.

Once inside, Max crouched behind a rusty I-beam and looked out. Ade was twenty feet to his left, behind another support beam. The room they needed was halfway down the right-hand side, a square of space bolted onto the wall, probably once reserved for the manager or floor supervisor. Max could see that the door was partially open. He pointed and Ade nodded.

They moved up cautiously, leapfrogging each other to the next beam. Now that they discovered the camera by the door, Max expected more resistance inside. There wasn't but he felt watched nonetheless. He was terrified and elated at the same time. He recognized the reaction. He always felt distinctly alive this close to death.

They reached the outer wall of the office and collected themselves beside the open door. Max took the lead. His friend, his risk. He listened hard, but couldn't hear anything other than his own heart beating. The gun's grip was slick in his hand as he tried to get his pulse under control. Despite the chill in the warehouse, sweat beaded on his neck and back. He swiped at his brow and took a quick peek through the door.

"Shit," he whispered.

He slipped through and stepped right. A moment later, Ade did the same but went left.

Julio hadn't set up an ambush. He'd taken a hostage. He had untied Lawrence and was standing behind him, using him as a shield. He had a gun pressed to Lawrence's temple. Lawrence didn't look good. His eyes were open but glassy. His pallor was gray, and blood soaked the left side of his shirt. He needed medical attention or to at least stop the bleeding soon.

Julio's eyes were wide and sweat dripped off his face. He was young and heavyset. The cloth belt was taut around his bulging middle. He was almost panting and looked to be right on the edge of panic. His hand was shaking. Max hoped the gun had a heavy trigger pull.

In the short time Max had been gone, they had added a

cheap folding table and a couple more chairs to the room's decor. Cans of soda and the two pizza boxes sat on the tabletop along with a laptop. The laptop was open and the screen cycled between two views. One from the front door. One from the rear door. They'd been lucky they hadn't been spotted sooner. Every ten seconds Max saw the two bodies stretched out on the pavement in grainy black and white.

Max edged a half-step farther right. "Easy. Just take it easy. It's Julio, right?" He saw Ade match his movements out of the corner of his eye. If they could open up the angle ...

"Stop. Don't move." Julio took a half-step back.

Max held up his hands, pointed his gun to the ceiling. "No reason for you to end up dead. No reason we all can't walk out of here alive. We just want my friend. He needs help." He slid forward and to the right again.

"I can't." He looked genuinely conflicted. "It doesn't matter. I'm already dead. You guys shoot me now or Tuco gets me later."

"Not true. There's always an out. There's always an option. Trust me, I've had some experience in tight spots." Another half-step. The guy swiveled his body toward Max and took a matching step back, but he was running out of room. The wall was coming up fast. "Listen," Max continued, "I've got some money. You let us get my friend some help and I'll give you the cash. You take off. Get free of Tuco. Start over somewhere else."

The guy was shaking his head before Max was halfway through his pitch. "Where would I go? Everyone I know is here. My family is here."

"Anywhere. You can go anywhere. It won't be easy, I won't lie, but better than being dead, right? Maybe Tuco goes down. Everyone does eventually. Maybe you get to come back. Live to see the next day, right?"

He wasn't lying. He thought that was important. Julio

would see if he was lying. Max would give him the cash in his pocket if he let them get Lawrence out of here. Lawrence was easily worth that much. The guy would probably blow through it within a week in a cheap motel down in Baltimore and end up right back in Philly, but that wouldn't be Max's problem.

He could see Julio wanted to believe, but years of experience told him it was all bullshit. It wasn't. It was ninety-eight percent crap, but there was a little truth in there, too. There was room for hope if he wanted it. Max watched him make a decision.

The gunshot was loud in the small room.

Max ducked on instinct, then ran forward and caught Lawrence as he stumbled forward.

"The next time he picks a human shield, he should make sure it's at least as wide as he is," Ade said and kicked the gun out of his hand. The caution wasn't necessary. Ade's shot had hit the guy above his right eye and left a splash of brains and skull fragments along the back wall. He was dead before he hit the ground.

"I don't think there's going to be a next time."

"I guess not."

He hooked an arm around Lawrence's shoulder. "I think he might have given it up."

Ade looked at him. "You were believing your bullshit?"

"You could have asked him about your sister."

She approached the table and grabbed the laptop. "I told you there's only one man I need to talk to. Besides, the result would have been the same, no? We could not have let him go. The only difference would have been an easier shot for me."

"That's cold."

"That's reality. Until this is over, it's us or them. No use trying to pretend any different."

· · ·

Max retrieved the Escalade from the self-storage parking lot across the street and drove it back to the warehouse. They pulled both bodies inside the warehouse. They'd be discovered soon, but the longer it took, the better. Max grabbed the camera from above the front door and stomped it to pieces and repeated the process around back. They had the laptop, so it likely made no difference, but why take a chance? He'd check out the laptop later. If it backed up footage to a cloud, they might need Eddie's skills. But would they really back up a kidnapping?

They laid Lawrence out on the back seat, put the weapons in the bag, and got out of there.

Max's hands started to shake, and his vision started to blur as he drove.

"You okay?" Ade asked.

"Yeah, just the adrenaline wearing off. Feeling the car accident, too. Plus, still recovering from a minor incident in an alley. I got jumped from behind." He looked over at her. She kept looking straight ahead.

"Sorry about that," she said. "I didn't know who you were at the time."

"That's what everyone keeps telling me. I should wear a nametag. But I'm just a driver."

"I think you are a bit more than that, no?"

"Maybe."

"But at the time, I was unsure. Why were you pursuing this? Why were you so insistent on finding me?"

"So mug a guy first, get answers later?"

He saw her lips curl up slightly at that. "Experience has taught me that is not a bad way to go."

"Rough life."

The smile dropped away. "Yes."

They both fell silent after that, and Max focused on

keeping his hands steady and the Escalade on the road. When they were back in the city proper, going west on Tasker, skirting Passyunk Square, Max asked, "Where to? Any ideas?" He glanced in the back seat. Lawrence's eyes were closed. He was breathing regularly, but Max thought he could smell the wound. That wasn't a good sign. "We can't take him to a hospital."

"Lorena's. She knows someone who has helped me in the past."

Lorena's someone turned out to be two people. A wizened old woman with a grooved face like a peach pit and her granddaughter. They made an effective pair that merged old traditions with modern medicine. Lawrence had passed out on the bed. Neither woman appeared concerned he was about to shuffle off this mortal coil. Max relaxed a fraction. The old woman was currently burning a fragrant bunch of herbs tied with twine over Lawrence's shoulder wound.

The granddaughter said something in rapid Spanish to Ade that Max didn't catch. Ade turned to Max. "She wants to know if you are hurt, too."

"No, I'm okay."

The grandmother glanced up and said something. Ade and the granddaughter smiled.

"What?"

"She says that asking for help doesn't mean you are weak; it shows you are wise."

"That's not what she said."

"She also said that she has seen dogs with three legs move with more grace."

Max put up his hands at that and sat down in the chair opposite the bed. "All right, it's been a rough couple weeks."

He cut his eyes to Ade. "Feel free to poke this three-legged dog and make sure nothing is out of place."

The granddaughter shone a slim penlight into Max's eyes and checked his pupils. She smelled like cinnamon and strong soap, and Max fought the urge to ask her name and where she worked. The less they knew about each other, the safer everyone remained. She cleaned his head laceration and applied some butterfly strips. After another five minutes, she declared nothing else wrong except bumps and bruises.

The old woman came over and ran her hands over him, squeezing and prodding, like she was inspecting a chicken at the market. Eventually, she nodded in agreement and gave him an almost toothless grin. "Lo siento, solo viejo."

He didn't need Ade for that one. Nothing wrong. Just old.

The granddaughter irrigated, cleaned, and bandaged Lawrence's shoulder. She left two bottles of pills on the nightstand before she and her grandmother left. He'd live, too.

Down in the kitchen, Lorena fed them both bowls of oxtail stew with poblano peppers, white rice, and warm tortillas. The food did as much to revive Max's spirits as the women's visit. He was reluctant to leave the warm kitchen but pushed back after finishing his second bowl.

"I need to get home and change clothes and get some sleep. We can start looking for your sister in the morning, okay?"

Ade didn't look happy about it, but he'd be no use to her in his current state. She could go out alone again if she wanted. She was more than capable of handling herself, but he'd been up since four a.m., had been interrogated by the police, kidnapped, been in a car crash, and raided a warehouse. It was a minor miracle he could stand at all.

He left by the back door and took a quick circuit of the

block. He saw nothing that worried him. He took Lawrence's SUV and made it across town and back to his apartment in fifteen minutes. Sleep turned out to take a little longer. Two cop cars blocked the street, their blue and red lights bouncing off the surrounding buildings. Ronnie sat on the curb with his head in his hands.

CHAPTER FORTY-TWO

Ash opened his eyes. He was alone. It was quiet. Where was he? The view out the windshield was of a ribbed metal wall. He looked left, out the side window, and saw a large open space covered with scattered leaves and random trash. A pile of rusting 55-gallon drums was stacked in one corner. The roof curved high overhead. An old warehouse or storage shed, Ash thought. It was roughly rectangular, the length and width of two football fields. There were a couple of large skylights in the ceiling letting in milky, diffused light. Through an opening at the far end, Ash could see skeletal trees and part of a white metal structure in the distance. There was the low hum of traffic noise, but it was faint.

He didn't remember driving the truck here. He tried to think back. Nothing. It was a blank. That scared him. He realized he was sitting in the passenger seat. Had he driven at all? He stood up and immediately felt the familiar headache hammer his temples. Stomach cramps roiled his guts and made him double over. He sat back down and held his head in his hands. His forehead was slick with flop sweat. The first few minutes were always the worst. If he could ride that out, his body grudgingly accepted what it had to do. He kept his head between his knees and took a couple of deep breaths. He could smell himself. He needed a shower. He sat up and tried to breathe through his mouth. It started coming back in bits and pieces. The man. The drugs. Oh God, the kid. The kidnapping.

He spotted the balloons in the cup holder and the two garish clown masks on the floor on top of a paper bag. He had a brief moment of hope. What if it was all over? What if they got what they wanted? He'd miss the money and the motel room, crappy as it was, but maybe he could sell the rest of the heroin. Find a program. He might have fallen off the wagon with that hit earlier, but it wasn't too late to keep his life going in the right direction.

The first step was getting out of here. That was simple. Drive back to the city. Dump the truck somewhere. Disappear for a bit. He'd lived rough for almost a year now. He could tough it out for a few more weeks until this all blew over. He slid over to the driver's seat and realized two things. There were no keys in the ignition and a security bar had been locked on the steering wheel. There was a dull thud from the back of the truck and Ash knew any thoughts of escape were fool's gold.

He stood. His stomach rocked and bile crept up his throat, but he swallowed it back. He moved to the coolers in the back. The thud came again from the ones on the left. The kid must have heard him moving. He reached out a hand but stopped short. He grabbed a mask from the front seat, pulled it over his head, then opened a lid. Two feet came flying out, and he dodged backward.

But feet were all he got. After a minute, Ash moved to the

side and peeked in. The kid's wrists were still cuffed, and tape covered his mouth. He'd managed to break the tape on his ankles, but couldn't do the same thing with the steel cuffs on his wrist. He was sweating and his eyes were wild with hate and fear. He kicked out again, but it was more protective, than aggressive. Ash was fine with that idea. His stomach bucked again. He flipped the lid closed and scrambled for the truck's door. This time, he couldn't hold it down. He managed to remove the clown mask a moment before he gagged up hot strings of bile and saliva. All the strength left his legs and he dropped to the floor, not caring how close he was to the steaming vomit.

He forced himself back to his feet. Okay, Ash, he thought, you can't drive, but you can walk. Simply walk away. He put the truck at his back and started toward the open space at the far end. He made it twenty feet before the image of the kid trussed up in the empty freezer came back to him. He stopped. Shit. He started back, then stopped again. Taking the kid would make them very visible. A lone white guy who already looked homeless could shamble along the sidewalk without being hassled. Most people would go out of their way not to see him. The same guy with a clean-cut black teenager could not. Ash knew if he left the kid, it would haunt him for the rest of his life. He thought about Maggie. His daughter would only be a few years younger than him. Would he walk away from her?

A sound came from his pocket. His pulse spiked when he thought they might have rigged him with some sort of bomb, but it was the mobile. His leash.

"Hello?"

"What are you doing?"

Ash spun around. Could they see him or was it a general question?

"Go back to the truck. Someone should arrive soon with food and water."

"Okay."

"356 Bentmore Drive, Danvers, Connecticut," the voice said.

"What are you—" But there was only dead air. The man was gone.

The threat was obvious. We have your parent's address. Try to walk away and it will cost you. He didn't know how long he stood there, his mind locked up, unable to comprehend how he'd ended up here, when he heard a car approaching. He spit, wiped his mouth, and walked back to stand by the side of the truck. A tan Camry pulled to a stop alongside the ice cream truck and a man got out. He was not the same man who had snatched the kid off the street. That guy had been a short, muscular black guy. This was a skinny Latino guy. He looked at Ash for a long moment. Ash glanced down at himself, worried that he'd thrown up on his shirt, but no, it was clean. Was the guy worried? Ash didn't come off as the best co-conspirator in a major felony. The guy said nothing, just turned back to the car, and pulled out two plastic bags. He walked over and held them out by the handles. Ash took them. He could see one was filled with plastic water bottles. The other held a variety of protein and granola bars.

"What's this? For the kid?" The guy still kept quiet. He tilted his head as if he was looking at a strange alien life form, then walked back to his car. "Where am I supposed to eat? Or shower? Or take a shit?" The man gave a strangely cheery wave as he drove off. "How long is this going to last?" Ash shouted.

Ash carried the bags back to the truck. He realized that the kid wasn't the only prisoner in the truck.

Can't leave. Can't stay. He let the bags drop and slumped into the passenger seat. The more his head cleared, the more he understood that his part in this kidnapping would not end well. What was the old saying? If you can't spot the asshole in the room, it's you. It could apply to any con or crime, too. If you can't spot the patsy ...

Ash opened a cooler lid and stepped back. Nothing happened. He inched closer and peered in. The foot came kicking out again, but this time he was ready. He caught it by the ankle and held on. "Stop. Just stop it." After a brief struggle, the kid went still. Ash dropped his leg. The cooler's lids were detachable to allow for easy product loading, and Ash pulled off three and tossed them on the nearby prep counter. He leaned back against the counter and waited.

The kid pushed himself up into a sitting position. The time in the tight cooler space had matted his hair with sweat. His face was greasy and dirty. His sweatpants were wrinkled, and his hoodie was torn on one sleeve. He didn't smell much better than Ash. At least they had that in common. His hands were still cuffed behind his back. The piece of duct tape over his mouth was peeling at the edges. He could hear the kid breathing hard through his nose. This time, there was no fear in the kid's eyes, just anger and frustration. He'd decided to fight rather than concede. Ash liked that.

Ash took a step toward the cooler and reached out a hand. The kid tensed up and moved his head away.

"Do you want me to take the tape off?"

There was a pause, and then the kid nodded.

"It's going to hurt either way, so I'll do it quickly."

The kid nodded again and kept his eyes on Ash as he stepped forward. Ash gripped the loose end of the tape and yanked it free. The kid winced but made no other sound. Ash backed off, and the kid started screaming.

"Help! Help!" He screamed for thirty seconds, as loud as

he could, the cords on his neck popping out. Ash let him get it out. Eventually, he stopped.

Ash shrugged. "No one around. And they've got a camera out there, I think. Not sure if it's just video or sound, too."

The kid stared at Ash.

"I can't do anything about the cuffs, sorry. The other guy has the key."

Still no response. The kid worked his sore jaw and stared at Ash like he was expecting it all to be a trick.

Ash grabbed the two bags from the floor. "Do you want anything to drink or eat?"

The kid nodded. Ash opened a water bottle and held it to his lips. The kid drank it down in one go. Ash pulled a granola bar out. He checked the label. Pulled another one out. Ran his hand through the bag. "I hope you like peanut butter protein bars. Doesn't look like they bought a variety pack."

After he'd fed the kid two bars and he'd drank another bottle of water, Ash helped him stand and climb out of the coolers. The kid was still wary but had reached some sort of decision with himself.

"What's your name?" Ash asked.

"Javon."

"All right, Javon, I'm Ash and unless we work together, I think we are both in serious trouble."

"You kidnapped me and now you want me to help you?"

"I'm sorry about that. I really am. If I could go back ... well, things got out of control quickly. I had no idea this was the plan. I thought I was driving a truck. That sounds weak, but it's the truth."

"It sounds like a lot of self-justification. Who did this?"

Ash looked away, embarrassed now at how easily he'd been duped. How little it had taken. Fifty bucks for a motel room and he'd been bought and sold. "I don't know."

"You don't know?"

"No. I was living on the street. A man came up to me and offered me money, good money, and a place to stay just to drive this old ice cream truck around for a couple of hours a day." Ash petered out. It sounded like wishful thinking even to his ears.

"I saw that old beater around lately. It was weird."

"I know. But then you forgot about it, right? It became part of the background."

Javon cocked his head but kept Ash pinned with his eyes. "Maybe," he eventually said.

"That was the point, I think. It was strange and creepy and memorable at first, but then it wasn't."

"So, you took the gig. And what? You thought it was your lucky day?"

"I guess. I don't know."

"What *do* you know, man? No such thing as a free lunch."

Ash did his best not to look away. The kid deserved that much. "I know a couple of things. I know I'm done listening to them, but I also know they are not done with us. They are coming back, and we need to be ready."

"A handcuffed fourteen-year-old and a homeless junkie? What are we going to do against them?"

"Catch them by surprise."

CHAPTER FORTY-THREE

Max parked the truck at the end of the block, a little leery of leaving the bag of guns with so many cops milling around but decided he had little choice. He walked over to Ronnie. It took a moment for the old trainer to notice him. He looked worried, angry, and confused at the same time. Max slipped under the police tape and sat down on the curb next to him. He observed the police activity down the street, past The Skyline. There were two vans and a knot of people combing the ground. A woman took a photograph of something on the curb.

"What happened?" Max asked.

"Someone snatched Javon."

"Javon? The kid who's always in the gym working out? With the fast hands."

"Yeah."

"Snatched? Like kidnapped? How?"

"No idea. He never showed up at home. Nobody can get him on his cell. They found his headphones down there by the diner. Not something you drop by accident. Best they can figure, someone grabbed him as he was leaving the gym. Maybe forced him into a car."

"This happened this afternoon?"

"Yeah, he left a little before four. Getting dark but still light out. No one saw anything." He spat out the last words.

A uniformed cop spotted Max and walked over. He had a small notebook out.

"Sir? You a friend of Mr. Shelton's?"

"Yes, I live in the building across the street and go to his gym."

"Mr. Shelton told you what happened?" Max nodded. "Were you home between three and five this afternoon?"

"No, I just got back now."

The cop didn't look surprised or disappointed. He nodded. "Can I have your name? We're canvassing the neighborhood."

Max gave his name and address and the cop wandered away. Max had a sense any canvass would be a haphazard door-to-door effort, unlikely to uncover anything unless they got lucky. One side of the street was Max's building. He knew most of his neighbors were single and out during the day. The other side of the street was the converted warehouse. Most of the people inside would be at work, focused inward, not looking out the windows. The Skyline was closed by four. It was a lonely spot. A good place for a kidnapping.

The late October wind knifed under Max's coat. He wasn't sure how long they'd left Ronnie on the sidewalk. But if he was this cold after only a few minutes, the old man must be freezing. "C'mon," he said, standing up. "I can make you some coffee and get you warmed up at my place."

Inside the apartment, the heat perked Ronnie up. Max took a mug off the shelf and rinsed it out. He didn't have visitors often; there were only two mugs on the shelf. He filled the clean mug with instant coffee.

Ronnie looked at the steaming cup. "Got anything stronger you can add to that?"

"Bourbon?"

"That'll do."

Max pulled out a bottle of bonded Old Grand-Dad out of the cabinet next to the refrigerator and added a slug to the coffee.

"Any ideas about what might have happened to Javon?"

Ronnie took a sip and looked at him over the top of the mug. "Why?"

Max frowned. "Why? I'd like to help if I can. He seemed like a good kid from what I saw. Certainly dedicated. He was in the gym almost every time I was."

"Yeah, he was a gym rat. I think it was a way to escape for him. Most of the other kids his age had already dropped it. It was a safe place."

"Problems at home?"

Abductions, especially children, made headlines but were actually pretty rare. Being grabbed off the street by a stranger was almost as rare as getting hit by lightning. Plenty of kids, some as young or younger than Javon, were reported missing each year, but the vast majority ran away or were taken over custody issues.

Ronnie said nothing as he took a long swallow of his Kentucky coffee. Max was happy to wait him out. He was too tired to do anything else. Ronnie made some sort of decision after three more sips.

"How would you help? What could you do?" It sounded like a challenge.

Now it was Max's turn to pause. "Maybe nothing, I'll admit. Depends on how the police are reacting. What are they doing already?"

Ronnie shrugged. "You saw them wandering around outside. They're covering their asses, doing busy work. Not exactly breaking their backs to practice community policing. You read the papers the other day. A Black kid got shot in that restaurant. I saw they pulled another Black guy out of the projects yesterday, dead in his apartment. Police are ready to write us off down here like it's the eighties and the crack epidemic all over. Pull up stakes and let us eat our own."

The stress and shock were winding Ronnie up. Max jumped in.

"I can bring a little energy, a little speed. Sidestep the police. Anytime a kid goes missing, speed is the biggest factor." Max didn't have any experience with finding missing kids, but he believed, like a heist or the recent murder investigation he'd gotten involved in up in PEI, achieving a certain velocity was critical. Move or die. You couldn't be out of control, but you needed to be constantly going forward. "You need to get some momentum and you need to keep it. If this thing drags out, two, three days, it might not end well."

"You going to do all this yourself?" Some of the anger had gone out of Ronnie's voice, but plenty of doubt remained. Max didn't take it personally.

"I've got some friends who might be willing to help." He wasn't sure how Ade would react to another diversion from finding her sister, but he thought he could get Eddie going on the computer side.

"All right, but there's something else you should know."

"What?"

"Javon is Deacon James's son."

Deke's house was on a corner lot in Gray's Ferry. He'd taken the last three row homes on the street and was in the process of combining them into a single residence. Scaffolding and construction materials were scattered around the outside of the house. Ronnie led Max past groups of young men chatting and milling aimlessly on the sidewalk and up a flight of brick steps. A massive pillar of a man stood by the door but silently stepped aside, with a nod to Ronnie, as they approached. They entered a long, well-decorated living room and dining room combo. The chaos of the construction outside didn't reach the inside. More people filled these rooms. Like the guys outside, no one appeared to know how to behave in the circumstances. A clutch of four women surrounded a younger woman on the couch. Max assumed the woman was Deacon's wife. Four men sat around a dining room table talking quietly and picking at beer bottle labels. Deacon paced by the bay window overlooking the street, talking on his phone, ignoring everyone else.

Deacon James did not look like a drug kingpin, gang leader, or real estate mogul. He looked like a man holding himself together by his fingertips.

Max saw Deacon's eyes pinball between Ronnie and himself, a mix of frustration, hope, and fear before they settled on something Max hoped was curiosity. Deacon said something into the phone and then disconnected.

"Ronnie, the cutman." They shook and half-hugged.

"Helluva thing," Ronnie said. "We'll find him."

"Gonna have to be us. Police aren't doing much."

"You expected different?"

"I hoped."

"We take care of our own."

Deacon nodded.

"Who's this?"

"This is my friend Max."

Max took a half-step forward and extended his hand. They shook.

"He wants to help," Ronnie added.

"That right?"

"I workout with Ronnie. Met your son a few times."

"And you're a what? A PI? A bounty hunter?"

"No, just a driver, for a car service, but I think I can help."

Deacon laughed and the room went silent. "A limo driver, huh? And a Good Samaritan? Came down to the Ferry to help the Black man who can't keep track of his son. That it?"

The man's rage at being rendered so helpless was palpable and Max could see himself becoming an easy release valve for that pent-up frustration. He played his trump card. If it didn't land, if Deke had no clue, Max would apologize and try to get out the door without catching a fist to the face. "I'm a friend of Lawrence Jackson from Boston."

"I'm not apologizing, but a quick warning. I'm going to have to ask some questions you might not like, but if this is going to work, I need information. You're going to have to be straight with me."

Deacon flipped a hand. "I won't mess with my son's life. Ask your questions. I'll answer."

Deacon had led them through the dining room and kitchen to a door that connected to the house next door. One guy had stood up from the dining table and followed. They walked up a set of stairs to an open third floor. If the other house was for family, this one was for business. There were no personal touches. It was tastefully decorated, but it was distinctly masculine. Dark leather, dark wood. There was an enormous desk with three computer monitors. Bookshelves lined one wall. The spines of the books looked cracked and well-thumbed. There was a grouping of furniture in front of the desk. Max and Ronnie had taken seats on a sofa. Deacon took a matching chair opposite. The new guy had leaned against the wall. Deacon introduced him as Len. Max took him to be a lieutenant or trusted advisor. Max noted with a little jolt of surprise that the big man from the front door was also in the room. He stood discreetly by the stairs. Max hadn't heard him. For a man of that size, he had light feet.

"First, you and your wife are okay?"

"What does that mean?"

"Your marriage? Any issues?"

Deacon's jaw tightened, but he answered.

"No issues. We're good. Ups and downs like any relationship."

"But nothing that would point at her?"

"No."

"No family on her side, no brothers or uncles, looking to come after you?"

Deacon ground his teeth some more. All marriages had secrets. Some were bigger than others.

"No."

Max would still check it out, but he thought Deacon was telling the truth. Family was always the first place to start with any crime. You start close and then you expand the circle outward.

"Did you talk to Javon's school? He's in what seventh? Eighth grade?"

"Eighth."

"Any problems there? That's a tough age. Kids can be cruel. Could this be a prank that got out of hand?"

"We thought of that, too. Tam—Tamyra—my wife, she called the school and talked to both the principal and guidance counselor. Both said they couldn't think of anyone who would do something like this. We called around to his friends and they all said the same thing."

Max nodded but made a mental note to double-check with both sources. The school would try to be helpful but also might be wary, and friends might tell another friend's parents some things but not everything.

He pushed the circle out further. "Business is good?"

This question caused Deacon to visibly relax. He sunk back in his chair, happy to talk profit and loss, leases, earnings potential, and more. Max was curious he never mentioned the word drugs. He couldn't decide if Deacon was delusional or lying to himself. He let him run on for almost five minutes, getting a solid overview of the man's expanding empire before he interrupted.

"Any, ah, rivals who might want to use Javon for an advantage?"

Deacon's eyes flicked to Len by the window. "Nothing major."

"What is it? Might not be major to you, but it could be for them."

"There's a little group over on 25th that's been kicking up a fuss lately."

"Got a name?"

"Bishop. Len can show you where they hang. We've been trying to work something out. It's been going on forever, since I was in diapers, believe it or not, and frankly, I'm tired of it. It's stupid and pointless. I want it to end."

"And they don't?"

"We haven't found a solution yet."

"Okay. Anyone else come to mind?"

Deacon shrugged. "Not in Gray's Ferry. We've got enough. Everyone does. Plenty to go around. No reason to expand. You got the Badlands up in the Northeast, but we don't mess with any of that. No reason anyone up there would bother us down here. I heard the cartels are tied in up there, at least for supply, and those guys aren't known for being subtle. I think we'd know if they were interested in our turf. You got the longshoremen and bikers down south by the docks and the airport. But it's the same thing as the Northeast. Geography doesn't make sense. Everyone sticks to their own thing. They run the corridor down to Baltimore. No reason to look north.

The mayor's made it hard to operate in Center City. He wants to make the tourists feel comfortable. He cracked down hard five years ago. No one, buyers or suppliers, wants to work there. Not worth the risk. The only other direction is east of us. That's Jorge and that FCM cult, but we've had no dealings with them."

"FCM," Max said. He didn't like how they kept popping up.

CHAPTER FORTY-FOUR

It was close to midnight when Max and Ronnie finished talking to Deacon and returned to their street.

"What are you gonna do now?" Ronnie asked.

"I'm going to get a friend started on some research, then I'm going to get some sleep." He'd been up for twenty hours straight, stressful hours, and each step now took considerable effort. "I need a couple of hours in the rack or I'll be no use to Javon, Deacon, or anyone else. You okay?"

"Don't worry about me. I'm old, but that's a blessing in this case. Life has worn me down to bone and gristle. Don't need much sleep to survive. Might as well open up."

He shuffled toward the warehouse entrance, pulling a keyring out of his pocket, then stopped and turned back. "Max?"

"Yeah."

"I'm old, but I'm not useless, okay? You let me know what I can do to help. All right?"

"I will."

"That boy don't deserve to pay for his father's sins."

He turned, opened the door with the key, and disappeared inside.

Max waited a beat, then double-backed to where he'd parked the Escalade. The street was empty. He opened the back door and pulled the bag out from under the back seat. He selected a Taurus 9mm, tucked it into his waistband and pulled his shirt over it. He was now fighting battles on three fronts: Ade's, Liam's, and Javon's. Better to be prepared.

He walked back to his building and made it up the three flights to his apartment. He stepped in the door and dropped the Escalade keys on the side table. He leaned against the wall, took out his phone, and tapped out a quick message to Eddie asking him to research Deacon Jones. Better to get him started and let him work while Max caught up on some sleep.

By the time he'd sent the text, Ronnie had turned the lights on in the gym and Max could see him through the windows as he sat at the small desk in the corner. Max left his lights off and watched for a minute, Ronnie didn't move. He sat and stared into space. Maybe he was trying to figure out his place in a world where kids get snatched off the streets.

Max finally turned and walked to his bedroom. He'd already wrestled with that question. He put the gun on the nightstand, stripped off his clothes, and slid into bed. He knew the world he walked in and he knew his place in it. It didn't make living in it any easier. He shut his eyes and thought about God. And fathers. And children. And the wages of sin.

He woke up to someone knocking on his door. From the sound of it, whoever was out there had been at it for a while. Max picked up his phone. No battery. He fumbled with the charging cable near the bed and plugged it in. He rolled out of bed with an audible groan. His bones felt like mismatched parts that all needed grease and oil. He raised his hand to touch the bandage on his head, but thought better of it. He carefully pulled on the jeans from yesterday and picked up the gun. He checked the window. It was still dark, but the horizon showed a thin line of lighter gray. He scanned the street and saw nothing unusual. He glanced across at the gym. Two guys were sparring in the far ring. Ronnie was still at his desk. It didn't appear that he'd moved. Bone and gristle.

The knock came again. Max walked toward the door. The green numbers on the microwave glowed 5:37 a.m. He'd slept for almost six hours. He needed at least six more to be halfway human. His shoulder ached the most, and the pain ran down his left side to his knee. He flexed it back and forth. It didn't get worse. Maybe the more he walked on it, the better it would feel. Maybe it would also feel better with six or seven aspirin. He liked that option better.

Few people had his address, so Max guessed it was one of two people. "Who is it?" he asked.

"You better have coffee in there."

Max opened the door and Ade and Lawrence walked in. Max felt a small sense of relief seeing his friend up and moving.

"Should you be out of bed?"

Lawrence's face was still ashen, and Max noticed small beads of perspiration at his hairline. No, you shouldn't, Max thought. Lawrence moved carefully, like an elderly man walking across a sheet of ice, and sat heavily on the sofa.

"Probably not, but from what Ade tells me you're going to need all the help you can get. Those pills will keep me going for a bit. Just try not to get me shot today and I think I'll be okay."

Ade took a seat at the kitchen table. Max sat across from her. That used up the seating options in the tiny apartment. The small worry lines still showed around Ade's eyes, but she somehow looked rested and alert. Max was feeling a lot less of both.

Lawrence looked around and shook his head. "Good to see you haven't lost your frugal ways."

Max shrugged. "All I need."

"Right. The humble monk, I forgot. And I wasn't kidding about the coffee. You spend any money on that?"

"I do." Max stood and filled the aluminum stovetop coffeemaker with water and grounds before setting it on the burner to boil. "What brings you guys here so early?" Max asked. "I was hoping for at least a couple more hours of sleep."

"Deacon James."

"Eddie told you?"

"This morning, Eddie sent me some files and intel I wasn't expecting. You didn't think one street gang was enough? You had to poke a stick in another nest?"

"Hold up," Max raised his hands. "This is a little different. Someone grabbed Deacon's son off the street yesterday. I knew the kid. Sort of. He boxes at the same gym across the street," he pointed toward the window, "I want to help." He quickly sketched in what he'd learned last night.

Lawrence frowned at the end, but his expression had softened. "Max, you need to learn to say no. You cannot save all the lost puppies in the world."

The water started boiling and Max stood again to pour the coffee. He carried a steaming cup to Lawrence.

"This isn't a lost puppy. It's a fourteen-year-old kid."

"I know that, and I know Deke a little. We've had some ... dealings in the past. Normally, I'd be with you. But damn, man, we're already stretched thin. Ade gave me the blow-by-blow from yesterday. Those FCM guys are going to be looking for some retribution and you're not exactly in hiding."

"About that—"

"Please tell me you didn't find some time to antagonize anyone else last night?"

"No, but FCM came up."

"With Deke?"

"I was asking about any enemies that might want to grab Javon for leverage. He denied it all. I think he's half-convinced himself he's a legitimate businessman. He ran through all the logical reasons that no one would have a beef with him, but guess who his closest geographical rival is?"

"FCM."

"They keep showing up like a bad penny."

"What do we know about them?"

"I talked to a community activist a few days ago when I had the problem at PPCS, and he told me they are relatively new but growing fast. Based mostly out of a place on Mercy Street. Calle Misericordia de la Familia. FCM. They started over on the east side, near the water, but are slowly pushing out. They get the Latin American immigrants that land in the city and are desperate."

"They hooked into the cartels?"

"No, not that I've heard. The head guy, Jorge Campos, has aspirations. He sees all the little parochial pieces of Philly, all these little ragtag groups dealing different pills and powders and protection rackets, and he sees a wide-open playing field."

"A man with ambitions can be dangerous."

"No doubt. He's also paranoid as hell. Does most of his business in a car. No one knows where he stays."

"And you think he's involved in taking Javon?"

"It's one possibility. He's got the means and motive if he wants to move in on Deacon and Gray's Ferry."

Lawrence tossed his phone on the table. "From what

Eddie sent, unless it's a random stranger, and what are the odds of that, Campos might be the strongest possibility."

"Nothing from Deacon's side? No family skeletons."

"Nothing that would make me think it could lead to kidnapping his son. They have no personal debt. His wife doesn't work. Her immediate family is also pretty clean. One brother likes to hit the casinos from time to time, but it doesn't look like it gets out of control."

"Okay. What about his businesses? He gave me an earful last night."

"I bet. He's a smart guy and well-diversified. You might question the source of his money, but the way it's being used, construction projects, various investments, tax shelters, is all legal and aboveboard. The white-shoe firms he's dealing with are unlikely to think that kidnapping someone is a viable business strategy."

"Doesn't rule out someone down on the street before the money gets washed."

"True, but in my experience as long as people are getting paid, they are unlikely to rock the boat. Cash flow has been steadily growing. He's keeping them happy. Not a lot of motive to go after the man at the top."

"What do you think then?"

"I think we put the immediate family aside for the moment. Javon hasn't been gone twenty-four hours yet. I think you hit the school and friends hard this morning. If this is some high school or adolescent thing that's gotten out of hand, we should be able to break it down fast. If that doesn't pan out, I think we move on and try to get a vibe on Deke's organization despite what I said. This feels personal, I think it comes from somewhere close. After that, we take a hard look at FCM."

Ade had been quiet for the entire exchange. Her head slowly pinging back and forth as Max and Lawrence talked but she spoke up forcefully now. "Tuco. We need to find Tuco."

"Right, I know. I haven't forgotten," Max said, "I need the FCM information, regardless. Even if they aren't involved with Javon, they are muscling in on the car service, already took a couple runs at both of us, and have Ade's sister. Can we get Eddie to dig there while we check out Javon's school this morning?"

"We can try—"

The knock at the door was loud and thumping. It carried the authoritarian quality they each recognized. They all froze for a moment, then Ade scooped up Max's gun from the table and quickly disappeared into the bedroom. Lawrence stayed seated. Max stood and opened the door.

Detectives Axelson and Diaz stood there, Diaz's fist raised to knock again. Max could see a door, two down from his own, cracked open, likely curious about the noise. The sun was up. The work-a-day world was moving. It wasn't obscenely early, but it was early enough that loud noises drew attention. Max was sure that was Diaz's point. Any kind of pressure you could bring to bear on a suspect helped. In a cop's opinion.

"Come on in, Detectives. Can I get you some coffee?"

They seemed surprised and a little put out that he was up and hospitable. They knew very well he worked nights and were probably hoping to roust him from bed again. They appeared even more surprised to find another man sitting on his couch.

Then it was Max's turn to be surprised. Lawrence broke into a big smile.

"Detective Diaz, such a pleasant surprise to see you again."

CHAPTER FORTY-FIVE

Diaz's face drained of color and he looked as if he wanted to bolt from the room.

"You two know each other?" Max asked.

"We've met," Lawrence said with a wide smile that was more icy than friendly. "How's your mom doing, Detective? Everything work out okay?"

Max watched Diaz's throat work and his mouth twist like he was biting into a lemon. "Yes, she's fine," he finally managed.

Max saw Axelson lift an eyebrow at her partner, but Diaz ignored her. She spoke up, apparently determined to rein back control of an interview that had veered way off the expected rails. "Mr. Lindell—"

"What is this? Our fourth date? You can call me Max."

"Mr. Lindell, we'd like to ask you about your whereabouts yesterday from the time you left the station until nine o'clock in the evening? Could you do that?"

"Sure. Do I need my lawyer?"

"That's up to you."

Max made a show of thinking about it and glanced at

Lawrence before responding. "Probably no need to call her if telling you now will get this done faster. My friend Lawrence here was kind enough to pick me up from the precinct. We had lunch at The Skyline Diner and—"

"What did you have?" Axelson was taking notes. He knew Nia would back him up. She had no love lost for authority, especially city police, and he only ever ate two things at the diner.

"We each had burgers. Cheddar cheese with fried onions. You ever ate there, Detective?"

"No."

"Well, you should. Sherrod is a maestro on the grill. After we ate, we came back here. I was pretty beat. You guys woke me up early if you recall. I took a nap. Later, we met up with my friend Ronnie, he runs a local boxing gym, and visited some friends in the neighborhood. Got back late. That's about it. Wait." Max snapped his fingers and worried he was laying it on a bit too thick, but Axelson just paused in her writing and lifted that eyebrow again. "There was a disturbance down on the street. I talked to one of your officers. Gave a brief statement. That should help with the timeline."

He saw something flicker across her face, disappointment maybe, then she flipped her notebook closed and turned to Lawrence. "That sound about right, Mr ..."

"Lawrence is fine and, yes, I think Max covered it."

"Why are you asking?" Max asked.

"Just following up on a few things," Axelson deflected.

Max guessed they'd found the FCM bodies by the docks. He hoped there were no cameras in the area that caught a clean shot of him. It wouldn't take much to bust the lies he'd told her.

"If that's all?"

"Mind if we look around while we're here?" she asked and took a step toward the hall and the bedroom.

If Axelson found Ade in his bedroom or the gun, it would cause him all sorts of issues. But he also didn't want to do anything that gave the impression he was hiding something. She took two more steps and stopped in the bedroom doorway. She glanced back. It was a game of chicken. He gave her a second to get a good look.

"Didn't think you'd be so interested in my bedroom, Detective."

She tucked her notebook into her jacket pocket and returned to the living room.

"Good enough?"

"For now."

"Good seeing you again, Detective Diaz," Lawrence called as the pair walked toward the door. "I'm sure we'll be talking again soon."

Max spent the rest of the day fruitlessly chasing down Javon's friends and trying to talk to some of his teachers. Everyone had heard about the kidnapping. The kids were mostly polite, but either wouldn't talk to a strange white man or really knew nothing. Max thought it was mostly the latter. He didn't push, but he could see the fear, uncertainty, and confusion under the brash fronts that most put up. There was nothing to know. Javon was in school one day and gone the next. Most of them found it spooky.

He didn't have much more luck with the teachers or administration either. It was a little trickier trying to get them to talk. They were all wary, even when he convinced them he was working in Javon's best interests and had the family's blessing.

A small, mousy woman who said she had had Javon in math the previous year gave him the most time.

"He was a quiet kid, not shy, really, more quietly confident."

"Mature." Max had detected something similar watching him in the gym. He didn't showboat or make a lot of noise, just went about his business. If he hadn't been so young, Max would have described him as a professional.

"Yes, that's a good word. So many kids at his age either retreat into themselves or go the other way, big and loud, to cover it all up. Javon wasn't like that. He was very comfortable with himself. He knew who he was."

"Lucky kid. Most people twice his age are still trying to figure that out. Did that bother people?"

"No, I don't think so. Javon was liked by most of the students, but he wasn't the most popular. He wasn't an outcast, either. He kept mostly to himself and a small group of friends."

"Was he happy?"

"I think so. As happy as teenagers filled with raging hormones ever are."

"No feuds, beefs, or arguments?"

"I'm sure some kids might have been a little jealous but nothing serious."

The people he talked to from the school all said similar things in different ways. It built up a nice portrait of a young man with talent and potential, but it didn't shed any light on what might have happened to Javon or who might be responsible. By the end of the day, Max was convinced that whatever had happened, it had not come from the direction of the school or Javon's friends. This wasn't a prank or retribution for some hallway slight. This was something else. But what?

Javon's disappearance wasn't the lead story on the news, but it was close. It was making waves around Gray's Ferry and beyond. Max could hear people talking about it as he went about his business. It was in the air. He checked in with Deke. He had his crew out trying to come up with any kind of line on Javon, but, so far, like Max's efforts, it was all for naught. The lack of leads and any kind of chatter gave Max bad vibes. He was sure he wasn't the only one. Deke must be fighting it, too.

Max returned to his apartment at six and found Lawrence still on the couch, now with a laptop open on the table. He looked tired, but there was more color in his face than there had been that morning. He looked up as Max came in and grabbed a beer from the kitchen. Max shook his head.

"Nothing. You?"

"About the same. Eddie and I have been poking around Deke's people, but not getting anywhere. We got plenty on Deke. He's got money and paper everywhere, probably more than we can find, but his boys are more old school. Mostly cash and very little footprint beyond social media."

"If this stretches out to a third day ..." Max trailed off.

"I know. I don't want to be in the same room, hell, on the same block, if they have to tell Deke."

"Even worse might be never knowing. That's what would scare me."

There was no response to something like that. Max finished his beer and picked up the keys again. "I'm going to go over and check on Ade."

Max drove the short distance across South Philly taking Reed to South Broad, then cutting across on Snyder. Traffic was light, he slowed and eyeballed Mercy Street as he drove past, but it all looked quiet through the glow of the overhead streetlights. It was full dark now, dinnertime. There were a few people out walking home from the bus stop or walking their dogs. Cars hunting for parking spots. Max drove past and made a left at the next block. He got lucky with a spot halfway down the street and managed to angle the Escalade in.

He'd texted her that he was on his way over and, when he crossed the street, he found a rock propping open the back door. He kicked it aside and went in. Ade had spent the day watching for Tuco from the second floor of the purple church across the street from La Champincita Grocers and the LCM's drive-through drug market. Max had been hesitant for her to do it alone. It was very close and very noticeable with the giant glowing cross in the front window, but Ade had been insistent and reminded him she'd been doing this on her own for six months, even if things had escalated in the last few weeks.

"Plus, it's perfect because it is so obvious. People only see the crucifix. It is all they remember. They do not look up. Besides, it is empty. I have been there before. Electricity is still on and plumbing still works."

"I wonder if God's covering the rent?"

She looked at him for a beat. "I do not need to know all the answers. Just that I can flush the toilet."

He climbed the stairs, being sure to make enough noise that she heard him coming. He didn't need any more bumps on the head. She sat a few feet back from the window, in a chair she'd likely salvaged from a nearby trashcan.

"Spot anything good?" he asked.

"A lot of drug deals, but no Tuco."

"Did you have any luck locating the boy?"

"No. Came up empty." He walked to the second window as a navy Honda CR-V slowed and turned into the lot. The order guy pushed off the wall and approached the car's window. "These guys must make a killing. I wonder what they're doing with the money."

Ade shrugged. "Nothing good. I already know all I need

to know. I have seen enough of what drugs and money do. I just want to find Tuco and then find my sister."

Max had no answer to that. They observed more deals go down and people enter and exit the small groceria. Some looked legit, others looked like they were part of the gang. It all felt very normal and very boring. Max knew surveillance was like that. When he was planning jobs, he'd sit and stare at a scene for hours, sometimes days, hoping to spot a piece of information that would give him an inch of advantage. That was all he needed. It was tedious, but sometimes resulted in extraordinary results.

He might have missed it if Ade hadn't spoken up.

The guy Max had beaten up in the storeroom on his last visit to Mercy Street exited the back door carrying a couple of plastic bags. His nose was bandaged, and he took the two short steps down to the parking lot gingerly. Max couldn't tell what was inside the bags, but they were full of something and hung heavy from the guy's hands. He must have called out to the guys in the lot as three of them soon joined him under the light by the door.

Max was about to push off the wall and tell Ade he was going to pick up food and head back when she broke the silence herself. "This is the second time this has happened today."

Max turned back to the window. "What?"

She gestured at the group. "This … meeting."

The three outside guys were arguing about something. It wasn't heated, but it was clear that whatever chore the inside guy had in mind, none of them wanted to do it. Eventually, the man thrust the bags at one guy. He grabbed at the bag handles but missed all of them. The bags tipped and bottled water and various granola bars spilled onto the ground. The guy barked something, and the kid quickly picked them up with a few additional words for his friends who had ducked the job. The kid climbed into a Camry with aftermarket rims and LED side panel lighting that was parked in the corner of the lot. The car started up and Max could hear the stereo's bass pulse through the night.

Something sparked in his mind, and he ran for the stairs.

CHAPTER FORTY-SIX

They spent the day talking, dozing, and hashing out a plan. A small, fragile partnership had emerged after their initial chat. Javon was still handcuffed, nothing Ash could do about that, but happy to be out of the freezer.

"Tell me again why we can't walk out of here?" Javon said.

"Because they have my parents' address. The threat was sort of implicit."

"So, no offense, you kidnapped me, why can't I walk off and leave you here to deal with it?"

"They got to you once. They'd do it again. Tomorrow? Next year? Whatever this is, they would finish it. You wanna wait? Wanna risk that?"

Javon thought it over and nodded. "Probably right. No need to go through this twice. So, what do we do?"

"I don't know who you are," Javon started to say something in response and Ash held up a hand to stop him, "and I don't want to know, either. We get out of this. I'm getting clean and getting out of this city." He'd said things like that before, but this was different. Even to his own ears, the words had weight. It only took kidnapping an innocent kid. Christ, this had to be different. He didn't want to see any further down the hole. "You got some value and that means eventually someone of value on the other side is going to show up here to deal with you. When that happens, we make our move and we get out of here."

"Won't killing or maiming a top guy of theirs only piss them off more?"

"Sure, but it will also make them a little more careful. We pick off a couple of foot soldiers, they will only send more. We pick off a lieutenant, it's going to make them pause."

"How's that any different from walking away right now?"

"It gives us time. We walk away now, they'll run us down like dogs. We make some trouble, they might start to ask themselves if it's worth it. We use that time. I get the hell out of dodge and make sure my folks are safe. You get to your people and figure out what the hell is going on. I'm not so stupid to think you're a random kid. You get back to your people and I figure that will give whoever's responsible for this a whole lot more to think about. You ever deal with bullies?"

"Some."

"How well does turning the other cheek and walking away work?"

"Okay, point taken."

"Plus, I really want to jam these guys up for the way they played me."

Javon smiled. "Now a little get back is something I can understand."

They waited until dark. Ash wasn't sure where the camera was or how it was activated or even if it was monitored. He doubted it was anything that sophisticated. Maybe the last

time he tried to walk away, the guy was watching and Ash got
caught by dumb luck and bad timing. He did a few tests. He
walked in circles around the truck and slowly edged out. He
waited for the mobile to ring. Nothing.

Javon peeked out the back window. "Probably stuck a
crappy nanny cam up on one of those posts. I doubt it's got
infrared or shit."

Ash was inclined to agree. "Let's give it a few minutes."

They sat, but the phone didn't ring. Ash got out of the
truck and this time he bent down and collected whatever
loose trash or debris he found on the warehouse floor. He
made two circuits and piled it up near the front of the truck.

"Explain this half-baked plan. What is that?"

"That," Ash said, "is kindling."

They'd searched the truck top to bottom earlier in the
day, hoping to find something they could use to get Javon's
cuffs off, but came up empty. They had found a few old ice
cream scoops and a dented napkin dispenser in one drawer.
Ash picked up one scoop now. "Let's see if we can get this
truck started."

Ash used the edge of the scoop to pry off a chunk of the
steering column. Javon sat in the passenger seat and watched
as Ash examined the exposed wires. He selected two,
stripped the plastic insulation with the sharp edge of the
steering column plastic, and twisted the ends together. The
truck's engine sputtered, once, twice, then coughed to life.

"Where'd you learn that trick?"

"They did some research on me, but not enough, I guess.
I was MOS 35 in the Marines."

"What's that?"

"Motor pool. People were constantly forgetting or losing
the keys to the vehicles. Knowing how to get a car or trans-
port going was something they taught you on the first day."
He looked over and caught Javon's expression. "Don't go

getting any ideas. This sort of thing only works on older cars. It will not do squat on any car with a chip key."

Javon shrugged. "Still interesting."

Ash popped the glovebox and took out the owner's manual, a flashlight, a small first aid kit, and other assorted crap that had accumulated over the years until he could see the black plastic cover of the fuse box. "We need to figure out which one runs the speaker system."

Ash liked the idea of using the diabolical music against his tormentors. He might have been leery to mess with the truck before, when envelopes were appearing inside his clean and warm motel room, but he had no such qualms now. If this worked, he wanted to see it go up in flames.

"You ever heard of Rube Goldberg?" Javon asked.

"No, who's that?"

"He was this old cartoonist who drew these ridiculously complicated machines to complete a simple task."

Ash paused and looked up. "You're saying my plan is over-complicated?"

"To put it mildly."

"You're probably right, but you deal with the hand you're dealt. Unless you have other ideas?"

Javon shrugged. "I'm still in favor of walking away and taking our chances."

"Might help in the short-term, but I don't see it working in the long-term. I really don't. At least not for me. I'd be constantly looking over my shoulder or worried about my family. It would wear me down."

"And you think antagonizing them further is more helpful?"

"I think it's what they will understand. These people are not subtle." Ash picked up the tweezers he'd found in the discarded first aid kit in the glovebox. Ash wasn't sure they'd be strong enough, but like the rest of his plan, he had little choice. He put them in his pocket along with the ice cream scoop. "The bottles ready?"

"Yup." Javon nodded his head at the empty water bottles now stacked in a drawer they'd pulled out of the truck's prep table. Ash picked up the metal drawer, stepped out into the dark warehouse space, and slid under the truck. If they were watching and could see, they would surely call now and ask what the hell he was doing.

Or maybe not. Maybe they'd shoot first and figure it out later.

CHAPTER FORTY-SEVEN

Len walked out the door and sat on the front steps. The night was bitter and the chill perked him up after the beers and the hours inside the stuffy living room. He was wrung out. He couldn't remember being more tired in his life. Or scared. The entire thing scared him. Bad. But he wouldn't let those feelings out. He couldn't. He knew where fear led. Nowhere good for him. He had to push through. Hell or high water, as his old man used to say. It was all so close now.

The women had convinced Tamyra to get some rest, or at least go up and lie down. They'd all gone home. A few groups of young men, dealers, and runners still milled about on the sidewalk, but the majority had also left. It was late. There was a sense in the air that nothing more was going to happen tonight. Len looked over his shoulder through the window and watched Deke, back on the phone, still pacing the living room. He wouldn't sleep until he found Javon or found who was responsible. Deke turned and peered out the window and their eyes locked for a moment and that worm of fear squirmed through his guts. For all his polish, Len knew Deke was also capable of violence when required. He would protect his family. If he couldn't do that, he would get vengeance. An eye for an eye.

Len turned back to the street and thought about the odd incident of that white boy showing up with old Ronnie Shelton. What had that been about? Len had paid no attention to the white boy at first. He figured him for another hanger-on. Len had expected Ronnie was paying his respects and they would be in and out. It had been like that all night. The first floor of the James' house was like the lobby of a funeral home before a wake. People saying hello and sorry in hushed tones. But that's not how it went down. Ronnie introduced the white boy, and they'd spoken briefly. Deke appeared on the verge of having Cherry toss the white boy out on his skinny ass when things took an unexpected turn. The white boy had dropped a name. Len hadn't recognized it, but it must have carried serious weight with Deke.

The white boy didn't look like anything special until his eyes flicked over Len as he leaned against the wall in Deke's office. A certain vibration passed between them, and he realized the white boy might be more threatening than he appeared. He was dangerous in the same way that Deke was dangerous. He kept it carefully camouflaged under a veneer of normalcy, but his eyes were cold. He let Len get a glimpse of something hard and menacing swimming below the surface.

And he'd picked up on FCM, too. That didn't sit well with Len. That couldn't come out. Not yet. He was thinking through it, working out what to do next, how best to play out the next twenty-four hours when the hulking presence of Cherry came through the door. He nodded at the man-mountain.

"Deke says to go home for now."

Len stood. "You going?"

"That's what the man wants. I'm going to shoo away the puppies down here and head out."

Len knew he'd likely go back to his mom's place, change clothes, and come right back. A loyal dog. "All right." He held out a fist and they bumped knuckles. "See you in a few hours."

His phone vibrated as he walked to his ride parked down the block. The phone in his left pocket. He waited until he was in his car to answer. He listened. "When?"

"Tomorrow night works."

Len stiffened and his hand drifted to the butt of the gun in his pocket. "Who's that?"

"Relax. It's a delivery," Tuco said.

Len didn't like the idea of more people seeing his face with Tuco. He was getting more and more anxious about the whole thing. He hadn't slept more than an hour at a stretch in weeks. He was exhausted. He couldn't take a deep breath. There was a rock, a boulder, sitting squarely on his chest. He'd spent the day in a semi-comatose daze. He'd sat with Deke and Cherry. He listened to various guys pass through and tell the same story. They had nothing. Eventually, he couldn't take it anymore. He said he'd get out there himself and left. He just had to hang on a little longer.

Len squeezed his eyes shut as the extra-bright headlights swept over them. A young guy, his hair slicked back and cheeks dotted with acne, stepped out carrying a couple of plastic bags and a puffed out chest. It didn't impress Len. Tuco said something in rapid Spanish. He guessed the posturing didn't work on Tuco either. The smile on the kid's face faltered and he deflated. He walked over and stood next to Tuco but a step back. Another dog brought to heel, thought Len.

"Look," Len said, anxious now to get back to business before anyone else showed up, "if you're going to hit him, you best do it soon. He's distracted and tired, and he's got most of his guys on the street looking for Javon. He's never going to be more vulnerable."

"And you'll never have a better shot."

Len shrugged. No use denying it. "That's the whole point, right? I get the big chair and out from under Deke's thumb and you guys get access to Gray's Ferry. Win-win."

Len knew, and he damn well suspected, that Tuco and his bosses knew it would not be that simple, but why bring up the side effects when the cure provided so many benefits?

Tuco looked at him for a long second. "Right. Win-win. Let's go see the kid."

"Whoa. Before we go, to be clear, the vagrant's got to go, but we leave Javon. He walks out without a scratch." Len had no qualms about killing a kid if he was in the game, but that wasn't Javon. He wasn't in the game. He was only connected because Deke was his father. A fluke of birth. He was a useful and expedient means to an end. Len was the kid's godfather, after all. Not his executioner. After FCM took care of Deke, and Len took over, he'd make sure Tamyra and Javon got out of Philly.

"Right," Tuco said, "just the vagrant."

CHAPTER FORTY-EIGHT

Max dug the keys out of his pocket and hit the unlock button as he ran across the street. He felt more than saw Ade coming up behind him. She slid into the passenger seat as he started inching the big SUV back and forth out of the tight parking space. The gun at his waist dug into his back and he pulled it out and dropped it in the door's side pocket. He could feel the other car getting farther away, and it took all his will not to punch the gas and muscle his way out of the tight space with the big SUV. Finally, he pulled free and hit the gas. Then had to stand on the brake immediately as a kid darted between the parked cars and across the street.

"Shit!"

He took a breath and drove more slowly down to the intersection with Snyder. Left or right? Max tried to picture the groceria parking lot. The car had been headed west, but was that a one-way road? Left was the highway, the river, and Jersey. Right was the city, the Schuylkill, and the suburbs.

"You've lived here longer. Left or right? Where would you stash a kid?"

Ade glanced both ways. The clock was ticking, the car racing away, but he didn't push.

"Left. The docks. They used it once, they might use it again."

He turned and started weaving through traffic. There wasn't a lot of road or turns before the river. Max figured they would know quickly if they'd made the right choice.

"You think he's going to the kid?" Ade asked.

"Yes, bringing food and water."

"So, he's alive?"

"For now."

They crossed under the 95 overpass and into the waterfront district, got lucky with a couple of green lights, had passed a Lowe's and were approaching Christopher Columbus Boulevard when Ade pointed, "There. Making the turn."

Max saw the blue and green LEDs on the side panel of the Camry as it turned right. Max got caught at the light but was able to close the gap quickly once on the wider two-lane avenue. Traffic was brisk along the commercial strip, and he settled three cars back. They followed for two miles, traffic thinned as the fast-food joints and box stores gave way to warehouses and the marine port. Max dropped farther back.

"You don't think they'd use the same spot, do you?" He wasn't eager to return to the warehouse where they'd rescued Lawrence. He knew from Diaz and Axelson's visit that they'd already found the bodies.

Ade shrugged. She echoed his thoughts. "Too risky. Especially if there's been police activity. They might have other properties nearby."

"That could work. Like hiding in the bank basement after a robbery. You wait them out. Cops are swarming a scene six blocks away, maybe they don't look all that closely at their immediate surroundings. Risky, but an option. Unlikely that they are doing a door-to-door canvass in this area. Half the buildings are abandoned."

"Perfect for stashing a kid."

Ahead of them, the Camry pulled abruptly into an empty lot on the right, underneath the 76 overpass. There was nowhere for Max to go. It was a desolate stretch of road. He couldn't stop or pull over. It would be too noticeable. He drove past. Two other cars were in the lot parked front-to-back near the overpass abutment.

A quarter mile later, he turned into the driveway of a recycling processing plant. The gate was open and pushed back, but the parking lot was empty. Max cut the lights and let the Escalade drift to a stop.

"We need to see this." He grabbed the gun. "If they have the kid, we gotta try to get him back." Ade said nothing, just nodded, and followed him out of the car. They crossed a strip of landscaped grass that surrounded the business's parking lot and into a thin line of trees the city's public works department had probably planted to provide the surrounding businesses a buffer from the noise and concrete of the highway overpass. It was scant cover. Anyone would have spotted them easily during the day, but Max hoped the darkness would be enough to conceal their approach.

The trees petered out fifty yards from the overpass. They knelt by the trunk of the last tree. The lot appeared to be a DPW staging area. Cones, barrels, drums, and orange signs filled the space along with a pile of gravel and sand. Four tall security lights at each corner of the lot provided enough light to see the men now standing in a rough triangle in front of their respective cars. The kid they'd followed from the groceria was standing next to another thin man in similar clothes. Max recognized him from the warehouse.

"Tuco," Ade whispered.

Max nodded. He also recognized the third guy. Short and stocky with thick shoulders and close-cropped hair. Several pieces clicked into place. "The third guy works for Deacon."

"What's he doing here?"

"Not sure. Deacon says they've had little to no contact with FCM."

"Maybe Deacon doesn't know."

They watched the men. Max took out his phone and snapped a few shots and added a short video. They were likely too dark and too far away to be of much use. But getting the two groups in the same frame was telling. Tuco was doing most of the talking. They were too far away to hear any specifics. Eventually, the kid handed the bags to Tuco and they all went back to their cars.

"I'll run back and get the car. You watch which way they go," Max said.

He jogged back through the trees and pulled the SUV back onto the main road. He kept the headlights off and drove slowly. Ade popped out of the trees and jumped in the passenger side.

"They split up. Looks like the kid is heading back. The other two stuck together and turned right up there." She indicated the next traffic light.

Max floored it to the light. The intersection was empty and he didn't slow as he took the turn. They were back on the access road, the one that led down to the marine ports that they were becoming all too familiar with. The road ahead was long and straight. And empty.

Max put the headlights on and pushed the speed up close to eighty. The Escalade shimmied under the strain, probably knocked out of alignment by the earlier crash. He gripped the wheel tighter. "You're sure they turned right?"

"Yes." She was scanning the nearby buildings and side roads as they flashed past.

They drove half a mile. Then a mile.

"Maybe we should turn around. We might have missed them."

"There." She pointed off to the right, and Max saw two sets of headlights carom and bounce off a tall, rusting, white oil or gas storage tank.

He followed and stopped short on the side of the road. Ghosted letters, now unreadable, wrapped around the large tank. He flicked his headlights off again. It was an isolated lot in a dead spot away from the water. The fence bordering the entrance was open and sagging. Inside the fence, there were four smaller pill-shaped tanks spaced apart that looked to be for filling or offloading. A low, squat building was off to the left beside the small tanks. It all appeared abandoned. The building's windows were broken, and a panel was missing from the entry door. The small tanks were corroding at the bottom. Farther back, beyond the white storage tank, Max could see the darker shadow of a larger building at the back of the lot.

"Some sort of old fuel processing plant," Max said.

The headlights had disappeared behind the large tank. He pulled in and drove around the far side of the filling station, close to the rounded bulk of the white tank, tucking the SUV out of sight from both the road and the building in back.

They shut their doors softly and kept close to the sagging fence on the lot's left. They stepped clear of the tank's shadow. A corrugated steel building similar to a Quonset hut, but five times the scale, squatted at the back of the lot. A large rolling door, wide enough for a tanker truck to pull through, was open and rusted into place. The headlights of

the two cars illuminated the distant corner and cast a spotlight on what appeared to be an ice cream truck. Max didn't
think this whole affair could get any weirder, but it kept
surprising him. The truck's running lights and accessories
were on, he could hear calliope music, but the truck itself
wasn't running.

They slipped inside the open door and crouched down
near a pile of old 55-gallon drums. Two hundred yards away,
Tuco and Deke's guy stood framed in their headlights. Deke's
guy's face was strange and distorted and Max realized he was
wearing some kind of mask. A moment later, Max watched a
third man climb out of the ice cream truck and stand ten feet
away by the passenger door, facing the two men.

"Both of them have guns," Max whispered. If Javon was
here, he didn't want to get in a shootout and have the kid
catch a stray bullet. "We need to get closer."

The space inside was large and open. The ice cream truck
was parked at an angle, front in, against the wall. The two
cars were perpendicular to the truck, pinning it in and
lighting it up. There was no simple way to get close to the
vehicles without being seen.

"Follow me," Ade said. She moved away, not waiting for
Max's answer.

They worked their way along the far side of the hut,
keeping Tuco and Len's backs to them. Ade walked silently
but excruciatingly slow. Max knew it was the right call, any
quick movement would draw the eye, but it was torture as
they inched along in the darker shadows where the hut's walls
curved and met the ground. Max's legs ached to sprint across
the open space and tackle the two men and find Javon. He
clamped down on his impatience and focused on following
Ade, putting his feet carefully down, one in front of the
other.

Halfway there, something caught Max's attention. He

stopped and held still. Ade took another step in front of him, and he reached out a hand to her shoulder. She turned and looked at him. He pointed. Someone was exiting the ice cream truck from the driver's side. The way the truck was angled, Tuco and Len couldn't see him, but Max and Ade could. He watched Javon carefully step down—he was hand-cuffed—and crouch by the front tire. What was he doing?

Then Max noticed something else. A small yellow and orange glow. The truck was on fi—

A sucking whomp interrupted his half-completed thought. A moment later, the entire other side of the ware-house was awash in flames.

CHAPTER FORTY-NINE

A sh's first idea hadn't worked. They hadn't been able to isolate the fuse for the speakers. It turned out, the speakers needed more amps, perhaps to get the spinning lights on the roof going simultaneously, and worked off an ignition relay.

They turned to plan B. Make the truck into a bomb.

Working quickly, but carefully by the muted light of his burner phone, Ash popped the hood and found the right relay. He'd pulled the relay, taken off the housing, and bent the arm down to force the switch to stay in the on position. If he could overheat the jammed circuit enough to cause the battery to spark with the starter, they might be in business. If the sparks were enough to get the trash piles burning, step two was to spread the flames with the help of the gasoline he was about to bleed off by putting a hole in the truck's gas tank. He had to admit, laid out like that, he agreed with Javon. It was a fragile, Rube Goldberg contraption. A lot of ifs.

He shimmied farther under the trunk until he was within

reach, but off to the side, of the gas tank. He reached back and dragged the empty bottles in after him, making sure he still had room to maneuver. Finally, he took out the tweezers and ice cream scoop. He almost laughed. Not exactly standard Marine issue tools.

"Semper fi," he whispered.

Sometimes the longshot comes in. Sometimes that scratch ticket pays off.

It happened slowly at first and then fast, all at once, like a boulder teetering, before catching gravity and rolling downhill. He smelled a whiff of smoke but didn't dare turn around. He kept talking, trying to keep the two men distracted. He saw the flames reflected in the Hispanic one's eyes. The man's mouth formed an O as his gun came up.

Ash had reconnected the wires when the pair of cars had entered the warehouse. The overloaded relay had caused enough sparks to ignite the piles of trash and now it was greedily lapping up the gas he'd spread in widening circles around the truck. The one good thing about the old truck was its large gas tank. There was plenty of fuel for the flames.

"Holy shit," Ash yelled and gave up any pretense of submitting to these men quietly. He ducked and ran back toward the truck. He felt like he was wading through puddles of fire. It was everywhere. He dodged left as something buzzed past his ear. He cut back in the other direction and squeezed around the front of the truck. The smoke was still heavy, but the fire was on the opposite side. He coughed. His eyes watered and made him almost blind. Someone pushed him.

"You're on fire, man. Get on the ground. I can't put it out with these handcuffs on."

Ash looked down and saw blurry orange flames on both of his shins and his left sleeve. He quickly dropped to the ground and smothered the flames. Wiping his eyes, he stood up to find two guns pointed at his chest.

CHAPTER FIFTY

Len stumbled back and fell. He felt like someone had slapped him across the face with a hot, heavy frying pan. He clawed the mask off his face. He was on his back, looking up at the ceiling of the warehouse in a daze. Someone screamed. He heard his nana's voice. Their old housing authority apartment was rife with poor electrical work and shoddy appliances. Sporadic fires in and around the complex were common. He remembered her raspy instructions as the flames licked his ankles and shins and tried to climb higher. He rolled back and forth in the dirt, and slapped at the cuffs of his jeans to put out the last sparks. Finally, he stood and looked around. It looked like he'd dropped through a hole into hell. Fire surrounded him. He didn't know where it had come from. It seemed to have sprung up from the ground itself. He saw Tuco running wildly toward the warehouse door, his back and legs on fire.

Thick smoke and more fire obscured the ice cream truck just yards away. Len had lost track of the homeless guy. Had he somehow started the fire? What about Javon? He took a step toward the truck, but the heat was intense and pushed him back. It was like walking into a gale force wind. He stopped. If Javon was still in the truck, he was as good as dead. Nothing Len could do about it now. It wasn't what Len wanted, but it had happened. Maybe it would help in the long run. Javon was soft, but who knows how he'd react to all of this. Maybe a few years down the road, he'd get ideas of revenge. Maybe it was better for everyone that it ended here.

He took another step back. He could smell the harsh pungent odor of the tires burning. Tuco's screaming suddenly stopped. Len turned. Tuco was fifty yards away. His hair now on fire. Another, sweeter, smell reached Len and he tried not to think about what it was. Tuco slowed, stumbled, and fell. The fire continued to consume him. He didn't get back up.

Len picked his way back to his car. Tuco was dead. He had to assume Javon was dead, too. He'd lost track of the homeless guy, but he was the least of Len's worries. As he backed the car up and drove around Tuco's body, he'd already stopped thinking about him. He'd left both cell phones in the cupholder. One rattled and blinked with a message indicator. Deke's phone. Len picked it up. Four missed messages. Len smiled. At least something appeared to be going right.

CHAPTER FIFTY-ONE

Max took a step toward the sudden inferno before Ade grabbed his arm.

"Wait."

He realized she was right. Javon was on the far side of the truck. He was safe for the moment, and the fire didn't change the fact that Tuco and Len still had guns. They might be distracted, but they were still armed.

They watched the fire spread and wash over the two men. Len dropped and rolled frantically to snuff out the flames, but Tuco tried to run and only made it worse.

"Tuco," Ade said.

Max could see she wanted to go after him. The best lead she had on her sister was going up in flames. It was hard to watch. Tuco staggered to the middle of the warehouse before he collapsed.

"You couldn't have made any difference," Max said.

Ade nodded.

A car started. Len drove past in a blur and out the open door.

The third man had come around the side of the truck and

was on the ground trying to smother the flames on his own body. He'd be up in another minute. The smoke was getting thicker.

"C'mon," Max said, "I need to get the kid." They dropped any pretense of creeping in and sprinted across the open space while Javon and the other guy were still preoccupied with the fire.

The third guy had dropped his gun or wasn't armed. Something else, too. Javon was still handcuffed, but he and Javon appeared to be on friendly terms. The guy stood and brushed off his burned cuffs and wiped at his watering eyes.

"Who are you two?" the guy asked. He didn't seem that put out by the guns pointed at him.

Javon spoke first. He didn't seem to mind the guns, either. Maybe getting snatched off the street and kidnapped in an ice cream truck hardened you to certain matters. "Wait, I know you."

"From Ronnie's gym. My name is Max. I'm helping your dad."

"A little late to the party, aren't you?"

The kid had a right to be angry. Max didn't take it personally. "Better late than never. Who's he?"

"That's Ash. He's ... it's complicated. I can explain, but can we get out of here first?"

The smoke was thickening as the fire died down. The place was off the beaten path, but the smoke would get someone's attention.

"Good idea."

They walked out. No one looked twice at Tuco's body.

At the SUV, Max pulled out Lawrence's supply bag and dug

around. He thought he'd find what he needed, and he wasn't disappointed. He pulled out a small leather portfolio with a zippered side. He opened it and quickly selected two slim metal picks.

"C'mere, kid," he said to Javon.

"What's that?"

"Turn around."

Javon did.

"Ade, can you hold my phone up, give me some light? Lift your wrists a little, kid."

Max bent over and worked the picks into the handcuff lock. Ten seconds later, they clicked open and fell to the ground.

Ade raised an eyebrow. "Just a driver."

Max grabbed the cuffs and threw them in the bag with the lock pick kit.

While they drove past the docks, Javon told his story. Max shook his head. It might have been the adrenaline high of the fire or being rescued, but Max thought Javon was in remarkably good shape for what he had endured. He was sure some type of reckoning would come later but, for now, he was relieved Javon was all right.

Ash remained silent. Nervous energy radiated off him. As Max turned left off Christopher Columbus, his phone vibrated with an incoming call.

"Lawrence? What's up? We have—"

"Max! You gotta get back here!"

Max pulled the phone away from his ear. It was loud. There was shouting, maybe crying in the background. "Lawrence, where are you? Was that a gunshot?" He pulled to the side of the road. He couldn't concentrate on the call and drive. He didn't explain to the others. He was sure they could hear most of it.

There was a long pause.

"Lawrence?" Max's stomach tightened, but Lawrence came back and the noise sounded more distant.

"Jesus Christ, it's like a war zone, Max. I'm close to Deke's. I was going over to talk to him about a few things Eddie found and it looks like someone is taking a run at Deke. A serious run."

More pieces fell into place. Javon's kidnapping wasn't the point. It was a distraction. A way to weaken Deke's defenses, knock him off-kilter, distract him before the take down. That was the real play.

"On our way."

Max disconnected and sent off a quick text message. Fathers and sons, he thought, then dropped the big SUV into gear and hammered the accelerator back toward Gray's Ferry.

What should have been a fifteen-minute drive through the congested center of South Philly, took six. Max used all the alleys and shortcuts he'd accumulated driving for PPCS and still broke at least eleven traffic laws. If they got pulled over, he planned to use Javon as his get out of jail card. But nothing happened except several angry horns and angrier gestures. He redialed Lawrence and slid to a stop outside a funeral home, three blocks short of Deke's house. He tried not to think about the omen that the building might represent.

Fifteen seconds later, Lawrence limped out of the connecting alley and climbed in the back seat. Max looked at him in the rearview mirror. He was sweating profusely and there were large, dark circles under his eyes. He looked hollowed out. Even worse, Max saw a dark patch on Lawrence's shirt. Lawrence caught him looking.

"I'm all right. For now. Let's get this done."

Max held his friend's eyes for a second, then nodded. "What's the best way?"

"You're going to have to go around and come back in from the west. The bad guys are coming from the east."

"FCM?"

"That's my guess."

"Cops?"

"Not yet."

"It's been almost ten minutes."

"I don't think they're in a rush."

CHAPTER FIFTY-TWO

He had never touched her before. Never. He had seen firsthand what happened to those that tried. When he touched her in the dark now, she stiffened but didn't pull away. The end was coming. It had been building like an electrical charge. It was a constant roaring in her ears that had built to a crescendo and now rushed toward her. His touch was an invitation, a mark. Here. Take this one.

She recognized the sound. She'd heard it before. It was death, and she welcomed it. She had been waiting a long time.

She climbed out of the car's trunk. It was dark outside. Her eyes didn't need long to adjust. After all the time spent in the black void, darkness was her natural habitat.

The man held out a hand. She looked at it and something must have shown in her eyes. "You'll get the good candy when you come back," he said. She knew that was unlikely to happen. Still, the urge was so strong that she didn't hesitate for long. She took the pill and swallowed, then shook the small vial of powder out on the back of her hand and snorted the whole thing up. She didn't know exactly what it was. And didn't care. Probably speed and coke. Her tolerance was so high that anything less than a full syringe to her heart was unlikely to kill her. It only took a moment. She didn't know which of the drugs hit her bloodstream first and, again, didn't care. It was like throwing a switch. Everything clicked on in ultra-detail as the stimulants revved up her motor. Her eyes swept the street and her mind raced ahead. The bag of bones that was her body was only slowing her down, holding her back.

The man did two more things before letting her off her leash. He took her arm and wrote a series of numbers on it in large blocky numerals. "For the door," he said. Then he held out one last thing. "Su hoja, mi hoja." Her blade. She was his weapon. His blade. He was always careful at this point and she saw his bodyguard tense. Her eyes watched his knuckles go white around the grip of his pistol. She took the short blade by the handle and a flood of images blew past her. Tio, the farm, slashing, cutting, bodies. He gently turned her by the shoulders so she faced the house on the corner. "Go around back, get inside, leave no one alive," he whispered.

She moved across the street. She was desperate for her body to catch up to her mind. The noise in her ears grew. The wave built higher. Death moved closer. She felt its breath on her neck.

The others had seen Jorge's car drop her off. She did not fear a bullet in the back. She did not particularly fear one coming from the front either. She had split in two. It was what always happened. She was just a passenger now.

She kept her eyes ahead, saw each pebble and hairline crack of asphalt. She slipped between the parked cars. A man appeared, a boy really, no lines on his face, barely any hair on his chin. She was on the balls of her feet, balanced, a constant whirl of motion. He stood no chance. He didn't raise his gun higher than his hip before she had sliced across three life-giving arteries. He stood, not sure what happened, not understanding that he was already dead. She moved past him.

CHAPTER FIFTY-THREE

Max turned the Escalade around, circled the block, came in from the west end, and stopped in the middle of the street. They all took in the scene. It looked like a riot or a war zone. Cars parked on the street had their windows shattered. People were screaming. The pop of gunshots was followed by more yelling. Max could see at least three darker shadows lying still on the sidewalk. He hoped they were only wounded and unable to move, not dead. He also hoped none of them were civilians, but it would take a miracle in these close quarters for an innocent not to get hurt in the crossfire.

The row homes on each side were old and packed next to each other, wall-to-wall. Other than Deke's place on the opposite corner, no one was gentrifying these. They were of uniform height and, other than varying facade colors, they all had the same look and feel. There were few places to hide.

"It's a box canyon. Everything's funneled to street level," Max said. There were two FCM groups that he could see, each slowly advancing and pinching in on Deke's corner lot. If Deke had one thing going for him, it was time. Maybe Jorge had paid the cops to be slow, but they had to show eventually. The FCM guys needed to push. Deke's side just needed to hold them to a stalemate. But could he do it? Did he have enough guys? He'd spread most of his people out looking for Javon. Even if he'd been able to call them back, most wouldn't arrive in time.

Max pulled the Escalade into a hydrant spot. "How do we help?" he asked.

No one said anything for a moment, then Lawrence said, "You could flank them by going down the next street or get behind them. Draw some fire away from Deke's corner."

"Could work, but I don't like the idea of introducing more bullets. The street is tight as it is. We don't need to kill anyone; we just need to slow them down. The first sound of sirens should end this."

"What are you thinking?" Lawrence asked.

"I think we go up. We get on the roofs. We walk. That way, if we have to shoot, we're directing it down, not across. You have anything in your cache that will help?"

Lawrence smiled. It looked tight and ghastly on his face.

They left Lawrence in the car with Javon. Lawrence was in no shape to climb stairs or run across rooftops. He didn't argue. Much. That told Max more than anything how badly he was hurting. They tried to leave Ash in the car, too, but he insisted on coming. "I've got a deep debt on this thing. I helped Javon escape, but if I'm going to come out close to even on this, I gotta keep paying." Max didn't fight him on it. They might need the extra hands.

They picked a dark house, opposite of where they parked, on the same side of the street as Deke's place. They stayed low, crossed the street, and used a Halligan bar, a short stubby piece of metal that resembled a crowbar, to pry open the door. It was the first of two things that Lawrence gave them from his bag. Max paused inside the doorway. The house felt empty. He picked up no movement or vibration. He waved the others in behind him. The stairs were directly in front of them. He took them two at a time.

There was a bathroom in the middle of the second floor and separate bedrooms at the front and the back of the house. After a quick search, they found the crawlspace up to the roof in the closet of the back bedroom. There were a pair of twin beds in the room, a desk in one corner, and a generic beach landscape on the wall. Nothing personal. No photos. Or loose change. Or charging cables. It was likely used for the occasional overnight guest. Max removed the stained plywood and piece of cut pink insulation before hitting the metal outdoor hatch. There was a cheap convenience store padlock looped through the steel hasp secured to the hatch. They pulled out an armful of clothes wrapped in dry cleaner plastic to give them room to work and threw them on the nearest bed. Ash pulled the desk chair over. Max stood on it and used the pry bar again and popped off the lock with a quick tug. He pushed up the hatch and the cold October air flooded in.

Max boosted himself through and then helped the others. The noise from the street drifted up, but their height muffled it. He glanced around. The roofs extending toward Deke's were flat and empty, save for the stub of a brick chimney and the round, covered tops of ventilation fans. There was a short, shin-high wall running around the perimeter of each roof. Every third home, there was a small gap, but it was less than six feet and they could jump across easily. The setup made moving along the roofs easy, but Max also knew it provided little cover or safety if someone spotted them or had the same idea and joined them on the roof.

The exposure made him jumpy and eager to move. "C'mon, let's go."

He stuck to the middle of the roofs and quickly made his way the length of the block, only stopping behind the crumbling chimney of the last home before Deke's double on the corner.

Now it was time to use the second piece that Lawrence had pulled from the bag.

"Got it off a SWAT guy instead of cash for certain services rendered," Lawrence had said as he handed over the gun and added an extra six-shot clip.

From a distance, it looked like a normal pistol except for the elongated grip and bright orange highlight running down the barrel. It wasn't a pistol. It was a CO_2 powered paintball gun that fired pepper spray balls.

"Is it going to have the range to reach?" Ash whispered as they peered around the edge of the chimney.

Three of Deke's guys were squatting behind a bullet-pocked car near the sidewalk leading to the front door. More guys peered through a couple of open windows on the first floor. Construction scaffolding covered the top floors or Deke likely would have put his guys on the roof, too. It was an obvious choice, and Deke didn't strike Max as a stupid man. Max would have to fire over Deke's guys to come close to hitting the FCM groups spread out on the opposite side of the street. Max put the distance at close to 150 yards. He'd likely be pushing the maximum range of the air gun.

"Only one way to find out. I don't think we have to be super precise. Close enough should do. The gas will disperse a bit." He extended his arm and braced it against the side of the bricks. He aimed a little higher to account for the drop and fired three shots toward the FCM group on the opposite corner, then emptied the remaining clip at the group trying to cross the street. One of Deke's guys was keeping them pinned, but if they made it across the gap, they would be sitting ducks.

Max saw the pellets hit, but nothing happened for five, then ten seconds. Finally, guys started to cough and shout. He watched the closer group, the one trying to cross, stagger back around the corner with their shirts pulled up over their faces. The other group stayed put, the gun didn't appear to have quite that much range, but the confusion of seeing their buddies running back had frozen them in place for the moment, which was almost as good.

Max popped the empty clip out and slapped in a new one.

"That might be enough. Should we head back down?" he asked.

He was about to turn away and find the hatch on this rooftop when Ade spoke up. "Look."

"What?"

A figure emerged around the corner from the FCM group and moved across the street. There was no hesitation. No fear. But a confidence and fluidity that felt familiar to Max.

One of Deke's guys broke away from behind the car and inched up the street. Someone must have alerted him to the movement and told him to check it out. He approached the next gap in the parked cars, gun in hand, and then the figure materialized out of the dark like a wraith. There was a brief flurry of movement before the wraith melted back into the shadows near the house. The man dropped like a stone. He never got off a shot. He never even raised his arm.

"What was that?" Ash asked, stunned.

"That was my sister," Ade said. She took two quick steps and jumped off the roof.

. . .

Max peered over the roof's ridge and watched Ade land softly on a narrow ledge and then launch herself across the open space and grab onto the construction scaffolding clinging to the side of Deke's house. She swung down to the ground and disappeared around the corner.

He looked over at Ash. "Stairs?"

"Yeah."

CHAPTER FIFTY-FOUR

They moved the girls around to keep buyers interested and inventory fresh. The third place that they took Ade and Sol was a new house somewhere. Ade remembered all the carpets were slick and smelled like plastic. It was brutally hot. The air outside was dry and crispy. It hurt to breathe it in for more than a few minutes. The air conditioning ran 24/7, not for their benefit, but for the clients. Ade later learned it was a small suburb outside Phoenix. None of the girls ventured outside often. It was too hot, but even if they did, no one would have seen them. The builders had finished the housing development right before the housing crisis got a stranglehold on the country. The homes were less than half-full with new foreclosures popping up weekly. Other than the clients coming up the driveway, Ade saw no one else on the surrounding streets. It was like living on a movie set.

The only time they went outside was to walk to the shed. The shed wasn't for clients. It was for Tru, one of their minders. She never learned his actual name. They all called him Tru, a truncation of the Spanish monstruo, or monster.

He never corrected them and appeared amused by the nick-name. He was a sadist. He didn't particularly have a fetish for young girls, like the clients, they were the available stock he had to work with. He would find imaginary transgressions or mistakes to mask what he was doing, but, as long as the girls kept working, the bosses didn't care. Or maybe they were afraid of him, too. A sadist on the payroll had pros and cons.

Tru took a special liking to Sol. He was the first one to give her drugs, and soon that urge overcame any fear or pain he could inflict. He took it as a challenge. So did Ade. She had to rescue her sister or risk Tru one day going too far. Ade was too naïve at the time to realize it might already be too late.

They had taken her blades, obviously, but they didn't watch the girls too closely. Why bother? The minders had guns and were much bigger. What could little girls do? She pocketed two small paring knives from the kitchen. They were dull and utilitarian things, but Ade methodically sharpened them against the rough metal leg of her bed frame in the basement and the next time Tru took Sol outside to the shed, Ade took her knives and followed.

The shed was flimsy and small, made of cheap pressed board that looked good from a distance. It would likely blow away on the desert wind within five years. An eight-foot by ten-foot rectangle, there was enough room for a worktable and a rolling chest of tools. There was nowhere to hide. She walked right in. A sharpened paring knife in her right hand. Tru was standing by the workbench, prepping a syringe. Sol was on the table.

He saw the knife in Ade's hand and smiled. "I enjoy it more when you fight back."

He stepped toward her, and she waved the knife wildly.

He dodged back and laughed. "Where did you get that little toy?"

He feinted one way. She swung again, off-balance now, and he reached in and swatted her arm. The knife flew away into the corner and he grabbed her by the throat. She kicked him in the groin, hit something fleshy and solid, but it had no effect. He laughed again and pulled her closer.

"Feisty. I like that this place hasn't broken you like your sister."

She smelled the fetid rot coming off his small pointy teeth. She slipped the second knife out of the waistband of her shorts and plunged it into the side of his neck. The hot liquid splashed across her cheeks. She held onto the knife's handle and pulled. His grip tightened on her neck, and she saw stars pop in the corner of her vision. She couldn't pass out. She kicked out her foot again but missed. She let go of the knife and gripped his wrist, tried to pry his fingers off. Her vision darkened even more. Just as a pleasant warmth spread through her limbs, his grip loosened and he let her go. She fell to her knees, gasping. He staggered back into his tool chest. He tried to stop the blood with his hands, but the wound was too large. He grasped the handle of the knife with slippery fingers but slid to the ground and died before he could pull it out.

She'd taken her sister from that house, but they hadn't lasted long. They were too young and too ignorant to survive on their own. It would take another two years and more damage to both of them before Ade escaped for good. Ever since, it had been a race against time to save her sister.

Ade shadowed her sister around the side of Deke's house into the backyard. It was quieter and darker there. Deke had concentrated his shooters in the front. Ade gave the space a quick sweep with her eyes as she came around the corner. She sensed no danger. The ground was trampled dirt waiting to be landscaped when construction on the house was complete. There was nowhere for anyone to hide. It was just a wide rectangle of dirt, weeds, and rocks that spanned the space behind the two houses. A windowless garage with space for a single car sat in the back corner of the lot. The other house had no garage, and the dirt ran down to a temporary cyclone fence at the sidewalk. The crew had parked a small Bobcat loader opposite the garage. A stack of rough-cut boards leaned up against the side of the garage next to two sawhorses.

She watched Sol creep along the side of the house, staying in the shadows. She stopped next to the bulkhead doors that led to the basement. A large chain and padlock hung from the handles. Sol knelt and spun the lock, glanced at her arm, and spun it the other way. She has the combination, Ade thought. She remembered what Max had said about Deke's man standing with Tuco.

Ade knew if her sister went into that house, she wouldn't come back out alive.

"Sol," she said and stepped around the corner.

Her sister looked up. In the dim light, Ade saw her eyes were black marbles with tiny pinpricks of pupils. She was as high as a kite. There was no recognition. Sol dropped the lock, adjusted her grip on the knife, and charged.

Ade had memories of Tio, but she took different lessons from their training. Sol liked to attack. She liked to push until she had an advantage and was confident she was better. Then she would let up. Ade knew a knife fight wasn't about fighting at all. It was about surviving. It was about patience, intelligence, and defending yourself until you found the advantage, slipping behind your opponent's defenses with precision. And then finishing it. There were no half measures.

Sol overwhelmed her opponents quickly. That was her strategy. Ade had witnessed it from the rooftop only minutes prior, but Ade wasn't just any opponent. She parried her sister's thrusts and kept moving. She stayed balanced and tried to stay out of the way. Her sister was fast, the drugs helped, but the chemicals also made her sloppy and overconfident. Tio always preached to stay out of striking range until you could end the fight with one blow.

Ade saw Sol tiring and getting impatient. Ade waited and kept moving. She sensed her opening was coming. She needed to be careful. And precise. Ade sidestepped and circled. Sol made an angry noise in her throat and thrust out quickly, her arm extended, slashing at Ade's neck. Ade tracked the arc of the blade and moved backward and to the side, in sync with her sister, like all those sparring sessions on the farm. The blade whipped past and she counterattacked. She brought her wakizashi up from her hip and pierced the underside of her sister's forearm. Her sister screamed and dropped her knife.

CHAPTER FIFTY-FIVE

Len didn't rush. The fire seemed to have seared away his fear and hesitation. The future was coming, and he was ready. He drove away from Javon and the warehouse and waited until he was off the access road and on the boulevard to pick up the phone.

"Where are you?" Deke asked.

He heard the stress in Deke's voice. No one else probably would, but Len knew. Deke was worried. Not panicked. Deke prided himself on not overreacting, on being cool and collected. And not about Javon. That was a deeper dread, a helplessness. This was different. Deke was thinking about the end. You didn't get into this business and not know how it ended for most.

"I'm on my way back. No sign of him. Did you hear anything?"

"No, and we got other problems. I need you back here. Fast."

"What's going on? What's bigger than Javon?" He tried to put some worry of his own into his voice. Some uncertainty.

"I've got everyone out looking for Javon and now there

are shooters outside my house. My house, Lennie! Tamyra is hiding in the bathtub."

"Who is it?"

"I don't know for sure. I think it's Jorge and the FCM making a play."

"Cheap shot when Javon is missing."

"Just get back here and help us take care of this."

Us? Deke didn't realize yet that there was no more us, but a part of Len couldn't help but respond. He'd had Deke's back since he was eight. He wanted to ride in and save the day like he used to on the playground or when they started on the corner. But he pushed that sentiment aside and let another rise, the part that had been twisted and left to rot on the vine. Help us. You mean be the hammer. Do the things you no longer want to do. Deke didn't need his help or opinion during those endless business meetings. But when things got real again, he asked. What a joke.

"I'm coming. Five minutes."

"Faster. It might be over in five minutes."

Len disconnected and eased the car to a stop at the next intersection. He glanced left and saw the yellow overhang of South Philly Chicken and Seafood half a block down. He couldn't remember the last time he ate. He turned left, and it was like providence. A van pulled out and a parking spot opened up in front of the restaurant. He parked and went inside to order.

The first time Len drove past, Deke's street was awash in cop cars, official vans, yellow tape, and news trucks. He saw Deke and Cherry standing in the yard talking to a detective. A cop waved him past and, after a moment's hesitation, Len kept driving. Deke was alive. It hadn't worked. He drove another six blocks and pulled into the parking lot of a Dunkin'

Donuts. He took out his phone and his finger hovered over the speed dial for Deke, but he stopped. He pulled out the second phone, the left pocket phone. There were only two numbers programmed in, no names. Tuco was dead, a twisted crisp on the floor of that warehouse, but maybe someone else would pick up. Before he met up with Deke, he needed to know what happened or what might still happen. He tapped the screen. He disconnected after twenty rings. He tried the other number and received an automated message that the number was no longer in service. He got out of the car. He snapped the phone's SIM card in half and dropped the card parts and phone into a garbage can.

He watched the night traffic pass and tried to think it all through. Any calm he'd felt earlier had been blown apart by seeing Deke alive. His mind felt like it was moving in thick oil. Could the dead-end phone numbers be a good thing? He'd been careful. They all had. The whole thing had to be sealed up tight if it was going to work. No one knew he was involved. No one who would talk. He might still be okay. He decided the best thing he could do was go back and take another run at Deke later when all this had cooled off. Do it on his own. Keep it simple. He'd let them overcomplicate things. If he could get his guts up and put a bullet in Deke himself that would accomplish the same thing. It would piss off a lot of people, he'd have to figure out what to do with Tamyra, but he also knew many people would respect it. Respect him. If you wanted the crown, you had to take it, not sneak in and steal it.

He entered the shop and bought a donut and coffee. He didn't want either, but it gave him something to do with his hands. He sat in his car. The coffee turned cold. He took a bite of the donut and regretted it. The powdered sugar was grit between his teeth. He waited another hour before he drove back.

The scene was still busy, but it had calmed down. The police had pushed the curious, or the bored, off the block or back into their houses. The cops had removed the bodies. Most of the news vans had gotten their clips and disappeared. Len parked a block south. He started walking then paused, went back to the car and took the gun from between the seats and slipped it into his waistband at his back. He approached the corner house from the rear. He slipped around the temporary construction fence and knocked on the back door. Deke himself answered and, as soon as Len saw the relief on his face, he knew he'd made the right decision.

"Shit, man, where you been? I was worried you were bleeding out on the sidewalk somewhere."

"Nah, I drove past, but the entire block was lit up with cops. I saw you and Cherry. I knew you were okay. Thought it might be better to stay clear."

"Yeah, all right, I hear that. It was crazy. First Javon," his voice cracked a little and while Len had never been a father, that he knew of anyway, he felt some small elemental ping in his chest at his friend's grief, "and then Jorge coming at me."

Deke stopped, and Len was afraid he might start crying. He spoke up instead, "You think Jorge took Javon?"

Deke raised his arms and let them drop. "Probably. Nothing else makes a lick of sense, you know? The odds of him going missing and the FCM trying to take me out at the same time are astronomical."

"You always said Jorge was a cockroach. He might take advantage of that situation. Javon, I mean."

Deke turned and gave Len a hard look, and Len again saw some of that old fire but then it disappeared, and Deke deflated. His shoulders slumped and his head dropped. "Cockroach. You might be right," he said to the floor. "God, I'm so tired. I can hardly see straight, never mind think. C'mon, let's go upstairs. I need a drink."

The house was quiet. The back stairs creaked as they climbed, and Len heard the boiler shudder and fire down in the basement.

"Where is everyone?" Len asked.

"The ones not in the hospital or at the morgue are back out looking for Javon. Cops said they'd be out there until morning. The safest place in Philly is probably right here, right now. Ironic, huh?"

Len sat in one of the leather chairs across from the dark oak desk. The curtains were drawn across the big window with the city skyline view. Deke filled two thick crystal glasses with scotch and handed one to Len. There was no toast. They each took a sip. The liquor burned. Len had never gotten a taste for it. When he wanted to relax, he preferred a beer and some weed. He took another small sip. He watched Deke take a long swallow.

"The thing I have the most trouble understanding, and if I have trouble reconciling it, having lived through it, I can only imagine the confusion others might have," Deke said as he swirled the liquid in his glass. "The only thing the streets have to offer is money, death, or jail. The last two are dead ends, right? So, if you're with us, living the life, it should be for the money, right? And you should want to use that money to get off the street and move up. That's what I always thought, but that was my big mistake, wasn't it, Len?" He looked up now and Len felt the first stirrings of unease.

"I'm not sure, Deke."

"But I am. It took a while, but I finally saw it. There's something else on offer. I always thought money was a solution, but I've concluded, based on recent experience, that this is not always the case. Not at all. You know I tried to use some of my money to buy up real estate, apartments, and to set up investment funds that would pay the guys dividends?"

"Yeah, I know. I'm in."

"Yes, I know. And you get a monthly check, right? You know how many others signed up?"

"No."

"Six. And I'm pretty sure five of them were only trying to curry some favor with me." Deke shook his head. "I couldn't get my head around it. I tried to offer opportunity and guidance, but it was always 'live by the gun, die by the gun.' That's stronger than getting off the street. That's what the streets offer. The rush of fighting, the risk of dying. Guys like it. They can't see anything else. But you already know that, don't you?"

He tossed a phone across the desk.

"What's this?"

"Take a look, I queued it up."

Len picked up the phone and tapped the screen. The video was small and grainy, but he could still pick himself out talking to Tuco under the highway overpass. He glanced up.

"Keep going. It's a double feature."

The second video was inside the warehouse, shot from a distance, but even with the clown mask on, he was still identifiable. And so was Javon.

"I was ..." he started, but there was nothing to say. The relief and camaraderie Deke had shown downstairs had been a mask. That mask was gone now. Cops were still crawling around outside, but that was almost a perfect alibi. Who would kill someone with cops right outside their front door? Deke stared across the desk at him with empty eyes and Len knew that no cops nearby, no history, no friendship would buy him a reprieve. Not from this.

"Listen," Len tried again, but no more words came. He moved his hand toward the gun at his back. Deke didn't flinch. Len never heard him. The big man had always been light on his feet. Len became aware of the sucking black hole presence a split second before a thick arm snaked around his neck and clamped tight. Len forgot about the gun. He forgot about anything except finding the next sip of air. He clawed at Cherry's forearm, but it was like trying to twist a piece of rebar. He was lifted out of the chair. His feet scrabbled for purchase on the polished wood. Cherry tightened his hold and lifted him higher. Time stretched out.

Len stopped fighting and let his arms relax. It wasn't so bad. It was like slipping into a warm pool. It was a better ending than he'd always imagined. Or deserved.

CHAPTER FIFTY-SIX

Max could see them across the street through the gym's tall windows. He pulled on a jacket and crossed the street. He stopped at the diner and got a couple danishes and two cups of coffee. The gym's door was open, like always, but the four of them were alone inside. At the opposite end, Max watched Ronnie put Javon through a typically merciless workout, moving from the speed bag to the heavy bag to the jump rope in one-minute intervals. Max felt winded just watching. Sweat poured off Javon's face, but the boy said nothing, only moved to the next exercise when Ronnie blew his whistle.

Deke sat behind Ronnie's desk in the corner. Max took the other chair and placed the coffees and rolls on the desk.

"Thanks," Deke said, taking a coffee. "But if you keep bringing me things, I'm going to lose track of what I owe."

"Seeing him back in here is enough, but there is one thing I wanted to ask you."

Deke shifted in the chair so he squared up to Max. "So ask."

"I drive nights for a car service based out of Fitler Square."

"The blue box?"

"That's it. An old school guy named Liam O'Brian owns it. Been around for decades. He and his wife run it. Solid guy. Treats people right. He also recently butted heads with the FCM."

"We got that in common."

"Looked like a protection racket. He didn't want to play along. But he didn't come out as well as you did. He took a beating and ended up in the hospital."

"You want me to put the word out that his place is off limits?"

"If it wouldn't put you in a tight spot, yeah, that would probably help, but a quiet word. He's a proud guy."

"Not my usual line of work, but not a problem. The least I can do. That's it?"

"Watching Javon pound that bag for Ronnie covers the rest."

They each watched for a spell, the gym silent except for the slapping of Javon's gloves on the leather.

"He's been in here a lot, I noticed," Max eventually said, taking a bite of a sweet cheese and fruit pastry.

"Therapy of a sort, I guess."

"He talking to anyone else? Professionally?"

"He's barely talking to Tam or me, never mind a shrink."

"He'll be okay. It won't go back to the way it was, but he'll be okay. He kept his head throughout. Give him some space. And time. He'll come back."

"Yeah? You think? Teenagers are so screwed up in general, and you throw this on top. I don't know. I tried to shield him from ... what I do. Maybe that was a mistake. Maybe I ended up making him a target."

"He was always going to be a target. You know that. Any

code of honor among thieves is bullshit. You've made it harder on yourself, no doubt, but you are hardly unique. You protect the ones you love as best you can when the reckoning comes. Every parent out there faces similar choices."

They watched Javon finish another round. He was breathing hard, but Ronnie wasn't letting up. You climb between those ropes and you couldn't expect your opponent to let up either. If you didn't know that going in, you were in trouble and probably in for a world of hurt.

"You going to workout?" Deke asked.

"Maybe. If Ronnie sees us eating these, he's going to make both of us get out there."

Max still felt sore from all the events of the last week. He realized it was taking him longer to bounce back, physically and mentally. A nick or niggle that would once take a day or two and be forgotten would now linger for three or four days, sometimes longer. He needed to rest more than he needed to workout, but he was also feeling a familiar restlessness. Not for the gym but someplace else. He couldn't explain it, even to himself, but he was coming to accept it.

He sipped the strong coffee and then looked across the dented, battered desk at Deke. "It's a young man's game, though, right? You stick around too long and the ending is always ugly."

Deke glanced over. "We still talking about boxing? Or something else?"

"Does it matter?"

Deke swept the pastry crumbs into his hand and dumped them in the garbage. "No, I guess not. I thought I had a good exit strategy worked out. I don't need the money, not anymore, I have enough stashed away, but getting loose from the ... machinery of it all might be more difficult than I realized."

"You can't outrun your reputation or your shadow."

"I guess I realized a little too late that I'd built prison walls up around myself."

"What are you going to do?"

"Long term? I still want out. Lawrence said he might have some ideas about how I could do that."

"Yeah? You should listen. He's a smart man."

"Yes, I don't doubt that."

"What about the short term?"

"To make things safe for my family, I think I need to attend to some loose ends."

"Police can't handle it?"

"Not all of it. They found some physical stuff, DNA, and video that tied Scootch's shooting and this other murder, a guy named Aaron, to Len. But some other parts, like who snatched Javon, are a little more difficult to pin down. Might never be enough evidence. Not for a court."

"Wasn't just Len? And Tuco? Or Jorge Campos?"

"I didn't know Tuco. Len had uses, but he was always more of a blunt instrument than a sharp scalpel."

"You think they had help?"

"Yes."

"Who?"

"I have some influence around Gray's Ferry. A bit of power, in a limited sense, but you know who really controls things? It's not Jorge Campos or me or the faraway cartels. It's the people up in City Hall. The people setting the budgets and the contracts. They will do anything to stay in power. So, yeah, I have an idea."

CHAPTER FIFTY-SEVEN

Max left Deke brooding at the old desk and walked back across the street to his apartment. If Lawrence was awake, they could hit up The Skyline for breakfast. The caffeine and the sugar from the danish had left him feeling jittery and even more hungry for some carbs and grease. Plus, Lawrence was slowly coming to appreciate the mysterious delights of Philly scrapple.

He walked up the stairs thinking about families, and parents, and the rippling effects of choices. Max believed current actions should ultimately define a person, not past decisions or destructive behavior. He was trying to be living proof of that. Judge the beating heart of an individual. But recent experiences had also made it clear that the sins of the parents leave scars that can be passed down to their children. Sin was rarely a solitary thing, Max decided. Especially in families. Children might not be responsible for the actions of their parents, but they could still suffer.

He pulled his key out as he approached his door and then heard voices. Lawrence was awake, and he had company.

"Max, you're just in time. The detectives here were about

to fill me in on some interesting events of the past few days. Go ahead, Detective."

Lawrence was on the couch surrounded by his laptop and a sprawling island of paper. A week of rest and antibiotics had done him good. Diaz sat on the edge of the coffee table, crowding into Lawrence's space. Lawrence seemed vaguely amused at the obvious tactics. Unlike the previous interviews, Axelson seemed to be riding shotgun on this one and letting Diaz take the lead. She leaned against the wall and picked at a hangnail. A shaft of morning sun coming through the window made her blonde hair appear almost translucent.

Max took one of the kitchen chairs and turned it around to face Diaz, then held out his hands. "Please, continue."

Now that the odds in the room had evened up, Diaz gave up the petty attempt at intimidation and paced the small room. "Where were you last Wednesday, Lindell?"

"Hell, I don't know. Probably working. I'm sure PPCS can provide you some records."

"We'll check on that."

"Look, is this still about the fingers and the missing woman? Didn't we cover all this already? This is beginning to feel like harassment." Axelson moved off the wall and took a few books off his cheap pine board bookshelf, riffled the pages, and put them back. "You guys have a warrant?"

"No," Diaz said.

"Then don't touch my stuff."

Axelson smirked but went back to her spot in the sun.

"What we have are more dead bodies at two different locations by the docks, forget missing fingers, one guy was practically cut in half, plus a burned-out truck, and a couple of eyewitness reports of a man and a woman near the scene."

Max realized they had all the pieces but hadn't sorted them out properly into the complete puzzle, yet. They hadn't connected Javon to the truck or the truck to FCM or Deke to Jorge or Ade to Sol. And maybe they never would. Maybe they would only get a piece. Only ever fill in a small corner of the jigsaw. But even a small piece might be enough to trip up Max. The longer they fixated on him, the more dangerous, and more likely, it became that they would get behind the Lindell alias and figure out who he really was.

"Do you think they mistook me or you for a woman?" Lawrence asked.

"You have slimmer hips," Max said.

Diaz stopped pacing and looked at Max. "Both incidents involved large crime scenes. There is a lot of evidence. A lot of ways for a perp to screw up. It will take time, but we'll sort it out. We move slowly, but we are good at grinding things down. I know you're mixed up in this somehow, Lindell. Someday I'll prove it."

Which was exactly what Max feared. And maybe part of what was stirring that restlessness in his legs. He suspected Diaz was right. The priority had been to save Lawrence and then get Javon. They had been careful but hardly spotless. Max was sure his DNA was out there, or his face was on some stray camera.

Diaz must have read the same look on Max's face and smiled. "We're coming for you, Lindell. Maybe for both of you. A matter of time." He nodded and moved toward the door.

Lawrence picked up the ledger book that Max had taken from the back room at La Champincita. "Hey Diaz, can I ask you a question?"

Diaz stopped and turned around. "What?"

"Do you know what a Caeser cipher is?"

Diaz and Axelson both looked confused.

"Clearly not," Lawrence said. "It's a simple technique for encrypting information. It's a type of substitution code in which each letter in the message is replaced by a letter some fixed number of positions down the alphabet. For example, with a left shift of 3, D would be replaced by A, E would become B, and so on. Even your feeble mind can probably grasp it. It's not tough to crack these days, even without the key." He tapped the laptop next to him. "A matter of time. And a little processing power."

"What's your point?"

"One thing kept bothering me in the last few days. After you dragged Max in to talk and he left your precinct, four guys grabbed him right off your front stoop. Not fifty feet from your shop's front door. I watched it happen. How did they know he'd be there? That was sloppy. Next time, you should tell them to wait until he at least turns the corner. Create some plausible deniability."

Diaz glared at him. Axelson took a step back into the room and said, "What exactly are you implying?"

Lawrence flipped through the pages of the ledger. "I'm not implying anything, Axelson. Unlike Diaz, I don't have to. I have actual proof. The FCM kept very detailed records."

Axelson looked at Diaz, but he remained silent. "What the fuck, Diaz?"

He didn't look at her but put up a hand. "Later."

Axelson's cheeks were red. She clenched her fists at her sides. She looked righteously pissed and, according to Lawrence, with good reason. Her partner had betrayed her. Max was glad he wouldn't be the one trying to explain why he'd been taking orders from the FCM. She didn't look remotely understanding.

"What do you want?" he said to Lawrence.

"Do what you have to do to close your case, Diaz, but Max wasn't involved."

Diaz left without saying anything else. Axelson followed more slowly. Max could hear Axelson's voice echo down the hall as she followed her partner. He turned back to Lawrence. "So, Eddie cracked the ledger?"

"No, he's still working on it. It's not a simple shift code."

"So that was—"

"An educated guess."

"Hell of a bluff."

Lawrence smiled briefly, then turned serious. "But only temporary."

Max knew he was right. He couldn't stay here. It was too dangerous. He'd made too many waves over the past few weeks. Rocked too many boats. Even keeping Diaz off his back didn't guarantee his safety, only bought him time. Axelson could be back knocking at his door in no time. She looked like she held a grudge.

"Know any good places to disappear?"

"I'll give you a ride."

CHAPTER FIFTY-EIGHT

In the end, Ash simply walked away. In all the confusion that night, it wasn't hard to slip away unnoticed. He walked back to his motel room, collected his small cache of belongings, and left. By dawn, he'd walked across the city to the Greyhound station near Reading Terminal and purchased a ticket for Connecticut.

His parents had been wary, he didn't blame them. It had been a long and painful road for them, too. They each took it slowly, but over time, a thin thread of trust built back up. He slept in his old room and kept himself busy doing chores and odd jobs around the house that his aging parents could no longer do on their own. It kept his mind focused and his body tired. For almost two months, he rarely slept through the night. He lay in bed, the gun he'd stolen from Max, secreted under his pillow, anxious and jumpy at any noise.

Then two things happened, and it was all over.

Each morning, he scanned through the online headlines of the Philadelphia papers. One morning, there was a story, a smaller one, in the Metro section that detailed the killing of a local businessman. Ash recognized the name. The *Inquirer* might be careful to call Jorge Campos a businessman, but Ash had learned from Max and Ade that he was the leader of the FCM gang who had taken Ade's sister and was at least partially responsible for Javon's kidnapping, too.

A week later, there was a bigger story. This time on the front page with the big headline type. Michael Youngblood, the chief of staff for the newly elected city council president and an early favorite to be the next mayor, James Watts, was found dead in his car. It appeared to be a suicide, though no one could understand the motive. The police expected more details soon. Everyone expressed shock. Watts released a statement talking about his dismay and how he'd looked forward to many more fruitful years of working together. There was an accompanying video that showed Youngblood giving an interview with a local reporter. It began to auto play before he could click away. Ash froze.

He knew that voice.

CHAPTER FIFTY-NINE

She knew where she was before she opened her eyes. She smelled disinfectant and desperation. Sol had been in different rehab facilities three times before and that noxious cocktail scent was unique. The thin chains rattled against the metal bed frame when she tensed her arms. Not the first time she'd been restrained, either.

She cracked one eyelid. Even the dim light hurt. She forced the other one open. She was alone but hooked up to an IV and other monitors. Someone would be in to check on her soon. The machines would give her away. She looked down at herself. Other than her arms, she was covered up to her chin with a beige blanket. There was a bandage wrapped tightly around her right forearm. It itched slightly under the white gauze. Three IVs were taped to the crook of her left arm. She noticed a tremor in both hands. She clenched her fists to make it stop.

She looked around. The room was small with a lot of blond wood and soft accent lighting. It looked more like a boutique hotel room than a drug rehab center. There was a side table, a small chest of drawers, and a half-open door leading to a private bathroom. She'd never had her own bathroom in the previous facilities. Her previous stays had all been barebones, almost industrial, more Army barracks than a hotel.

She laid back. The primary smell might be the same, but this place also carried the whiff of money. And that was a problem. She couldn't recall the details. Didn't know how long she'd been here. Ever since the trunk lid opened until now, there was an empty spot in her memory. But she knew who must be responsible for this room and her treatment. Her sister had spent all her life, since they fled the family farm, trying to first protect her and then to rescue her. It was no kind of life at all.

The squeak of rubber as footsteps approached from outside. Sol closed her eyes and laid still. She didn't need to have her eyes open to see the mixture of sympathy and condescension on their face. High money or no money, the staff were also all the same.

She went back to thinking about her sister. Ade would never let it go. She would follow Sol to the ends of the earth. She would always try to rescue her. Sol needed to put an end to it and free them both.

It took almost two months. The first month, she got clean. Her hands stopped shaking. The urge was still there, but it was a dull ache more than a sharp need. Sol's sobriety was fragile, like walking on a thin skin of ice but it was holding. She spent the next month searching. She woke up each day lying next to her sister in the bedroom they shared. She would force herself to eat and then she would walk. It helped to have a focus each day. One step in front of the other. One block to the next. If she was concentrating on searching, she wasn't thinking about that ache. She left early because she needed to be near the water in the morning. Her mind was still splintered but she remembered that much.

She found him on a Tuesday morning. Not him, Jorge, she reminded herself. Jorge Campos, head of the FCM, and both her jailer and her savior. The man with the drugs. Sol had spilled so much blood for him, but had never known his name until Ade filled in the blanks. Jorge thought his paranoia made him safe, but it only made him blind to his impulses. He'd grown up near the sea like she had grown up near the mountains, and he liked to start each day near the water, even if it was a different ocean from his boyhood. Maybe it made him nostalgic. Some days, while her eyes watered and she sipped her water, he'd tell her stories from his childhood. It was the only time she'd ever witnessed him show any shred of humanity. She had no qualms about using that against him.

On Wednesday, she woke up very early. She kissed her sister on the forehead. She took her sister's short sword from the closet and slipped it in her bag. Their father's box was already gone. The sword was a shackle her sister didn't need either. She would end that, too. She slipped out of the room and walked to the water.

She arrived before dawn. It had snowed lightly the night before but the wind was on her side. It quickly covered her footsteps. She moved down close to the water's edge, below the bench where he always sat, and settled in a crevice between two large rocks. She pulled her coat tight around her and watched the sunrise.

The commuters glided past on the ferry. She heard him sigh as he sat, and then she smelled his strong Veracruz coffee. He imported the beans, he'd told her. He thought all American coffee was little better than wastewater. She gave him a minute to get comfortable, then she rose from the rocks like a siren. As she climbed into view, she saw his confusion, then his comprehension. She stepped onto the gravel path and drew the blade back. He stood, spilling the coffee, and finally, she saw his fear. The bodyguard was running toward them, drawing his gun, but he was too far away to make a difference. He would get her but not save him. She brought the blade down. Blood bloomed across his white shirt. This time, she didn't stop.

ABOUT THE AUTHOR

Mike Donohue is the author of four previous novels in the Max Strong series. He lives with his wife, two daughters, and Dashiell Hammett outside Boston. Dash is the family dog.

Mike doesn't think reading during meals is particularly rude. Quite the opposite.

You can find him online at mikedonohuebooks.com.

 facebook.com/mikedonohuebooks

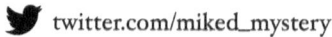 twitter.com/miked_mystery